"I'll tell you

He ached to touch her. Just holding her hand would be enough. It seemed impossible he had once taken the hundreds of small, day-to-day moments they'd shared for granted.

"There isn't a day I don't think about you. There are times I see a woman walking alone on the beach and let myself believe it's you. Some days someone will knock on the door. And for the seconds it takes to answer I tell myself you're the one waiting for me . . ."

GEORGIA BOCKOVEN

ANOTHER SUMMER

HarperTorch
An Imprint of HarperCollinsPublishers

Cassidy, Gina, and Michael—
a special, joyful welcome to the family!
Marge—a sad farewell. We miss you.

A big thank you to Alan Koch for his generosity in time and spirit.
He answered a hundred questions when he only had time for two
and took the mystery, but not the beauty, out of orchids.

This is a work of fiction. Names, characters, places, and incidents are
products of the author's imagination or are used fictitiously and are not
to be construed as real. Any resemblance to actual events, locales,
organizations, or persons, living or dead, is entirely coincidental.

❦

HARPERTORCH
An Imprint of HarperCollins*Publishers*
10 East 53rd Street
New York, New York 10022-5299

Copyright © 2001 by Georgia Bockoven
ISBN: 0-380-81865-5

First HarperTorch paperback printing: December 2001

HarperCollins®, HarperTorch™, and ❦™ are trademarks of Harper-
Collins Publishers Inc.

Printed in the United States of America

Visit HarperTorch on the World Wide Web at www.harpercollins.com

10 9 8 7 6 5 4 3 2 1

Prologue

THE BEACH HOUSE NOW STOOD EMPTY, PA-tiently waiting for another summer, when its shutters would be removed and sunlight would once again fill its rooms. Built in 1905, it has been silent witness to nearly a century of love and hatred, and withstood fierce storms, violent earthquakes, while hosting generations of visitors.

Location tied the house and the Santa Cruz boardwalk as much as longevity. Though neither was visible from the other, they had formed a symbiotic relationship: one drew the children, the other drew the adult the child would one day become.

Several small cities separated them. The largest, Santa Cruz, was California condensed to its purest form. To live in a place where high surf took precedence over work required tolerance, liberal thinking, and a love of the unusual. To visit such a place, T-shirts and shorts and sandals sufficed.

Considered useless property by the man who had inherited it, the five acres of rock and forest abutting the ocean changed ownership in a poker game at the Hard Luck Saloon during a turn-of-the-century celebration. The next year a farmer traded a team of horses for the land and that winter began clearing the ground at the edge of the fifteen-foot cliff. He built a rustic, one-room cabin, where a few years later he took his bride on their honeymoon.

Farming was good, and the farmer added rooms to his vacation home as his family grew. Three of his five children were conceived in the cabin. He instilled a love of the land and ocean in them all, filling their heads with stories of a future when they would bring their children and grandchildren to this beloved cottage.

The farmer was nearing sixty when the Great Depression settled across the country. The price of crops dropped below what it cost to produce them. To pay the bills, the farmer sold the five acres that surrounded the beach house to a developer. The developer divided the land into lots and sold them at a 300 percent profit.

The Depression lingered, and the farmer's children and grandchildren left to find work in the city. He fell behind on his taxes. To save his farm he sacrificed the seed for the next year's crop, hoping for a miracle. His "miracle" arrived in the form of a traveling salesman who offered to trade the beach house for a season's seed and fertilizer.

The salesman repeated the story of his incredible good fortune to the other farmers on his route in the long, fertile Salinas Valley. However, he failed to note how those farmers stared at the ground as they listened to his bragging. They put in a call to his competitor as soon as he drove away, and eventually the salesman had to add another territory to earn enough money to keep his bounty.

With two territories to work, the salesman was too busy to spend much time at the beach house. Rather than sit alone at home, his wife spent all her time there. At her insistence, the salesman added another bedroom to accommodate her mother. The next year he added a larger kitchen and new fixtures for the bathroom.

Adding yet more territory to his route to pay for the improvements, the salesman went for weeks without seeing either the house or his wife. Five years later, his wife divorced him, telling the judge his long absences made her feel as if she'd been abandoned. She asked for and received the beach house in the settlement, living there until she was killed in a cable car accident on a trip to San Francisco several years later.

Joe and Maggie Chapman were in Santa Cruz celebrating their anniversary when they took a walk one afternoon and happened on the island of houses in the sea of forest. It was Maggie who first

saw the real estate agent take a FOR SALE sign out
of his car. They stopped to talk and struck a deal
before the sign made it into the ground.

Joe and Maggie put the love into the house they
had saved for the children they had failed to conceive. Looking forward to the day Joe would retire
and they would live there full-time, they ex-
panded the living room and added a deck. Then
Joe had a stroke, and it was everything Maggie
could do to take care of him and the house in San
Jose. They found a renter, a young man named
Ken Huntington, who'd hitchhiked from Kansas
because it was his dream to swim in the Pacific
Ocean.

Ken was a mystery to Maggie, unfailingly cour-
teous and always on time with the rent, but forever locked away in the house playing with
something he called a personal computer. She
tried to listen when he told her the magical things
that she would be able to do with her own computer one day, but it was impossible for her to
summon anything but polite interest.

Joe's slow recovery from his stroke wiped out
his and Maggie's savings. They were left with the
beach house and their home in San Jose and a desperate need for income. Ken offered to buy the
house, but only if Joe and Maggie would carry the
note. In exchange, he would give them the summer months to do with as they pleased.

Unaware that Ken was one of the original Silicon Valley computer geniuses, Joe and Maggie

entered the agreement, believing they were help-ing a fine young man buy his first home while solving their own money problems. They kept July for themselves and rented June and August, proudly presenting the checks to Ken at the end of their first summer, "to help with the mortgage payments."

For the next seventeen years, even as Ken's business grew to be one of the world's leaders, the summer rental agreement continued. The beach house acquired new windows and paint, hard-wood floors and a laundry room. Dry rot was dis-covered in the bathroom and the fireplace chimney developed a crack. Repairs were made, appliances replaced, and a new brick path in-stalled through the garden.

Then Ken met and fell in love with a woman who opened the world to him. They were the cou-ple written about in love songs and sonnets and romance novels. They were forever. Only death could separate them.

Ken left Julia on an ordinary commute to work. Julia blindly passed him as he lay dying on the side of the road, oblivious to all but the massive traffic jam Ken created when he lost control of his car during a heart attack.

A sadness settled through the house. Over the near century it had stood sentinel on its rocky out-cropping, there had been times when weeks had passed with no one in residence. But not once in all those decades had the doors remained locked and the windows shuttered for so long as they did that year.

During those desolate eight months a timer kept the garden watered, but no one tended the flowers or cleared the cobwebs. The bleeding-hearts, foxglove, cosmos, plume poppy, and alumroot spilled from their beds and collapsed onto the brick walkways. Worn-out, abandoned spiderwebs filled with wind-strewn debris hung from eaves and fence posts, shutters and lights.

As if through an unspoken agreement, the neighbors steered clear of the beach house that winter. When they did happen by on their way to somewhere else, they kept their heads dipped, their eyes averted.

Finally, on a warm May evening, a car appeared on the narrow asphalt road that led to the house. The woman behind the wheel drove slowly, passing houses with unshuttered windows and families gathered around dining room tables for the evening meal.

She pulled into the driveway but didn't go inside. Instead, she took the public path beside the house that led to the beach, stood at the top of the stairs, and stared out to sea. Finally, she removed her shoes, set them under a boxwood sorely in need of trimming, and descended the stairs. She walked south, away from the houses toward the rocky outcropping that marked the southern end of the cove. When she returned, the sun rode low on the horizon.

With windblown hair, eyes swollen from crying, and designer clothes damp and wrinkled from sitting on a lichen-covered rock, she did not look like the woman of wealth who had driven there in a Mercedes to say good-bye to the man she'd loved well, but not long. Believing the memories too poignant for her to keep the beach house, she'd come there to ready it for a final summer of renters before putting it on the market.

It would be Joe and Maggie's last July. That summer they would say good-bye to each other and the house that had given them shelter through a lifetime of joy and sorrow. Their leaving seemed to mark the end of the long season of love lavished on the beach house.

But Julia couldn't sell. The lives of those who had gone before permeated the walls and reached out to her when she tried to walk away. One more summer, she told herself, convinced another season would give her distance and make it easier to let go. It would have to be an ordinary summer, one without life-altering changes to the people who came there, one without the magic that had touched those who came before.

When that happened, she would sell.

May

1

THE ODDS WERE AGAINST HIM. ANDREW Wells knew this as well as he knew his chances of winning the California state lottery. Of course, you had to play to win, which he didn't. He figured the lottery was on a par with tossing money in a fountain and expecting good luck.

He was, however, willing to gamble something far more valuable to see Cheryl Cunningham again—his pride. The slim possibility she might attend their twenty-year class reunion was all the encouragement he'd needed to return the invitation, a check attached. Now, an hour into the meet-and-greet portion of the evening, it was almost impossible to sustain the hope that had brought him there.

Andrew took risks as a matter of course, always willing to live with the consequences. Some considered the risks he took lunatic. But from his perspective, hang gliding off a mountaintop, running class-five rivers in a kayak, chasing tsunami-size waves with a surfboard, and sailing around the world with only a stray dog for company had more to do with philosophy than danger. He believed if he wasn't living on the edge, he was taking up too much space.

He looked at the melting ice in what was left of his gin and tonic and tried not to show the strain he felt listening to a group of his old football buddies trying to top each other with exaggerated stories of financial success and brilliant progeny. Glancing first at the door where he'd registered and then at the glass slider that led to the deck overlooking the eighteenth green, he began planning his escape route.

"First liar doesn't stand a chance."

Andrew smiled, immediately recognizing Roger Blanchette's wry sense of humor and halting voice. Best friends for eight of the ten years they attended school together, the paths they'd taken afterward never seemed to cross at a convenient time for either of them. Turning, he clasped Roger's outstretched hand with genuine pleasure. "Which is why I'm still waiting to add my two cents."

Roger laughed. "You'd think their biggest problem was finding a space to park their Learjets."

If anyone from their Santa Cruz High School class of 1981 could lay claim to a Learjet, it was the man standing in front of him. The years had been good to Roger. No longer plagued by acne or a mother who bought his clothes at garage sales and thrift stores, he could easily pass for exactly what he was, one of the startlingly rich computer moguls of Silicon Valley. He was still new enough to his riches to wear an obscenely expensive watch and bargain wedding band. "You're the last person I expected to find here."

"Exactly what I was thinking about you."

"Well?"

Roger nodded toward a stunning blonde holding court with a cluster of ex-cheerleaders. "Mary wanted to come."

Andrew did a double take. "That's Mary?"

"Shows you what a bitchy magazine writer and a willing plastic surgeon can do to a perfectly fine woman." He shrugged it off and changed the subject. "So, what's keeping you busy these days?"

"I'm back in the orchid business."

"Back?"

Even though no one new had arrived in the past fifteen minutes, Andrew compulsively glanced at the door before answering. "I thought I had the nursery sold a couple of years ago, but it didn't work out."

"Wholesale or retail?"

"Wholesale. Mainly to high-end retailers and florists. The shows are my bread and butter."

"Mary has an arrangement with a nursery in San Francisco. They take care of the plants when they aren't in bloom and bring them to her when they are."

"I thought about setting up part of my nursery for boarding plants but decided it was too labor intensive." Again, Andrew glanced at the door.

"Expecting someone?"

"Not expecting," Andrew admitted. "Hoping."

Roger tossed him a questioning look. "Anyone I know?"

Andrew hesitated. He could evade the question or lie, but what was the point? "Cheryl."

"I thought you two went your separate ways in college."

"I've grown older and wiser since then."

"In other words you finally realized what a jackass you were, and you're hoping it's not too late."

"That's one way to put it."

Roger slapped a hand on Andrew's shoulder. "It's the only way to put it where Cheryl is concerned."

Andrew had broken her heart. He'd known he would, but it hadn't stopped him. At the time he'd honestly believed his reasons for leaving outweighed the inner voice that compelled him to stay. For a while he'd even managed to convince himself he had done her a favor. The man she'd fallen in love with was whole and healthy, one who could fulfill her dreams of home and hearth and family. He stopped being that man his junior year. Selfishly saving himself the look of pity he was sure he would see in her eyes if he told her, he'd simply walked away with what now seemed a callous explanation.

The calculated selfishness of his leaving was what had kept him from coming back when he finally realized how big a mistake he'd made. Then he'd heard through a mutual friend that Cheryl had moved to Montana and married a state legislator with eyes on the governor's job. Over the years he'd found a way to let her go intellectually, but not emotionally.

"—don't know where I'd be without Mary," Roger said.

Realizing he'd missed most of what Roger had said, Andrew forcefully snapped himself out of his thick fog of memories. "My guess is that she's over there saying the same thing about you."

He shook his head. "A while back it hit me that, at best, love is lopsided. As long as a relationship is balanced out in other ways it—" He stopped, plainly embarrassed by what he was about to reveal. "Don't get me wrong, life's been good to me. I've got nothing to complain about." A good-old-boy mask slid into place. "How's your drink? Can I get you a refresher?"

"No thanks."

Roger held up his empty glass. "My first—not near enough to get through the rest of this evening. I'll catch up with you later."

Andrew watched Roger make his way to the bar, knowing it was the last time they would talk to each other that night. While Roger might not have come to the reunion to impress anyone, he hadn't come to embarrass himself with personal revelations either.

Sending one last look around the crowded room, Andrew absently noted how kind twenty years had been to some of his classmates and how cruel to others. With a mental shrug of acceptance, he acknowledged the depletion of his store of small talk, the lack of desire to search for more, the smile that had grown as uncomfortable as the overheated room, and the diminishing hope that had brought him there. While contemplating an unobtrusive escape through the exit next to the bathroom, he glanced up and saw Cheryl Cunningham standing at the registration desk talking to someone in an orange-and-pink polka-dot dress.

She stole his breath with the same gut-punch intensity she had that cold November morning when she'd first walked into his French class. He'd fallen in love with her that day—head over heels, illogical, down-to-his-toes love. He remembered that moment as clearly as he remembered the fog that had accompanied high tide that morning. The feeling was the first rock to tumble in an avalanche of emotion. Finally, he understood why he'd never been able to fill the emptiness with the freedom he'd sacrificed everything to attain. Only one person could cure the loneliness and ease the longing.

Still, one thing eluded him, one thing he would never understand. How had he left her? What words had he used to convince himself it was the right thing to do?

—WITH THE VETERAN EASE OF A POLITICIAN'S wife, Cheryl Cunningham glanced around the crowded ballroom, hiding her desire to escape the woman who had rushed up to greet her behind a practiced smile. She had no business being here, had even had sense enough to throw away the invitation when it arrived. But two days later a compelling blend of curiosity and desire and a sense of unfulfilled destiny overrode her normal good sense. She retrieved the invitation and sent in her check that same day, knowing that if she waited even a couple of hours, she would change her mind.

The check was the key. She lived too frugally to pay for the reunion and not attend. Or at least that was what she'd told herself, and any excuse that worked was a good one. She would rather spend a year on the campaign trail, a job she hated more than any she'd ever had, than have anyone discover the real reason she was there. She'd lived through humiliation: pity she couldn't handle.

"You haven't changed," the woman gushed. "Not one bit."

Cheryl struggled to connect a name with the face. Her family had moved to Santa Cruz her junior year, which left her little more than a year and a half to form these lifelong bonds with her graduating class. Twenty years was a long time to remember pass-in-the-hall friends.

"You haven't either," Cheryl ventured.

The woman laughed. "Tell that to my bathroom scale. But I'll bet you haven't gained a pound. How do you do it?" Before Cheryl could answer, the woman added, "Do you have kids?"

"No," Cheryl said without elaborating. Finally, she managed to catch the name tag on the woman's ample breast. Lynn Littrell Sawyer. It didn't help.

"I have five." She brought up her hand to display five fingers, hitting her other hand and sending a piece of ice sailing from her highball glass. "I did okay with the first three. But everything went to hell in a handbasket after the twins." She bent to retrieve the ice. "Max said he's going to trade me in for a couple of twenties when I turn forty if I don't do something to get the weight off. I told him there wasn't one woman—let alone two— who was going to have anything to do with him once she discovered he was paying alimony to me and child support to five kids." She grinned. "Shut him up real fast."

Lynn put her hand on Cheryl's arm. "So tell me about you. Still making those clay things?"

"I gave up sculpting when I got married." She glanced toward the bar and saw a man looking back. Not the right one. Why was she doing this to herself? What did she hope to gain?

"No time, I'll bet. I'm not surprised. A bunch of us girls got together a couple of months ago, kind of a prereunion thing, and Julie Thompson said you had to be the most famous person in our class. She said she saw a picture of you in *USA Today* at some party and that you were there with Tom Cruise."

Cheryl knew the photograph. It was five years old. "I wasn't actually with him, we—"

"What's he like? Is he as handsome in person as he is in the movies? I read somewhere that he's really short. Is that true?"

The moment captured by a photographer as she and Jerry entered an award ceremony at the Kennedy Performing Arts Center was as close as Cheryl had come to a conversation with Tom Cruise. But that wasn't what Lynn, or others who asked such questions, wanted to hear. "He's very nice," she said.

"Is your husband parking the car?"

"Jerry isn't with me," she said, resigned to what would follow.

"Oh." Lynn tried, but couldn't hide a look of disappointment. "When I saw you I was hoping he'd be here, too. It's not every day someone like me gets to meet someone like your husband." As if realizing how insensitive she sounded, Lynn quickly added, "Of course seeing you again is wonderful, too."

"Jerry and I are divorced. *USA Today* wrote about that, too. You must have missed it."

Lynn's jaw dropped. "You're kidding. When did that happen?"

"Two years ago."

She recovered enough to sputter, "How awful. Goodness, I'll bet you were devastated."

She had been, but not for the reason Lynn undoubtedly believed. The assumption was that no woman in her right mind would walk out on Jerry Walden, a man whose publicity photos made him out to be the Marlboro Man without the cigarette. Movie-star handsome, charismatic, powerful, rich, he looked as good in jeans as in a tuxedo, was adored by women over sixty, lusted after by their daughters and granddaughters, and drooled on and over by the stroller set.

But Jerry hadn't walked out on her; the decision to divorce was hers. The telling clue to his own apathy over the marriage was how quickly he agreed, not even ordering a poll to see how it would affect his career until she'd made an appointment with an attorney.

When they'd met, Jerry was on a calculated search for a young, vibrant woman he could marry who could help jump-start his stalled political career. She had to be someone who could pull in the male voters without seeming threatening to their wives. Without knowing she was being tested, Cheryl aced the exam, even winning the approval of the political consultants who hovered around Jerry like gulls around a shrimp boat. Caught up in the frenetic excitement of his campaign for reelection and the heady ego of not only being needed but told so nightly, she mistook passion for love and ignored the inner voice that warned about the long fall from such heady heights.

She'd anticipated an adjustment period after the divorce, a time to settle into the cocoon of solitude. It never came. Sadly, she realized she'd been alone the entire time she and Jerry had been together.

Lynn's eyes narrowed. "Oh, now I know why you came here tonight." She smiled like a *Jeopardy!* contestant who knew the final answer. "I told Margo I thought it was strange that you and Andrew were both coming to this reunion when neither of you have ever come before." She moved in closer. "Who told you he would be here?"

"No one," she answered truthfully, feeling a momentary sense of violation at having her motive so easily exposed.

"But you were hoping."

"Of course," she admitted. "Isn't that the reason we all come to these things? It's an opportunity to see old friends." She couldn't tell if her attempt at casualness had worked and wasn't sure if she cared. Did it really matter if a woman she hadn't seen in twenty years and would likely never see again knew she'd come to the reunion to find the man who'd broken her heart and never bothered to find out if she'd survived?

Lynn swung around to study the crowd. "I saw him by the pool talking to Joan earlier."

"Joan Beatty?"

"It's Joan Fisher now—or at least it was last week. She's either on her fourth or fifth husband. I lost track at three. Wait till you see her. She's every woman's nightmare—buns of steel with boobs to match. I hate her. I'm going to take charge of the invitations next reunion and make sure hers gets lost."

Cheryl laughed harder than the comment deserved. She needed a drink, something to hold in her hands beside her purse to keep them busy, something to put to her mouth to bridge awkward silences, something to bolster her flagging courage. "And she says such nice things about you."

"Yeah, I'll just bet she does."

Cheryl's gaze settled on a man standing at the bar with his back to her. He was the right height, weight, and hair color but was wearing a plaid jacket she knew Andrew would never wear. She should have questioned knowing this: seventeen years was a long time. People changed. Knowing Andrew as she had, having him so integrated into her mind and heart that thoughts of him still intruded into the most ordinary moments of her day-to-day life, was a burden she had come there to shed.

Slowly, she began to sense a change in the air around her. It was as if it had grown heavy, sending gentle, insistent ripples charged with electricity against her skin. Unbelievably, she was still in

tune to Andrew's presence, could still feel him before seeing him, was still drawn to him without a
word being spoken. The feeling was so compelling, so powerful, so deeply familiar that she
knew she'd been right about seeing him again. It
was the only way to find a way to forget him.

"I was afraid you weren't coming," Andrew
said softly.

In a room echoing with talking and laughter
and raised voices, Cheryl heard the whispered
words as if he had shouted them.

She turned.

He was no longer the boy she'd held frozen in
the recesses of her mind, but a man she had not
accurately imagined. His lean body and confident
posture, the premature wrinkles on his forehead
and at the corners of his eyes, the threads of gray
in jet-black hair were all expected. What she
hadn't foreseen, what nearly stole her composure,
was the pain and loneliness she saw in his eyes
and in the unguarded way he looked at her.

"I almost didn't," she said.

Moving to Cheryl's side to turn what had become a one-on-one into a triangle, Lynn said,
"Twenty years seems to be a magical number. The
reunion planner who helped us said we could expect a lot of people who'd never attended."

Andrew studied Lynn. "Lynn Littrell? Didn't
we have chemistry together?"

She nodded, a smile showing she was pleased
that he'd remembered.

"You married Max Sawyer."

"Eighteen years this October. And five kids," she added. "Have you seen him yet?"

"Only for a second. He was looking for you."

"Really?" She glanced around the room. "I wonder why." Obviously torn between going and staying, she said, "I guess I'd better find out what he wants."

When Lynn was gone, Cheryl said, "Max wasn't looking for her."

Andrew gave her a questioning look. "What makes you think he wasn't?"

"Because I know you." The simple truth was an acknowledgment that cut through the years. For a time after Andrew left her she'd managed to convince herself that love wasn't singular, that the belief two people were destined for each other and no one else was poetic fantasy.

When she married Jerry and still dreamed of Andrew, she'd dismissed those dreams with the reasoning that a first love was never forgotten. Then, after the divorce, when she was alone again and found herself looking for Andrew in every man she dated, she accepted that he would always be a part of her. Acceptance gave an illusion of peace. . . . until the invitation arrived. She knew then that she would never have any real peace until what had once been between her and Andrew was resolved.

"I heard you were divorced," he said.

"I heard you never married," she countered.

He looked at her, his gaze a connection. "A long time ago I made a mistake. I've had to live with the consequences."

"Am I supposed to know what that means?"

"Are you saying you don't?"

"How could I possibly know what consequences you've lived with?" She shifted her weight from one foot to the other. "But then, I didn't come here to listen to how hard your life has been."

"What did you come for?"

"An apology. Better yet, an explanation—one that I can believe this time."

"You deserve more than me telling you how sorry I am," he said with heart-stopping humility. "And I don't know how to explain something I no longer understand myself."

"Why did *you* come here tonight?" She fought to maintain her emotional footing, to remember the pain he'd so easily inflicted on her, to remind herself that if she let him, he would have the power to hurt her that way again.

"I wanted to see you."

"Just me?"

"Just you."

In the background she heard someone announce that dinner was being served. Panic set in at the thought of spending the next hour making small talk between bites of salad and prime rib. Cheryl glanced at the double doors leading to the dining room. "Do you want to stay?"

He shook his head. "Do you?"

"No."

"Let's get out of here."

"Where?"

"I don't care. Anywhere we can be alone to talk."

She didn't know anyplace. She'd only been back to Santa Cruz twice since her parents moved sixteen years ago. So much had changed since the earthquake, she hardly recognized what had once been favorite haunts. "The Last Wave?"

"Closed down a couple of years ago."

"Wilson's?"

"Never reopened after the earthquake."

"You choose."

"What about my place?"

"You live here?"

"Twenty minutes away."

Her immediate thought was to say no. But then she questioned her reasoning. Why not his place? "I'll follow you."

She turned toward the door. He put his hand in the small of her back. The casual, intimate gesture stole her breath. She stopped and stepped away from him.

"What's wrong?"

"I don't want you to get the wrong idea. I'm not going with you for anything but conversation."

"It's me, Cheryl," he said softly. "I know why you're going with me. And no matter how much I wish it were different, I know what to expect."

If so, he was a step ahead of her.

2

CHERYL LEANED AGAINST THE RAILING that surrounded the small, flagstone deck at the back of Andrew's house and tasted the Chardonnay he had poured for her. She stared at the ocean from the vantage point of being on top of a fifteen-foot cliff, took a deep breath, and let a sense of homecoming fill her mind. She knew this beach; it was one she and Andrew had come to when they wanted to escape the crowds at Santa Cruz. Every memory they'd created here was a good one. Nothing painful had happened that she could summon to use as a shield if she felt herself slipping too close to forgetting the years between then and now.

The beach beckoned. She could almost feel the warm grains of sand between her toes. She knew exactly how the water would feel as it hit her legs, how free she would feel if she dove into a wave and released herself to its power. From the day her father had moved the family from the mountains of Idaho to the beaches of Santa Cruz and she saw the ocean for the first time, she knew she'd found her spiritual home.

Andrew came to stand beside her. "I can see it still holds you the way it used to." He put his hand on the railing next to hers, close but not touching, and turned to face her.

She both loved and hated that he knew her so well. "How long have you lived here?" More than that, she wanted to know why he lived there. Why this house on this beach?

"Twelve years, off and on. When my grandfather died I wound up with a great deal of money that no one knew he had."

"Your grandfather was still alive all the time you were in foster care?"

"He and my mother were estranged. Or at least that's the way the lawyer put it. Seems he didn't know I existed until the detective I hired to find my mother showed up on his doorstep."

Andrew had refused even to consider the possibility of looking for his mother when Cheryl had suggested it. What could have happened to make him change his mind? "Did you find her?"

"There was nothing to find. She died of a drug overdose when I was two."

"What about your father?"

"He could have been any one of a dozen men she hung around with at the time, or a stranger passing through with drugs and willing to trade for sex."

She winced at the flat retelling of something that must have devastated him at the time. "I'm sorry."

"It wasn't what I'd hoped to find, but I've learned to live with it."

"Did you get a chance to know your grandfather?" She told herself that she was asking as an old friend, nothing more, that she was interested more out of politeness than caring.

Andrew let out a short, harsh laugh. "He didn't want anything to do with me. At least not while he was alive. I guess it satisfied some hidden sense of family to leave his money to me when he died. But then it was either me or the local men's club if I decided I didn't want it."

"Are you happy?" This came from curiosity and a raw need to believe he hadn't walked away unscathed.

"I have my moments." He turned to look at her. "What about you?"

"Most of the time." The truth would make her too vulnerable.

They slipped into an awkward silence. Cheryl turned her attention to a man racing a small boy across the sand. They were headed toward the stairs that led to the path beside Andrew's house. Laughing and out of breath when they reached the landing, they paused for one last look at the ocean.

"I don't wanna go yet," the boy said, tugging on the man's hand, trying to lead him back to the water.

"Mom's waiting for us."

"She won't care," the boy coaxed. "She likes us to have fun. She told me so."

"How's this for fun?" He reached down and lifted the boy, swinging him around and up to sit on his shoulders.

Not trusting herself to look at Andrew, Cheryl watched the man climb the stairs, the boy hanging on to his ears as he twisted to have one last look at the ocean. "I always imagined you with children," she said.

"And I thought for sure that you would have a houseful of your own by now. You and Jerry must have been happy in the beginning. Why didn't you—" He leaned forward, resting his elbows on the railing, staring at the palate of oranges, pinks, and reds coloring the horizon. "Forget that. What happened between you and Jerry is none of my business."

Jerry had told her up front that children were a part of the package. He insisted he wanted them even more than she did. Only later did she discover he wanted them for completely different reasons. Along with producing an heir, he saw the media attention and photo opportunities that having children would bring. She saw an end to her loneliness. As disheartened as she was when all their physical and medical efforts to conceive failed, she was glad the end of the marriage was uncomplicated and she could walk away without ties.

"I do have kids in a way," she said. "They don't go home with me, but I get to see them almost every day."

"You're a teacher?"

"A social worker with a private agency. We're funded by endowments and a trust."

The man stopped at the top of the stairs and turned to face the ocean. "Say good-bye," he told the boy.

"We'll be back," he said instead, leaning over and pressing his cheek to the side of the man's face.

"I know how he feels," Cheryl said, anger rising in her like bubbles in a pot of boiling water.

Andrew looked at her. "I'm sorry."

She avoided his gaze. "For what?"

"Everything."

"That covers a lot of territory." She wasn't going to make it easy for him. She'd waited too long for an apology, needing one even though it would change nothing. "Are you saying you're sorry I dropped out of school for two years before I went back to get my degree, that I married someone I didn't love because I wanted to prove to myself I'd gotten over you, or that I've wasted half my life wanting something I can't have. Just what is it you're sorry for, Andrew."

"That I was such a coward."

At last she looked at him. "Oh, is that what happened?"

"I'm not the man I was then."

"Too bad, I really liked that man. Actually, I loved him. With one small exception, of course."

The anger didn't bother him. The pain did. How easily he'd convinced himself the wounds he'd inflicted would heal and that she would be whole again and happy without him. "Do you ever wonder—"

She turned on him. "Don't you dare ask me that. What I wonder, what I think about, what I feel are none of your business anymore."

"Then I'll tell you how it is with me." He ached to touch her. Just holding her hand would be enough. It seemed impossible that he had once taken the hundreds of small, day-to-day moments they'd shared for granted.

"There isn't a day I don't think about you. There are times I'll see a woman walking alone on the beach and let myself believe it's you. Some days someone will knock on the door, and for the seconds it takes to answer I tell myself you're the one waiting for me."

"How long has this been going on?"

"I can't say. I'm not sure when it started."

"I know exactly how long it's been with me." She stared at the liquid in her glass, brought it to her lips, and finished the wine in two long swallows. "What happened that finally made you realize you'd made a mistake?"

"One day I took a hard look at myself and all the other men I knew chasing the endless summer and realized we'd bought into something that doesn't exist."

Her eyes flashed an antagonistic challenge. "I was hoping for something better."

"I had to grow up to understand what I had lost. By then it was too late."

"Lost? You didn't lose me, Andrew, you discarded me."

He flinched. None of the arguments he'd used to justify abandoning her made sense anymore. In hindsight he understood the fear that had consumed him the day he was told he had cancer. He remembered the growing, desperate need to grab hold of whatever time was left to him. Most of all he remembered the shame that came with the prospect of losing his manhood. Facing testicular cancer hit him harder than anything else ever had, stealing his youth and with it the belief that he was invincible.

He'd reacted the way he had reacted to every crisis he'd faced before he met Cheryl, pulling into himself and closing out those who would have helped him. He battled the cancer and chemotherapy and radiation alone, dropping out of college, coming up with excuses at the last minute not to meet Cheryl for holidays and birthdays, lying to her about difficult classes and intractable professors. He came through the experience so completely focused on himself all he could think about was his determination to savor every moment left to him, to experience everything life had to offer, to refuse ever again to settle, or compromise, or bargain.

Cheryl turned back to the man and boy and watched them until they went inside a house at the end of the block. "If you realized you'd made a mistake all those years ago, why did you wait until now to look for me?"

"You were married. Happily, I thought."

She nodded. "For a while we actually managed to convince ourselves that we were the perfect couple portrayed by the media." She paused as if struggling with what she would say next. "But a marriage gets a little crowded when another person becomes involved," she said finally.

"Jerry was unfaithful?"

She held up her empty glass as if to ward off the question. Andrew reached behind him for the bottle of wine. As he poured, he said, "I know you. There's no way you would ever—"

"You *knew* me, Andrew," she reminded him. "The breakup was my fault."

The revelation stunned him. "There was another man? What happened? Why aren't you with him now?"

She stood motionless, her gaze fixed on the horizon. "I am."

"I don't understand." And then it hit him. "Me? I'm the other man?"

Instead of answering, she took another long, deep swallow of wine.

Andrew reached for her glass. "Talk to me."

She pushed his hand away, looked at him, sighed, and then handed him the glass. "Liquid courage isn't all it's cracked up to be. It's never worked before, I don't know what made me think it would work now."

A childhood spent in foster homes where he'd been on display like merchandise for childless couples had taught him that dreams were for others, for those who had the right looks, the right smile, the right words. Those who were left behind, the kids like him, learned to play the cards that were dealt them.

Still, he couldn't stop the swell of hope that filled his chest. A lump in his throat, he took a chance. "I never stopped loving you," he admitted. "You have been the standard I used to judge every other woman I met."

Her smile was tinged in a bitter sadness. "I've dreamed of this moment. So many times I've lost count. It's always the same. You tell me you love me and take me in your arms and all the hurt and confusion simply disappear."

"It can be like that."

"No, it can't. It's not why I came, Andrew. I don't want to start over. I want to put you behind me. I want to forget I even knew you."

"I don't believe you."

"Don't you see? We can't go back. We can't even start over. You can't have a relationship without trust, Andrew. Or do you have a magic wand you can wave that will bring that back the way you think you can bring back everything else?"

He didn't have an answer, at least not one good enough. "What would it take for you to trust me again?"

She considered the question. "I'm not sure that's possible. Even if I were willing to take a chance."

"Time?" he prompted.

"I don't know."

"It's yours. As much as you want."

"What if it took years?"

"I'm not going anywhere."

"Seems to me I've heard that before."

He put his hands on her shoulders and brought her around to look at him. "I let you go once, there's no way I'm going to do it again. At least not without a fight."

She started to say something. He put his finger to her lips to stop her. "Do you still love me? Even a little?"

"It doesn't make sense for me to love you, and I don't do things that don't make sense anymore."

"I don't care whether it makes sense or not—do you love me?"

For long seconds she looked into his eyes, trying to decide whether it was the man she loved or the memory. "I'll give you this much—there's something unfinished between us."

He nodded. "That's enough—for now."

It wasn't enough for her. "So where do you see us going from here?"

"If it were truly up to me, I would have you move in with me tomorrow."

"Just like that?" she snapped. "What about my job? My friends? My life in Oakland?"

He gave her a slow grin. "Like I said, if it were *truly* up to me."

She was at a place she'd imagined, but never truly believed she would be. Andrew loved her and wanted her. Wasn't this the answer to her dreams? Or was it a reminder that she had to be careful what she wished for?

He could break her heart again as easily as he had broken it before. She wasn't the tower of strength, the battle-scarred worldly veteran she wanted to believe she was, that she wanted him to believe she was. "I don't know. . . ."

"Where we go from here is wherever we feel comfortable going." He stepped back and hunkered down to look her directly in the eyes. "Right now, a walk on the beach would be nice."

It was exactly what she needed—time. He knew her as well as he'd ever known her, and it scared her as much as it connected her to him.

"Of course, unless you have a suitcase in the car or are willing to wear something of mine, you probably don't agree."

She'd spent an entire week's salary on the midnight blue designer dress she was wearing. The narrow strapped high heels had set her back another two hundred. Sand would ruin one, salt water the other. "My suitcase is at the motel." He looked the same size he'd been in college, and his shirts had swallowed her then. "What did you have in mind to lend me?"

"Shorts and a T-shirt?" He looked at her waist. "And a pair of suspenders?"

ˣ—ALONE IN ANDREW'S BEDROOM, THE PROMised clothes on his bed, Cheryl questioned what she was doing. Doubts assailed her. She could feel her defenses slipping. How long would it take to recover if he walked out on her again? Would she ever recover? If not for her mother and father and their persistent efforts to get her on her feet again the first time, she wasn't sure where she would be now.

Andrew's power over her had been complete. She'd looked to him for her happiness, her dreams of the future, even her career, which she'd chosen to accommodate the children they would have one day.

She'd been so young and trusting and filled with conviction. Other couples might fight and break up and go their separate ways, but not her and Andrew. They were the perfect match. Everyone said so.

What was she doing? Was she out of her mind? She'd come to the reunion to put Andrew behind her, not start over again.

What made her think it would be any different this time? If she had any sense, she would thank him for the stroll down memory lane and get out of there as fast as she could.

Instead, she slipped out of her dress and into his clothes, tucking the T-shirt with San Jose Firefighter's Chili Cookoff emblazoned across the back into the khaki shorts and rolling up the sleeves. She shortened the bright red suspenders and snapped them onto the waistband of the shorts, then went out to meet Andrew on the deck.

Andrew looked up. He'd taken off his jacket and shoes and socks and rolled up his pant legs. "Ready?" He held out his hand. She hesitated just long enough to let him know she still wasn't sure about what they were doing. Andrew let the moment go, taking her hand as he would a friend's, leading her out the gate and down the stairs.

A full moon had followed the sun into the western sky, marking its position with a silver trail across the water. Along the shoreline, waves deposited shimmering arcs of bubbles that glistened with moonlight. A gentle breeze tugged at a strand of Cheryl's hair. She tucked it behind her ear.

They crossed the beach to the water in silence, the only sound the soft roar of the tumbling waves. Andrew stopped at the edge of the shore. Cheryl continued moving forward. She closed her eyes, listened to the wave break and roll into itself, and waited for the rush of water. When it hit, she put her head back and looked up to the stars. *I'm home*, she told herself.

The receding wave pulled the sand from beneath her feet. She dug in her toes to maintain her balance and laughed when she teetered to one side. Opening her eyes, she discovered Andrew beside her.

"I'd forgotten how much I love your laugh."

She put her hand in his again and started walking toward the south side of the mile-wide cove, where a rocky promontory isolated the area from the next beach. Only twenty-five private homes and the state of California shared this cove. With the state the primary landowner, the dense forest of pine and eucalyptus surrounding the houses had remained undeveloped. Only a small parking lot at the trail head that led to the beach intruded on the sense of isolation.

She and Andrew had come there when they wanted to be alone, their friends preferring Santa Cruz beach and the boardwalk, where the action was. This was where Andrew had told her he loved her the first time, where their teenage petting had moved to something more serious, and where he had asked her to marry him.

"Why did you buy a house here?" she asked.

"I would have thought you'd figured that out by now."

"Tell me anyway."

He stepped out of the path of a wave, pulling her with him. "In the beginning I told myself it was to be as near the water as I could. I wanted to be able to grab my board and be the first one to catch the big waves. It seemed the ultimate endless summer when I cared about such things. Turned out the big waves invariably hit when I was tied up at the nursery. And even when I wasn't, the thrill I thought would be there, wasn't."

"You could have been close to the water a hundred different places. Why here?"

"I didn't understand that myself until I became friends with the guy who was renting the house next door. Ken Huntington was a lot like you. He came here from the Midwest, took one look at the ocean, and never looked back."

"Ken Huntington . . . wasn't he the computer guy who died in a car wreck?"

"It wasn't a wreck, but it was on the freeway. Ken had a heart attack on his way to work. He made me realize it wasn't just the ocean that held me, it was this cove. I had my choice of beachfront property, some of it a lot nicer than what I wound up with and at the same price, but it had to be here."

"And how did he make you realize the reason you had to be here?"

He stopped to brush windswept hair back from his forehead. "He fell in love. Seeing him was like looking in a mirror at the man I once was."

She stared at him until the silence grew awkward. "Was there someone else, Andrew? You can tell me now. I'm stronger than I was then."

He'd started to say something when she added, "Don't tell me what you think I should hear. I deserve the truth."

"There was no one else, Cheryl."

"I could understand if there were. You were half a state away. You were bound to get lonely."

Even after all this time, the pain was still there. He could see it in her eyes. She wanted there to be another woman because it was something she could understand. "Would it be easier for you to forgive me if I told you that I left you for someone else?"

She folded her arms across her chest in a protective gesture. "Did you?"

"No."

"Then why? Make me understand. At least give me that much."

His reasons for not telling her now were as valid as they had been then. He didn't want her to feel sorry for him or make decisions based on what he'd gone through. "Something happened to me that I couldn't share with anyone, not even you. It changed me, Cheryl. Suddenly I was looking at the world through a narrow tunnel of time. I thought and acted in ways that seemed logical to

me then but now seem like irrational acts commit-
ted by someone scared out of his mind."

"Why were you scared?"

She was right. She deserved the truth. "I had
cancer."

"Cancer?" She frowned, her expression going
from confused to disbelieving. "How could that
happen without me knowing? I saw you every—"
She peered into his eyes, questioning, remembering. "That's why you didn't come home for
Christmas. And why you wouldn't let me go
down there for spring break." Still struggling to
understand, she added, "How could you have
had cancer? You were never sick. You never even
had a cold the whole time we were together."

"That's how I reacted, too. At least in the beginning."

Her confusion turned to anger. "You had no
right not to tell me."

He started to reach for her; she slapped his
hand away. "You *bastard*. How could you do that
to me? How could you let me believe there was
someone else? You had to have known that's what
I would think no matter what you said. All these
years I've doubted myself, believing I wasn't
good enough."

She was wrong. He hadn't known. "I'm so
sorry." The words sounded hollow. "If I had it to
do over . . ." What did it matter what he would do
differently now? "I made a mistake."

"A mistake?" she echoed. "A mistake is when

you show up for an appointment on the wrong day or when you put the wrong check in an envelope—not when you destroy the reason another person gets up in the morning."

"I thought I was doing you a favor. At the time it was something I believed with all my heart."

"How could you have had cancer? You were so young."

Finally, he understood. He'd had eighteen years to come to terms with what had happened to him, she'd had less than a minute. "Testicular cancer happens to young men."

She started to cry, angry, frightened, accusing tears. "Make me understand why you didn't tell me."

"I couldn't."

"But we told each other everything."

He led her to a log that had washed up on the beach during the last storm, brushed the sand from its smooth, gray surface, sat down, and brought her down next to him. She tried to pull her hand free, but he hung on. "The cancer was happening to *me*, Cheryl, not to us," he said as he gently wiped tears from her cheeks. "No matter how hard you tried, you couldn't have understood what I was going through, and I didn't want you to have to try. It was my problem." He looked down at their clasped hands, and then up to meet her eyes. "And to be honest, it was easier for me not to talk about it. Not even to you."

"I might not have understood exactly what you

were feeling, but I could have helped. How could you have excluded me? You didn't even give me a chance. You didn't give *us* a chance." She turned her face to the sea.

"As I started to say before, if I had it to do over again, I would do it differently."

"But you don't," she said with finality. "What might have been is gone."

Fear traveled his spine like a sharp-clawed cat. He'd barely found her. He couldn't lose her a second time. "The years we would have had together are gone, but there are a lot of years left."

"I have a good life, Andrew. I like my friends, my job, where I live. It took me a long time to get over you the first time. Why would I want to take a chance on being hurt again?"

He reached over and took one of the suspender straps between his thumb and forefinger and slowly moved from her shoulder to her waist, feeling her tense when the backs of his fingers lightly brushed her breast, hearing the quick intake of air. "Because you're not over me," he said. "Any more than I'm over you."

3

CHERYL ROLLED TO HER SIDE AND STARED at the narrow line of light coming through the drapes in her motel room. She'd planned to drive home this morning, taking the coast route and stopping in Half Moon Bay to have lunch with her cousin and do some shopping. That was before Andrew talked her into staying another day. She still wasn't sure staying was wise. Too much had happened. Too fast. She'd come for closure and had been broadsided by openings she hadn't dreamed existed.

She was scared. She'd expected to feel a mix of emotions if she saw him again, but had been unprepared for the raw power. Thank God for the fear. Without it she would have been in his arms and in his bed and ready to start over.

He was the man she remembered, the man she

had loved, the man she would have followed to the ends of the earth. Being with him again was as easy as if they'd been together the day before.

Nothing real was that easy.

If only he'd told her about the cancer. How different their lives would have been. Even if, in the end, he'd still chosen to leave, she would have understood and could have gone on with her life.

Or so she wanted to believe in hindsight. But could she have gone on as easily as she imagined? No matter how they parted, she would still have loved him, would still have dreamed about him, would still ache for what might have been. Her heart would always be heavy with thoughts of their lost years. Nothing could change it or make it go away.

She glanced at the clock. Ten after six. She was to meet Andrew back at his house at nine for breakfast. Over two and a half hours. Too much time to think.

She got out of bed and headed for the shower.

An hour later she was standing on his front step, her hand raised to knock, when he came up behind her wearing jogging shorts and shoes and nothing else. Her heart skipped a beat and then raced as a wave of pure, naked lust washed over her.

"So you couldn't sleep either," he said.

There was no use denying the obvious. "I was hoping you'd be up. We need to talk."

He reached around her to open the door. "Hungry?"

She caught a hint of shampoo and aftershave and something spicy and masculine mixed with the saltiness of sweat. She flashed back to the illicit mornings they had spent together when she'd sneaked off to spend a weekend with him in San Diego, telling her parents she was off with a girlfriend. They'd pooled their money for a motel room and had stayed up all night then, too, only together. They'd made love and talked and made love again until hunger drove them from their cocoon.

To save money to see each other, they limited their phone calls to twice a week, late Wednesday evening, after the rate change, and Sunday mornings. In between they wrote letters, his long and poetic, hers filled with details of her day. Later, compulsively, she had read and reread what he had written, looking for clues to help her understand why he left. Her darkest moment came the night she burned the letters, one by one, in the backyard at her parents' home.

Two days later she was in the hospital with pneumonia. While there she realized she needed to either start going through the motions of living again or curl up and die. The next month she started school, graduating with honors two years later.

"All right, so you're not hungry," he said, when she didn't answer. "How about some coffee?"

She looked up into his gaze. "I don't know if I

can ever forgive you for not telling me the truth about your cancer."

The light left his eyes. "Is that what you came to tell me?"

"One of the things."

"Can we go inside and talk about this?"

"Yes," she conceded.

"Can I get cleaned up first?"

The question brought a smile that surprised them both. "Actually, I would prefer it."

"Sorry. I smelled a lot better an hour ago." He backed away, indicating she should go first. "I thought maybe you were having trouble sleeping, too—actually, I hoped you were—and figured you might show up early so I got up and did the spit-and-polish thing. And then when you didn't come I went jogging. It was either that or pace a path in the carpet."

It was the "too" that reached her. "I was awake; I just didn't think you would be."

"Come on, Cheryl. You know better than that."

"All right, maybe I just didn't want to admit that I couldn't sleep."

"Give me five minutes."

"Take as long as you want. I'll make coffee." She shouldn't have volunteered. Making coffee was too familiar, too domestic.

He disappeared down the hallway. A minute later she heard running water and the click of a shower door. Slipping her purse strap from her shoulder, she dropped the bag on a table beside the sofa and looked around, something she hadn't done the night before. As always, Andrew chose comfort over style. The eclectic furniture ranged from a futon that was a step past its prime to a magnificent, custom-made bookcase that ran the length of one wall. Two Mission-style chairs faced a stone fireplace; the table in between held a fanned stack of orchid journals. Specimen seashells lined the mantel, each an exquisite piece of nature's art. The paintings were watercolors of local scenes, beautiful in their simplicity and execution, the artist, Peter Wylie, one of the most sought after painters of the decade. She was impressed, not because of the small fortune Andrew had hanging on his walls, but because he had settled enough to actually collect something of value.

She realized with a sinking feeling that instead of freeing her mind of him she was filling it with new, fiercely compelling images.

She went into the kitchen and spotted the coffeemaker on the counter beside the sink. She found the coffee in the refrigerator, and with her stomach reminding her that she'd not only skipped dinner the night before, but lunch, too, she tucked a carton of eggs under her arm and dug around for something to add to an omelet.

If making coffee was too domestic, cooking was over the top. He'd invited her to breakfast. Would he get the wrong impression if she—

What was the matter with her? Did it matter what

impression she gave him? Wasn't it time they moved past playing games and were honest with each other?

⌐NOT CARING THAT SHE WOULD KNOW HE didn't want to waste a minute of their time together, Andrew skipped drying his hair and applying cologne, even skipped putting on shoes and socks. He did grab a comb to run through his hair as he walked down the hall, tossing the comb on the futon before entering the kitchen.

In a glance he took in the eggs in the bowl, the green onions on the cutting board, and the cheese beside the grater. He was about to protest that he'd invited her to eat breakfast, not to cook it, but couldn't get the words out. Seeing her working in his kitchen as if she belonged there, as if she wanted to be there, left him speechless with hope.

Without turning, she asked, "Who lives in the house across the path?"

Andrew's kitchen had large picture windows on two sides, one facing the ocean, the other the Chapman house. He moved to stand beside her and picked up the cheese. "No one right now. The friend I told you about who died a couple of years ago used to live there. His widow married another friend of mine, and they lived there until his ex-wife moved to Virginia. He and Julia followed to be close to his kids."

"So the house just sits empty now?"

"They get here as often as they can in the winter, but with a baby on the way and Eric's writing career taking off, they're never here in the summer. Instead of selling, they've decided to try renting it out again, a month at a time. If that works, they'll keep it, if it doesn't, they'll put the house on the market this fall."

"You said 'again.' If they've done it before, why would they think it wouldn't work this time?"

"The couple who owned the house before Ken were the ones who did the renting. The people they rented to came back every summer for over ten years. They were more like extended family who loved and cared for the place as if it was their own."

"And none of them want to come back?"

Andrew took a plate from the cupboard to catch the cheese as he grated it. "That last summer turned out to be pivotal for all of them. Their lives changed dramatically. One actually became a movie star."

"Anyone I would know?"

"Chris Sadler."

Her eyes widened in surprise. "You're kidding. The girls I work with at the clinic would go crazy if they knew I was even this close to a house Chris Sadler had lived in."

"He's a terrific kid. Or at least he was when I knew him. I can't imagine he's changed."

She finished cutting the onions and scooped

them into a bowl. "How long have you known him?"

"As long as I've lived here."

"There's so much I don't know about you. It seems so strange that I came here thinking I knew everything."

"Whatever you want to know, just ask." Anything to close the gap, to fill in missing pieces.

"Seventeen years . . ." She gave him a lost look. "I don't know where to begin."

"I told you about finding my grandfather." What he hadn't told her was that after six months of cancer treatment, the less-than-wonderful meeting had nearly delivered an emotional knock-out punch. Knowing better, he'd gone in with high hopes that someone had been looking for him, too, that someone, somewhere cared.

"When that didn't work out, I took off and hitchhiked across country, and ended up in Virginia Beach. I figured one ocean was as good as another and tried to settle in, but it didn't work. A year later I was on the road again, headed home.

She started to say something. He waited, finally prompting, "What?"

"Nothing."

"Tell me."

She opened drawers until she found a whip to beat the eggs.

"Cheryl?" He put his hand over hers.

Without looking at him, she asked, "Did you miss me? Did you ever think about me?"

He didn't know the words to tell her how hard it had been to wake up to a sunrise and know she would never share another morning with him or how many times he'd composed a conversation telling her about something new he'd seen or experienced that day. Would she care how many letters he'd written and destroyed? Or how, slowly, he came to recognize that she was more than a habit he could get over, she was an integral part of him, the best part.

"Always," he told her. "Every moment of every day."

"Just not enough."

"At the time I believed I loved you more than any man had ever loved a woman. My inflated sense of nobility kept me away, but not so far I didn't secretly hope we would run into each other if I came back."

"No one told you I moved?"

"I couldn't ask about you and still maintain the self-sacrificing fantasy that I'd left for noble motives. I know how hard this is to understand all these years later, but I believed it was only a matter of time and the cancer would be back. I didn't want to put you through that. Even if I'd somehow managed to beat the disease, I was only half a man. I could never give you the children you wanted."

She let out a harsh laugh. "*I* can't give me the

children I wanted. Turns out I'm only half a woman, and I don't have cancer as an excuse. I was just made that way."

Andrew did something he'd sworn he would not do. He reached for her and brought her into his arms. "I'm sorry," he whispered into her hair.

She held herself stiffly, resisting the comfort he wanted to give. And then, with a soft moan of letting go, she wrapped her arms around his waist. "I promised myself I wouldn't let this happen."

"Me too."

"It doesn't mean anything."

He closed his eyes and nestled his chin against the top of her head. "Nothing."

"I'll give you this much—even though I shouldn't. I've never felt as if I really fit in anyone else's arms."

A fire raced through his midsection, settling in his loins. It was everything he could do to resist a sudden, nearly overwhelming urge to taste the lips he remembered as if he'd kissed them the day before. Only knowing he was embarking on the most important journey of his life kept him from giving in to that urge. It wasn't momentary satisfaction he was after, it was a lifetime.

"Welcome home," he said tenderly.

With more effort than he would have thought possible, Andrew released her. Then, needing something to do, he took out a pan, put it on the stove, turned on the fire, and added a pat of butter.

Cheryl stood back and watched him. For the

first time she allowed a glimmer of hope to take root in her heart. She'd seen the hunger in his eyes and felt a reciprocal hunger in herself. She knew she wouldn't have, that she *couldn't* have, resisted him, but she also knew that later, when she was alone, she would have questioned whether they were building something real or if they'd simply been caught up in physical longing.

His back to her, his hands planted on the counter, staring out the window, he said, "I want you to know that letting you go just now was one of the hardest things I've ever done. I meant it when I told you I was playing for keeps this time." He turned. "We have a lot of years ahead of us—and a lot of years to make up."

"How do we do that, Andrew? How can we possibly make up for seventeen lost years?" She feared if they tried to go back, they would end up mired in what might have been. "Wouldn't it be better if we just concentrated on the here and now and see where it leads us?"

"Do you really think you could fall in love with me again without dealing with the past?"

Falling in love with him again was a moot point. She'd never stopped loving him. Unexpectedly, tears welled in her eyes. "If only you'd told me."

The butter crackled in the heated pan and started smoking. Andrew reached to turn off the burner.

"No, don't," Cheryl said. "We'll save it for later.

I'm not ready to go over it again now anyway."
She was mentally exhausted and needed a break.

"You're sure?"

She nodded. "Want me to do that?"

He smiled, plainly trying to make the transition
easier. "I know you'll find this hard to believe, but
I've become a pretty good cook."

She wiped her eyes and summoned a smile.
"You're right, I do find it hard to believe. So, just
this once, why don't you indulge me and let me
make the omelet?" More than issuing a challenge,
she wanted something to do.

He yielded the skillet. "You do realize you've
put me in an untenable position. Now I actually
have to prove to you that I can cook."

She eased the eggs into the pan. "You make me
sound so . . . I don't know . . . insensitive."

"I was thinking more along the lines of
'clever.' "

She laughed. He was wrong, of course, but she
basked in the gentle teasing. She tilted the pan to
let the eggs cook evenly. *Andrew was right—she
was home.* She just wasn't ready to admit it yet.

⌒AFTER BREAKFAST THEY DID THE DISHES TO-
gether, then went down to the beach. Through
the morning fog they could see groups of brown
pelicans, mostly made up of five or six but some
with as many as a dozen, skim the waves, heading

north for a day of foraging. Sanderlings raced across the sand ahead of incoming waves, then dashed back again as the water retreated, stopping to search for the tiny mollusks and crustaceans the water left behind. Conserving their energy, gulls patiently waited in the dry sand for the waves to bring something more substantial.

When the fog cleared, the beach would fill with Sunday visitors, but for the moment Cheryl and Andrew had only a few intrepid fishermen for company. Without giving details, Cheryl had canceled lunch with her cousin, promising they would get together soon. Cheryl sidestepped her cousin's questions, unwilling to listen to the lecture about getting involved with Andrew that her cousin would relish giving.

Having him in her life again would not be easy. The friends and family who'd seen her through the rough years were not people who forgave or forgot easily.

"You're drifting." Andrew stepped in front of her and walked backwards. "I can see it in your eyes."

"I was thinking about my family and what they will say when they find out that I'm seeing you again."

"Are you?"

She stopped. "What?"

"Seeing me again?"

"Is that a trick question?"

"No, just one we need to talk about. Among others."

She folded her arms across her chest, stopped, and dug her toes in the sand. "Like where do we go from here?"

"I ask you out on a date, and you say yes."

"What kind of date?"

He shrugged. "Dinner? Movie?"

"Don't you think we're a little past that?"

He cupped her face with his hands and looked deeply into her eyes. "I'm not sure what you have in mind, but I think we should get something clear right from the start. I'm not one of those guys you pick up in a bar and have your way with—at least not on the first date. You're going to have to spend some time getting to know me before you get me to agree to anything more than a good night kiss."

Her heart skipped a beat. Here was the man, the boy, she'd known, the one who could touch her heart and make her laugh and convince her she was safe in his arms. But here, too, was the man who had left her. How could she trust them both?

Instead of responding to his teasing, she said, "Tell me something about you that I don't know."

The question threw him. He thought for several seconds. "I sailed around the world a couple of years ago."

"By yourself?"

He nodded.

"Couldn't you find anyone to go with you?"

"I wasn't looking for company."

"What were you looking for?"

He took time to gather his thoughts before answering. "I never did decide. It took hindsight to figure out that selling my business and leaving had nothing to do with knowing I was about to turn thirty-five. It was something I did out of a gut reaction to Ken dying so young. His death destroyed the shield I'd managed to build around myself—the belief that all the years of being cancer-free actually meant something."

This was not what she wanted to hear, certainly not something to shore up the fragile sense of confidence she had started to feel that they might be able to make it this time. "If thirty-five did that to you, what are you going to do when you turn forty?"

"Have a small, private party on the boat with just the two of us toasting our future." He grinned. "Now for presents, I see one about five feet six inches tall wrapped in Saran Wrap with a red bow placed—"

She wasn't going to let him off that easily. "How long did it take you to sail around the world?"

The grin faded. "Sixteen months. But that's not what you really want to know, is it?"

She shook her head, unable to find the words to express what she was thinking.

"You want to know if you can believe me when I tell you it will never happen again."

"I just keep thinking actions speak louder than words."

"I celebrated my birthday with a group of strangers in a bar in Darwin, Australia, silently toasting my freedom while they toasted the things that held them down. I was convinced I felt sorry for them. Then for some reason I stuck around until closing and watched the couples peel off to go home. They walked away hand in hand, and I was left to walk away alone. I've never been as lonely as I was at that moment, nor been more aware of what I lost in you. I guess you could say it was one of those life-altering moments."

Seeking to ground herself in the ordinary, she glanced down the beach and focused on a fisherman packing his gear. "What did you do then?"

"I finished the trip thinking I could fill the emptiness with new places and people. It took several thousand miles before I was ready to admit there was only one person who could make me feel whole again."

"All that time alone," she mused. "I could never do it."

"I had a dog, a stray I picked up in Darwin the morning I left. Because I didn't want to burden him with anything as prosaic as a name, he became Dog. It was amazing how well we fit together. I started wondering if there wasn't something to this reincarnation business and Ken had come back to keep me company." He stopped and took a deep breath. "I had no idea how much he'd come to mean to me until the day after I passed through the Panama Canal and woke up the next morning and he wasn't there. I spent a week looking for him, long past any reasonable expectation that he could still be alive. When I got home, I put ads in all the Central American newspapers and even a couple of sailing magazines offering a reward in case someone had come across him and picked him up."

She could hear the grief in his voice and see it in the way he held himself. "You used to say you never wanted a dog."

"Yeah, I remember."

"But you would never say why."

"It's easier not to want something you can't have. No foster family was going to take in a kid *and* a dog."

How could she have known him so well and not known this? "What kind of dog was he?"

"Black. About two feet tall at the shoulder. Long, silky hair. He had a funny way of tilting his head to the side when I said something to him, almost as if he really understood me."

Slowly, but with inexorable force, Cheryl began to understand she wasn't the only one taking a chance on being hurt again. Andrew might have been the one who walked away, but he hadn't left unscathed. She looked at him long and hard. "I really do want this to work," she finally told him. "But you're going to have to give me some time."

Andrew nodded. "I can do that."

If he put his mind to it, he might even manage to wait a day or two before he called her.

June

1

"IF THIS THING FALLS, IT COULD DECAPITATE me," Donna Anderson grumbled.

Kelly Anderson felt her locked hands slipping as she strained to hold her sister's 120 pounds three feet off the ground. Donna had been at the double-hung window a good three minutes, long enough to have climbed through and back out again. "If you don't get a move on, *I'm* going to decapitate you."

"Hey, it's not my fault we're locked out." Obviously deciding she'd studied the situation long enough, Donna finally stuck her arms through the oversize window and hiked herself higher. "Push," she commanded.

Kelly did and immediately felt resistance. "Now what?"

"I've changed my mind," Donna said. "Let me down."

"What? You can't be serious."

She wiggled back out the window. "I said, let me down."

Kelly let go and Donna slid to the ground. "But you were almost inside," Kelly protested.

"Yeah, and it just occurred to me that we could be arrested for what we're doing. What if someone is watching us? What if they call the police? What if Walter found out?" She shuddered. "I'd lose my promotion. Never mind that, I'd lose my job."

"Donna," Kelly said through clenched teeth, her patience strained to breaking. "If you recall, we decided to go in through the window because it's after midnight and everyone around here is asleep."

"Just because their lights are out doesn't mean they're sleeping."

She let out an exaggerated sigh of frustration. "All right, if you're going to be such a weenie about it, I'll go in." She moved Donna out of the way. "Give me a boost."

She took a step back. "If I do, they could still get me as an accessory."

"To *what*?"

"Breaking and entering."

Donna had graduated at the top of her class at the University of the Pacific, was considered a brilliant analyst at her brokerage firm, and was being groomed to sit on the board of directors before she was forty. She made more money than both of her other sisters combined, and had the basic common sense of a gnat—which made it easy to say what came next. "There is no such thing as breaking and entering."

"Since when?"

"Since forever. If you're going to read mysteries, would you please read the ones written by people who know what they're talking about?"

"Well, I might not have the name right, but that doesn't mean we can't be arrested for what we're doing."

Kelly backed into a bush. A pointed branch jabbed her hard in the thigh. She grimaced. "Think about it, Donna. We couldn't even be taken in for trespassing." She felt for blood and stuck her hand in a tangle of spiderwebs. Shuddering, she tried to fling the sticky mass off before wiping her hand on her shorts. "We have a legal right to be here. Now, if you can manage to keep yourself from snatching a towel rack and breaking the window as you toss it outside, we'll be okay."

"What has a towel rack got to do with anything?"

"That would be vandalism, which is a crime."

Donna considered Kelly's statement. "If you're lying to me about the breaking and entering part, I swear I'll—"

Before she could finish, Kelly slapped her hand over her sister's mouth. She'd spotted the dark figure of a man at the corner of the house. The moon at his back, a flashlight in his hand, he loomed large and menacing.

"What's going on here?" he demanded, his voice as menacing as his appearance.

Unaware they'd been discovered, Donna jumped at the sudden sound of the man's voice and let out a scream that shattered the quiet night like a piece of crystal hitting a tile floor.

Kelly shoved an elbow into Donna's ribs. "Get a grip," she hissed. To the man, with as much authority as she could summon, she said, "Who are you? And what are you doing here?"

"Oh, good one, Kelly," Donna said.

"You first," he countered.

"Kelly Anderson."

"And?"

"And what?"

"What are you doing here?"

"I live here. Or at least I will be for the next month, providing I can ever get inside, that is. I'm the June renter."

He moved the flashlight, studying Kelly and then Donna and finally shining the beam against the house to provide reflected light. "You weren't due until tomorrow. And I was told you'd be alone."

"I decided to come a day early. And my sister—" Wait a minute. Why was she telling him this when he still hadn't told her who he was? "It's your turn. Who are you?"

"Sorry." He came forward, his hand extended. "I'm Andrew Wells. I live next door."

Kelly recognized the name from the list of instructions she'd received with the rental agreement. Relieved, she shook his outstretched hand. While she'd told Donna the truth about not committing a crime, she'd left out the part about the possibility of having to prove their innocence from a jail cell. "Boy am I glad to see you. I forgot the key the rental agent sent when I told her I'd be coming in late." She knew exactly where the key was—tucked in the side pocket of the purse she'd decided to change at the last minute.

Andrew took a step back to give her room to extricate herself from the bush she'd trampled.

"I remembered her telling me that you had an extra key if I couldn't reach her," Kelly said. "But your lights were out and I didn't want to disturb you so we decided to try the window and, well, you know the rest."

Donna wiped her hands on her navy blue slacks and stepped in front of Kelly. "Hi," she said, her voice just short of a purr. "I'm Kelly's sister, Donna."

"Pleased to meet you, Donna." Andrew gave her a quick smile. "I'll get the key and meet you out front."

Gingerly making their way through thick plantings while trying not to do any more damage than they already had, they barely beat Andrew to the driveway. He opened the door and stuck around to help them inside with their luggage. As he turned to leave, Donna invited him to stay for a drink. He declined, telling her he had an early-morning appointment and agreed to make it another time. She saw him to the door, leaned against it when it was closed, and grinned at Kelly.

"He's *gorgeous*. Those eyes, that smile—that *ass*. Oh, little sister, if you don't have the best four weeks of your life, you're no sister of mine."

Kelly picked up her suitcases. "No man who looks like that is unattached. His kind have women on waiting lists." She headed down the hall. "Besides, if you remember, I'm not exactly free myself." Donna didn't believe in long-term relationships and didn't think Kelly should either.

Kelly checked out the three bedrooms and settled for the one with the queen bed that faced the ocean. Donna took the one with the connecting bathroom, unpacked the essentials she would need for the two days she would be there, and joined Kelly to help her unpack.

She picked up the conversation where they'd left off, not missing a beat or giving an inch. "You're on vacation for crying out loud. Live a little. If you think Ray is going to stay home and watch The Learning Channel while you're gone, you're nuts."

"He's so tied up with that tax case he has going to trial next month he hardly makes time to eat. If I didn't occasionally take dinner to him at the office, we'd never see each other." Not the complete truth, but close enough. There was always time for baseball. San Diego Padre season tickets were a company perk, and Ray insisted that attending the games was a part of his job.

"And who does he have lined up to do that little chore for him while you're gone?"

"Cut it out, Donna." She was more annoyed than angry. Donna subscribed to the belief that monogamy had been devised by men to hide their inadequacies. She also believed the only true way to determine the worthiness of the product inside a tight pair of jeans was to sample the package. And sample she did. But with rigid guidelines— never with a coworker, never with someone who was dating a friend, and never anyone who was married or newly separated.

"This place is a lot nicer than I expected." Donna opened a drawer and lined up a rainbow of Kelly's cotton tees and matching shorts. "Especially considering it's a rental. How did you find it?"

"Dad knew someone."

"Dad *always* knows someone. Last month we were at a party at the club and I foolishly mentioned that I was thinking about putting crown molding in my dining room. The next morning a contractor called with a bid."

"There is no such thing as a casual conversation where Dad is concerned. He does the same thing to me if I don't watch what I say around him. And I'll bet if you asked Alexis, he does it to her, too."

"It must be the lawyer in him."

"I'm a lawyer." But not the lawyer her father was. Harold Anderson never equivocated. He understood himself and his goals and beliefs with a single-mindedness that was breathtaking in its intensity. No matter how Kelly tried to emulate him, she fell short. Even this trip, a job most would consider a no-brainer, had her questioning herself, doubting her goals, and concerned about her real beliefs.

Donna feigned a surprised look. "So you are. Somehow I keep forgetting. Maybe it's because I can still vividly remember changing your diaper and it's hard for me to imagine that you've gone from that to—" Her gaze swept her sister. "This."

Kelly knew how disheveled she looked dressed in a pair of shorts she'd had since high school and a San Diego Padres T-shirt she'd retrieved from a box Ray had packed to go to Goodwill. She'd opted for comfort over style for the seven-hour drive from San Diego. "Ray doesn't seem to mind."

"Oh? And on what do you base that bit of wisdom?"

She smiled. "Some things you're just going to have to take on faith."

Donna laughed. "It's nice to know he has that much going for him."

Kelly glanced at her watch. It was almost one. She should have felt exhausted but was wide-awake. "I could use that drink now."

"What drink?"

"The one you offered Andrew."

"Oh my poor little naive—"

"Do you have something to drink or don't you?" she asked, cutting Donna off.

"It was a setup. I knew he would say no. I also knew he would say yes if I offered to make it another time. Now all you have to do is name the time and place and you've got your first date with the handsome man next door."

Kelly was impressed. "I have to hand it to you. You're good."

"The best."

"No, if you were the best, you would have had a bottle of something tucked away—just in case Andrew said yes."

"Oh my poor little naive—"

Laughing despite herself, Kelly threw a pair of socks at Donna. "I don't want to hear it."

⟋⟍AT DONNA'S INSISTENCE, SHE AND KELLY were on the beach by nine-thirty. With their chairs set in the path of the stairs, the two sisters slathered sunscreen on their bodies and toasted their weekend with tall, plastic glasses filled with Donna's special Bloody Mary recipe. Donna's flesh-colored one-piece suit suggestively showcased her athletic body while Kelly's practical Speedo simply made her look athletic.

"Wait," Donna commanded when Kelly started

to take a drink. "I almost forgot." She dug in her canvas bag and withdrew two limp celery stalks, plunking one in Kelly's drink and the other in her own. "Now, it even looks right."

Kelly fingered her celery suspiciously. "I'm not going to ask where this came from, I just want to know how long it's been in your bag."

"Some questions are better left unanswered."

Kelly wished Donna had stopped at a grocery store instead of a liquor store when she went to pick up the key from the rental agent that morning, but as Donna had pointed out when she dragged Kelly from the house, they could do mundane chores anytime. The morning was too beautiful, the beach too serene, the company too special to be put off to another time.

Donna took a long swallow, smiled, sat back, and closed her eyes. "This is going to be a terrific weekend. I can feel it down to my toes. I'm really glad you talked me into coming with you."

"Hold that thought." Kelly made a show of digging through her bag. "I want to get that in writing."

"Save it for Alexis. She's the one who never goes anywhere. I think someone told her F & L Construction would fall apart if she weren't there, and she believed them."

At thirty-two, Alexis was the oldest of Harold's three daughters and the most ambitious. She'd acquired her job with the third largest new home construction company in California through connections and was constantly trying to prove herself in the male-dominated business. "Do you think she's going to get the vice president's job?"

Donna took another sip. "Sure I do—when she grows a penis or hell freezes over. Doesn't matter which comes first."

"I wish we could have talked her into coming," Kelly said. "It feels like years since the three of us did something fun together."

"Four to be precise."

"Has it really been that long? That's awful."

"If it weren't for Dad's birthday and holidays, I don't think we'd ever see her."

"Nobody should work that hard."

"Oh, you're one to talk. When was the last time you took a vacation."

The longest she'd been away from the office was four days, and she'd started feeling anxious by the third. The thought of being away an entire month actually made her hyperventilate. Only her father's flat insistence that she go had managed to get her out the door. What scared her the most, what she could admit to no one, was the fear she might discover she could have a life away from the pressure-cooker world she'd convinced herself she couldn't do without. "What do you call this?"

"Work—with a couple of free days thrown in."

Kelly settled in her chair before taking a sip of her drink. When she did, she reared back and choked. "What did you put in this thing?"

"A little of this and a little of that. Good, huh?"

"Maybe—to an alcoholic."

"It'll grow on you. I promise."

Kelly used the glass to make an indentation in the sand, propped it up, and left it there. After several seconds, hunger won out, and she reached for the celery. As much to try to convince Donna as herself, Kelly said, "I'm beginning to think taking a little time away from the firm wasn't such a bad idea after all."

"I wouldn't tell Dad if I were you." Donna studied the people on the beach as if she were looking for someone special.

"Why?"

"Wasn't this his idea?"

She thought about the question before answering. "I see what you mean."

"Give him a little encouragement and he'll be trying to run your life full-time." Donna reached for her hat and adjusted it to keep the sun off her face. She'd be thirty in a couple of months and had started paying attention to such things.

"He's getting better."

"I still think you were an idiot for joining Dad's firm when you had all those other offers."

"You wouldn't say that if you could have seen how excited he was when I told him I was going to turn them down."

"Actually, I shouldn't complain. Having you at the office with him all the time has taken a lot of the pressure off me and Alexis. He's down to only calling twice a day now."

Kelly laughed. "He doesn't do that."

"Oh, yes he does."

She gave her sister a mischievous look. "Well, he always did love you the best."

Suddenly serious, Donna said, "You know the whole time we were growing up I never sensed he favored one of us over the other. Think how hard that must have been."

"Especially when you were in high school and thought Brian McMurphy was the love of your life." Kelly's attention was drawn to an old man slowly coming toward them. Keeping to the hard sand near the water's edge where the walking was easier, he paused every few steps to study the treasures brought in with the waves. The way he walked with his hands in his pockets reminded her of her grandfather. She watched him for several more seconds before picking up their conversation again.

"I hope I'm half as good a parent as Dad has been," she said.

Donna shuddered. "Let's not go there, okay?"

"Why not? You'd make a terrific mother."

"I would make a terrible mother, and we both know it." Turning, she sheltered her eyes from the sun with her hand and studied the people behind them.

They'd been down this road before, and Kelly

was as confused by it now as she always was. Instead of pushing for an explanation, she picked up the book she'd brought with her and did what she always did with a new book, looked at the dedication, the copyright date, the reviews, and the acknowledgments—everything, including advertisements if there were any, before she turned to the main text.

Minutes later Donna came on point. "Hello . . . what do we have here?"

Kelly glanced up. "Where?"

She pointed. "That guy out there on the surfboard."

Kelly squinted, trying to see what Donna was seeing. At a hundred yards away, all she could make out was someone wearing a wet suit, sitting on a board, waiting for a wave. "How do you even know it's a guy?"

"Trust me."

Kelly went back to her book. She wanted background on Matt Landry before she started his class on Wednesday, and reading his book seemed a logical way to get it. She agreed with her father's philosophy—know thine enemy—and for any law firm that represented aggressively expanding businesses, Landry was considered the enemy.

Although there were more than a dozen marine biologists and environmental radicals in the San Diego area she could have approached for the same information, none of them testified in court as frequently or as successfully as Landry. The class was a unique chance for her to judge his effectiveness and look for signs of weakness. According to the background information her father had included in the file he'd had his assistant prepare on Landry, he was a frequent guest lecturer, but he rarely taught classes anymore. This one at the University of California Santa Cruz lasted four weeks. Then he was off to Brazil for a symposium on global warming.

It was an opportunity her father had insisted she take—for the sake of the firm. Those magic words never failed to bring her around.

If accolades mattered, there were enough in the first six pages of Landry's book to impress anyone, even her. Of course she only recognized a couple of the names connected to the effusive praise. She was still too new to the field to know who counted and who didn't, but the titles looked impressive.

Although she wasn't going into the project kicking and screaming, if given a choice, environmental law wouldn't have been on the top of her list. At least not from the position the firm's clients would assume. Too often she found herself leaning in the wrong direction, and she still found it difficult to argue for something or someone she didn't believe in, a flaw she hoped time and experience would overcome.

Despite her doubts, the opportunity to open a new division in her father's law firm was simply too good to let pass, the implication obvious—she would prove herself to the other partners, letting them know that, on occasion, nepotism could be a good thing.

She glanced at Donna and saw that in between sips of Bloody Mary and surveys of the beach, her gaze returned to the surfer.

"Mark my word, Kelly, this guy is something special."

"Uh-huh." Kelly closed the book and flipped it over to see if Matt Landry's picture was on the back. "Whoa," she said softly. "Now here's an example of what a great photographer can do with ordinary material."

Dressed in khaki pants and a black shirt, Landry was posed with his back to the ocean, the waves colored a deep bronze from the setting sun, the sand a soft, glistening tan. He was settled on his haunches, a baby seal's nose barely a foot from his outstretched hand. His black hair windblown, his shirt pulled tight across well-defined muscles, he looked more like a *GQ* model than a respected scientist. "I wonder how old this picture is."

Donna leaned forward. "Let me see."

Kelly handed her the book.

"Nice," she said appreciatively. "What makes you think it's doctored?"

"Oh, please. People who run around like Chicken Little shouting the sky is falling don't look like that. If they did, they wouldn't have to use scare tactics to get attention; they'd be regulars on all the morning shows."

"Now the sky is falling?" She dropped the book in Kelly's lap. "Last I heard it was some ozone layer thing they were upset about."

"Do you ever read anything except the *Wall Street Journal*?"

"*People*—once in a while, at the doctor's office or when I'm getting my hair done." She put her drink aside and sat up. "Now pay attention," she told Kelly. "My surfer guy is about to catch a wave."

With seemingly effortless grace, he lifted himself onto the board, shifted position, and stood with his knees slightly bent. He ran the face of the wave, cutting sideways as it began to break. The ride was clean, but not spectacular. Instead of heading out again, he sat on the board and rode it toward shore, jumping off at the last minute and reaching down to unsnap the safety line from his ankle. He unzipped the top of his wet suit and let it fall to his waist before he tucked the board under his arm and started their way.

Kelly's eyes grew wide with appreciation and then alarm as she watched him approach. "My, God, it's him."

"Who?"

"Matt Landry."

Donna retrieved the book from Kelly's lap. "So it is," she said with suspicious confidence.

"What's he doing here?"

"Who cares?" As he was about to pass, Donna held up the book. "Excuse me, Mr. Landry."

He didn't seem surprised to hear someone calling his name. "Yes?"

"I don't mean to impose, but do you have a minute to sign your book for my sister? She's a real fan, but she's too shy to ask herself."

Kelly could have killed Donna, easily, happily, right there, right then. It was the how she wasn't sure of, only knowing whatever it was had to be slow and excruciatingly painful.

Matt glanced longingly at the stairs behind them that led from the beach to the houses. With a resigned look, he came over. "I have to make it fast. I have an appointment in ten minutes."

"Please, don't let us keep you," Kelly said. "This can wait." She reached for the book, but Donna was quicker and moved it out of range. Even through the haze of mortification she could see the photographer hadn't made him look better—he hadn't done him justice.

Matt laid the board on the sand and waited while Donna dug for a pen.

"Really," Kelly insisted. "You don't have to do this now. I'm sure we'll run into each other again." And when they did, she would do everything possible to keep him from remembering, including wearing a disguise if necessary.

"Here it is," Donna announced cheerfully. She handed him the book and pen.

"And who should I make this out to?" Matt asked.

"Kelly—with a 'y,' " Donna said. "And just say something about how you're looking forward to having her in your class."

He stopped to glance at Kelly and offer her a quick smile. "Easy enough." When he finished he handed the pen and book back to Donna. To Kelly he said, "I'll see you Wednesday."

Kelly summoned a smile. As soon as he was out of hearing, she turned on Donna. "Why did you do that? You know you just made it impossible for me to get through his class with any kind of anonymity."

"Is he or is he not one of the best-looking men you've ever seen in your entire twenty-seven years?"

"I don't care. That's not the point."

"Then what is the point?"

"I'm here to learn how to tear him apart in a courtroom. How am I going to do that after my sister practically threw me at him?"

Donna had the grace to look chagrined. "You never said anything about facing him in court."

As frustrated as she was furious, Kelly sat up and grabbed the sunscreen, squirting a thick, long line along her leg. "I can't believe this happened."

"What?"

"With all the beaches in Santa Cruz, we wound up on the same one at the same time as Matt Landry."

"Coincidence."

"I don't believe in coincidence."

"If it never happened, there wouldn't be a word for it."

Something in the way she answered made Kelly ask, "You arranged this, didn't you?"

Donna gave her a sheepish smile. "Now what makes you think that?"

"How—*why* would you do this to me?"

"The how is easy. The real coincidence happened when I was leaving this morning and saw Andrew and Landry coming out of Andrew's house. Landry was wearing a wet suit, and there was a surfboard leaning against the house. It wasn't too hard to figure out where he was headed. In my defense, if I'd known who he was or how you would feel about meeting him, I wouldn't have set it up. But, my God, Kelly, would you really have wanted to miss seeing that body stuffed into that wet suit?"

She ignored the question. "Why are you throwing me at every guy you see when you know I'm not interested? Ray and I are almost engaged."

Without saying anything, Donna held out her hand for the lotion.

"Well?" Kelly demanded.

"If I tell you, you'll just get mad."

"*Get* mad?"

"All right, madder."

"Right now, I don't think that's possible."

Still Donna hesitated. She stopped rubbing in the lotion long enough to give Kelly a sideways glance. "All right. Just remember that this was your idea. I don't think Ray's the right guy for you."

Kelly wasn't surprised. Donna had dropped hints over the past year that she had doubts about Ray. "In what way?"

"I don't know. I can't put my finger on it."

"You started this, now finish it."

"Have you ever noticed how Ray stares at me when we're together, like I'm candy and he's a diabetic?"

"You're a beautiful woman, and Ray likes beautiful women. What's wrong with that?"

"I'm your *sister*, Kelly. He has no business looking at me that way. Even Alexis noticed."

Kelly didn't know what to say. She took the lotion from Donna and laid a narrower line on her other leg. "Has he ever said anything to you?"

"No."

"Done anything?"

"No—it's just a feeling I get. One I really don't like. Besides . . . never mind. It isn't important."

"Don't stop now. I want this out and over with."

"There's something inherently wrong in a relationship where the woman acts like a wife and the man acts like a boyfriend."

"I don't know what you're talking about." But she did; she just didn't want to admit something had been bothering her, too. She'd even tried talking to Ray about it, but he'd refused to listen.

"You cook and clean and do laundry and make his life a hundred times easier than it would be if he were alone. He reciprocates by demonstrating his independence with his regularly scheduled, sacrosanct nights out with the boys. I've seen him in the bars with these guys, Kelly. Nothing slows them down, not even a hint of a conscience."

"That's not fair."

She let out a sigh, obviously pleased that Kelly finally understood what she'd been trying to tell her. "You're damn right it's not."

"That's not what I meant." She only wanted to deal with one issue at a time. "Ray does his share of the cooking and cleaning."

"And that share is what? Ten percent? Fifteen?"

"It's my apartment. I can hardly expect him to come over to clean it when he has his own place to take care of."

"But does he? Be honest, Kelly. When you're over there don't you do most of the work?"

"We have an open relationship, no strings, no long-term commitment. It's what I told him I wanted, and he agreed." She would never admit the real reason she'd laid the ground rules she had—she'd known they were the ones Ray wanted.

"Do you love him?"

"Yes." At least that was what she told herself.

"An over-the-moon kind of love?"

"Is there such a thing?" There had been for her mother and father, but they were the exception.

She was afraid if she lived her life looking for something even her father knew he would never find again, she would wake up one morning and realize she had nothing.

Donna thought about the question. "For you there should be. You're special. You deserve someone who's special, too." She paused. "I'll tell you something I do know. There's no way I'm going to wash any man's dirty underwear for anything less than that kind of love."

Kelly leaned forward and hugged herself, turning her gaze to the sea. She saw that the old man was still there, but he wasn't alone anymore. He had been joined by a woman as old and silver-haired as he was. They were holding hands, passing words and looks that bespoke a lifetime of familiarity. Their smiles were warm and intimate, and Kelly felt like a voyeur watching them. She was hit with a stab of longing so intense it stole her breath.

She touched Donna's arm to get her attention. "That's the way I imagine Dad and Mom were together."

Donna watched them for a long time. "I think Dad loves her as much now as he did when she was alive. It may be beautiful, but it's sad, too. He'll never find anyone else because no mortal woman could ever compete with his memory of Mom."

"I can't imagine what it would be like to be loved that way," Kelly said.

"Me either," Donna answered. "I'd go out of my mind if someone told me I had to be with the same man for five or six decades. That is not my idea of a lifetime well spent."

It was bravado. Kelly knew it, and she knew Donna did, too. "Just wait. When you meet the right man you'll sing a different song."

Donna laughed. "But I have met the right man, thirty times at last count. And I loved every minute with every one of them because I knew I didn't have to stick around through the bad times as well as the good."

"Whatever," Kelly said, ending the conversation. She opened the book and turned to the first chapter. She was curious to see what Matt Landry had written to her but wouldn't give Donna the satisfaction of looking.

Donna leaned back and closed her eyes. "You're not fooling anyone, you know."

"Someday I'll get you for this," Kelly promised.

Donna laughed.

2

As Donna packed her overnight bag to leave on Sunday evening Kelly tried to talk her into staying another day. Their visit, even with its rocky moments, had served as a reminder of how much Kelly missed being with her sister. But it was too late. The executive in Donna had overtaken the sister, and she was already engaged in a mental battle with the office manager she was scheduled to meet the next morning.

"Remember what I said," Donna told Kelly, giving her one last hug before she got in the limo the company had hired to take her the final leg to San Francisco.

Kelly laughed. "Which time?"

"Don't be a smart-ass. You know what I mean."

"Yeah, yeah, yeah."

"I don't want you closing any doors in your

life. Who knows, there might be a drop-dead gorgeous, sexy, man-of-your-dreams guy standing on the other side."

"I've got to start writing these things down."

Donna climbed into the car and rolled down the window. "You do know that there's a special place in hell for little sisters with smart mouths."

Kelly smiled, put her fingers to her lips, and blew Donna a kiss. "Take care of yourself."

"You too."

A thought struck. One she liked a lot. "Why don't you have Grace work that magic she does with your schedule and come back for a couple of days on your way home?"

"I suppose I could check with the other passengers to see if they would mind dropping me off and then see what the pilot thinks."

"You don't have to fly, you could rent a car. Or I could pick you up. It's not that far."

The limo started to pull away. Donna signaled the driver to stop. "What's up, Kelly? Why are you suddenly spooked about being here by yourself?"

Until that moment she hadn't known she was. "It's not that," she lied. "I've loved being with you. We need to do this more often." At least that was the truth.

Donna smiled. "I know." She signaled the driver it was all right to leave. "We'll get together with Alexis when you get home and plan something fun for this winter. I've been thinking about a skiing trip to Colorado."

"Alexis doesn't ski."

"We'll teach her," she called, as the limo pulled away.

"Fat chance," Kelly said softly. She had her hand in the air for a final wave when she spotted Andrew's car on the forest road. Instead of going inside, she waited for him.

"I have your key," she called, as he got out of his car. "If you'll wait a minute, I'll get it for you."

She retrieved the key and met him on the pathway between their houses. "I tried to return it a couple of times yesterday and this morning but couldn't catch you at home."

He added the key to a ring with a small, round photograph of a dog on it. "I was in Oakland this weekend."

"I thought about leaving a note but decided you might not want people to know you weren't there."

"You don't have to worry about things like that around here. Half the time I don't bother locking the door." He grinned. "We've only had one attempted break-in that I know of. A couple of suspicious characters tried getting into one of the houses through an unlocked bathroom window."

She liked Andrew Wells. "I take it this 'break-in' wasn't successful?"

"Amateur stuff."

"Probably kids with nothing better to do."

"Undoubtedly. By the way, I meant to tell you that if you ever need help with something and I'm not here, Paul Williams lives in the house a couple of doors down with the green shutters."

"Thanks, but I'm sure I'll be okay."

As if he'd read her mind, he added, "He's a great kid and loves being asked, so don't hesitate because you think you might be imposing."

She'd been on her own long enough to know how to take care of most problems or how to find someone who could. Still, it was good to know the neighbors here looked out for each other. "There is one thing."

"Yes?"

"The yard. Am I supposed to take care of it or does someone come in?" She'd discovered a lawn mower and edger in the garage and wouldn't mind doing the work. While growing up she'd loved taking care of the corner of their property where her father had planted her mother's favorite flowers. The living tribute to the woman he'd lost in a car accident the year after Kelly was born was the closest thing Harold Anderson had to a hobby. Whenever Kelly felt the need to be alone with him, she helped him with the garden.

"There's a service that comes in on Wednesdays and the watering is automatic."

"Oh."

Picking up on her disappointment, Andrew added, "But I know Julia wouldn't mind if you had the urge to get your hands dirty and did something with the planters on the back deck. The oenothera and phlox are years past their prime."

"Julia?" Kelly remembered seeing a corporate name on the rental agreement and had assumed the house belonged to an agency.

"She and her husband, Eric, own the house."

"As an investment?" She was curious because she'd looked into buying a condo at Lake Tahoe near one of the ski resorts. The tax rules were specific on investment property. The owner had two weeks a year for personal use and slightly more time for upkeep. She knew the beach house was only rented during the summer and found it hard to believe that it stood empty most of the rest of the year.

"Julia and Eric lived here for a year after they were married, then moved back East to be near his kids. They thought about selling but weren't ready to let the place go. Too many memories, I guess. The house has a long tradition of summer renters. Julia liked the idea of that happening again. If it doesn't work, she'll probably sell."

"If beachfront property here is anything like it is in San Diego, they're sitting on a gold mine. I can understand why she would want to see a return on her investment."

"It's more complicated than that." He started to explain, stopped, and said, "You want to come in for a drink? I think there's some iced tea left, and I know there's wine."

She hesitated, not knowing if the offer was as spontaneous as it sounded or a result of Donna's clumsy matchmaking attempt. She didn't want to spend the next month correcting a wrong impression. "I'm expecting a call from my boyfriend." She hated the term "boyfriend." It sounded so high school, but she didn't know what else to call Ray. They weren't engaged, he wasn't a significant other, he wasn't even her roommate.

"Another time then."

His lack of reaction to her having a boyfriend encouraged her. "He said I shouldn't expect him home from the baseball game for another hour yet. And I'd love to hear more about the house. I have a feeling if those walls could talk, they could tell some amazing stories."

He smiled. "I don't know about the first eighty-five years, but the last ten have given me some of the best friends I've ever had."

⌁THEY SETTLED ON COFFEE AND DRANK IT, SITting on teak chairs on Andrew's flagstone patio, facing the setting sun. "I can't believe anyone could get used to living in a place like this," Kelly said. "But I wonder if that's true."

"After all the years I've lived here, the first thing I do when I get up in the morning is look out the window. The only thing better would be to have someone looking out there with me."

"Anyone in particular?" Kelly asked carefully.

"Well, this is embarrassing. I was thinking out loud. Yes, there is someone in particular."

"The weekend in Oakland?"

"That's her."

Relieved, Kelly settled back in her chair and changed the subject. "You were going to tell me about my house," she prompted.

Andrew gave her a brief history, beginning with the couple who'd sold the place to Julia's first husband, Ken Huntington. "When Joe and Maggie died a couple of years ago, no one could remember a time when they weren't here. They were married sixty-five years and still lit up when they were with each other. I can't look at the house without picturing them there."

"Sixty-five years . . . that's amazing. It's hard to imagine that kind of relationship." Although she knew without question that her mother and father had loved each other that way. Unbidden thoughts of Ray intruded. Was she the love of his life? *Was he hers?*

"They were going through a rough time financially when they sold the place to Ken. As part of the deal, he insisted the summer months were theirs for as long as he owned the house." Andrew chuckled. "Somehow they got it in their heads that Ken was stretched pretty thin financially, too, so they rented the house two of the three summer months and gave him the money."

"I take it Ken was doing okay?"

"Does the name Huntington mean anything to you?"

"Of course." She shook her head in amazement at the poignancy of the misunderstanding. "That's a great story. Did Joe and Maggie ever find out that Ken was one of the world's richest men?"

"I'm sure they did, but they never stopped giving him the rent money, and he never made them feel foolish by refusing."

"How did Eric come into the picture?"

"He met Julia while I was off sailing, a year after Ken died. He was taking care of this place for me."

"It's easy to see why the same people would come back year after year. I've fallen in love with Julia and Eric's house and I've only been here two days."

"She'll like hearing that."

"I take it she was the gardener?"

"It started with Maggie. At first Julia kept it up just to please her, but then eventually she developed a real passion for flowers and plants and turned the yard into the English garden that it is today. Eric told me that Julia had the outside of their new house landscaped before she bought the first piece of furniture for the inside."

"I see your personal preference runs more toward simplicity." Nasturtiums were everywhere, circling the house and lining the walkways, their round, bright green leaves and orange and yellow blossoms the only landscaping.

"It's more that I don't like yard work, and nasturtiums pretty much take care of themselves. I work with plants all day, I'd rather not do it at home, too."

"You do landscaping?"

"I have a wholesale nursery."

Ray's father was in the nursery business in Santa Barbara. "Plants or cut flowers?"

"Mostly plants, but we do some seasonal cut flowers, too."

"Orchids?"

Surprised, he smiled. "How'd you guess?"

"A friend who's in the business once told me that, with the exception of orchids, most commercial growers either sell plants or flowers, not both." Kelly reached for the insulated carafe and poured them both another cup of coffee.

Andrew had started to add cream and sugar to his coffee when he was distracted by a sound on the other side of the railing. He went to investigate. Finding nothing, he explained, "There's a stray cat in the neighborhood that I've been trying to get to trust me. As terrified as it is with strangers and the way it bolts in front of cars, I don't think it's been an outside cat. I have a feeling there might be a collar under all that fur."

"If it's the gray-and-tan one that looks like it's part lynx, I saw him sleeping in the chair on my deck yesterday morning. I scared him when I opened the door. He took off, and I haven't seen him since."

Andrew doctored his coffee, then sat down again. "What brought you here for a vacation?"

"I'm taking a class at the university."

"Work or pleasure?"

"Definitely not pleasure. Environmental ethics is pretty dry stuff."

"And you're doing this because?"

"We're opening a new division at my law office."

"For or against?" he asked.

The question wasn't unexpected. Few people were neutral on environmental issues. Either you sided with evil corporate empires or valiant crusaders. "I like to think I'm against extremism and for reason."

"So you're here to check out the enemy."

She automatically went on the defensive. "I'm here to learn from a man who is a professional witness for environmental causes."

"Meaning he's someone who is paid to testify during court cases?"

"Yes." She had to stop taking these kinds of questions personally. She was supposed to be neutral about such things. Passion clouded judgment and lost cases.

"Aren't all expert witnesses paid?"

"Most of them," she acknowledged.

"So by calling him a professional witness you're not denigrating him."

Neither his voice nor demeanor appeared judgmental, but the statement was enough to let her know she'd crossed some invisible line. "Donna told me you and Matt know each other."

"We go back a few years."

She liked loyalty in a friend. "If he's as good a teacher as he is a witness, it should be an interesting four weeks."

"I've never taken one of his courses, but we've had more than a few 'lively' discussions over beers. Something tells me you might be in for a surprise or two."

"Glad to hear it. I like surprises." That was better. At least she sounded professional—the kind of lawyer who shook hands with the opposing council after losing a tough trial and walked away without a crushing sense of defeat. Law was like a game, sometimes you won, sometimes you lost, but you never—at least not at her firm—became personally involved.

Kelly stayed another hour, the time passing so quickly she was stunned when she saw that it was almost ten. Remembering Ray had promised to call at nine, she thanked Andrew for the coffee and company and rushed home.

Ray didn't answer his phone. She tried his cell number, then his pager, but he didn't respond to either. Hoping he was in the shower and not purposely ignoring her, she waited fifteen minutes and tried again, with the same results. She made two more attempts before she gave up and left a breezy message on his machine that she was sorry she'd missed him and would call again in the morning. By then he would have a story to cover his absence, and she would go along with it because it was easier than confronting him with his childishness.

His behavior was understandable, if annoying. He was an only child who'd been doted on by a mother with too little to do and a father who saw in his son a second chance to live the life he'd been denied by his own father.

Kelly had no doubt Ray eventually would grow out of his desire to be the center of attention. He needed time, and she needed patience. She just had to keep reminding herself that Ray's good qualities more than balanced his bad and that if she held out for a perfect relationship, she would live her life alone. She wasn't like her mother or Maggie, but neither were millions of other women. Real soul mates were about as easy to come by as fifty-carat diamonds.

Wide-awake, she turned on the television and clicked through a dozen channels before giving up and turning it off again. She glanced around the room and thought about the women who'd lived here. She wondered if Julia had chosen the furniture and curtains and colors out of preference or if there had been a nod to Maggie's influence. They weren't anything she would have picked, but they seemed to suit her in a way she never would have anticipated.

To celebrate passing the bar, she'd redecorated her apartment in an expensive retro fifties style that had seemed wonderfully clever and funky at the time, but now seemed dated. If Ray weren't so adamant about liking the look, or if she had some real idea what she wanted in its place, she would sell everything and start over.

The fact that she felt more a sense of home here than she did in her apartment might be the prod that she needed. She liked being somewhere she could kick off her shoes and curl up on the sofa and not worry what it was doing to the symmetry of the cushions. The drapes could be opened and closed without adjusting pleats, and nothing was finished to a high gloss that showcased dust.

She loved that someone had thought to put binoculars in every room that faced the ocean and that the bookshelves in the living room held everything from a rock collection to children's literature to popular fiction. There were restaurant menus from Aptos, Capitola, Soquel, Watsonville, Santa Cruz, Monterey, Pacific Grove, and Carmel in a kitchen drawer. All had handwritten reviews that ranged from a simple "yum" to "heartburn likely, but worth it if you're adventuresome" to "not to be missed" to "try the grocery-store deli first." There were ordinary shells in a basket on the coffee table and expensive hand-loomed rugs in the bedrooms.

The only photograph in the house was in an ornate pewter frame on the mantel over the stone fireplace. She'd picked it up a half dozen times to stare at the couple standing outside in the garden under the rose arbor. The condition of the photograph, the clothes the people were wearing, and the car parked in the driveway led her to believe it had been taken sometime in the late forties or early fifties.

The man had looked directly at the camera, making a connection she could feel through the years that separated them. He had his arm around the woman, and his smile was a beacon of happiness he plainly wanted the world to see. The woman had her arm around the man's waist. She was gazing up at him, her joy so complete and intimate that being a witness almost seemed an invasion of her privacy.

Kelly had planned to ask Andrew about the couple when she saw him again—who they were, why theirs was the only picture in the house, and what had happened to them. Now she knew. They were Joe and Maggie.

Settling deeper into the sofa, she picked up Landry's book and turned to the first chapter. She'd barely made it through the opening paragraph when the phone rang. Happier than she wanted to be that Ray had given in and called her, she reached for the phone. "I was worried about you," she said in lieu of hello.

"Why?" Donna asked. And then, "Oh, I get it. You thought I was Ray."

She could deny the assumption, and Donna would let her get away with it, but they would both know it was a lie. "I missed his call earlier and left a message for him to call back." Donna hesitated long enough that Kelly could almost hear the wheels turning.

"Oh? And what were you doing that made you forget he was supposed to call?"

"Did I say I forgot?"

"Same difference," she said.

"If you must know, I was out on the deck having a cup of coffee."

"Your deck or Andrew's?"

Kelly didn't stand a chance. Donna was too good. "Andrew's. We were talking about Matt Landry and his girlfriend."

"Matt's girlfriend or Andrew's?"

"Andrew's."

"Damn." Half a heartbeat later, "Did he happen to say whether Landry was seeing anyone?"

Kelly laughed. "This can't be why you called. You should be in bed by now."

"I need some legal advice."

Kelly groaned. "Please tell me you're not in trouble again."

"It's not for me, you nitwit, it's a friend. He just found out his ex never put through the papers to take his name off the condo they owned together, and the bank is coming after him, threatening to turn him over to a collection agency unless he makes up the back payments. He doesn't have the money, and he's scared to death his credit is going to be ruined." She paused. "And what do you mean *again*? I've never been in trouble. Or at least not lawyer kind of trouble."

Kelly ignored the last part. "Where is this friend?"

"Right now?"

"No, you nitwit," she countered. "Where does he live?"

"San Diego."

"John Murdock's the man he wants to see. He's tenacious and loves this kind of thing. I'll contact him first thing in the morning and tell him to expect your friend's call. I assume he's in San Francisco with you now but will be back in San Diego by the end of the week?"

"I could let him go as early as Wednesday, if necessary."

"Call me when you get a break tomorrow, and I'll let you know what John's schedule is like. Your friend can take it from there."

"I knew there would come a time when I was glad I pulled you out of Lake Morgan."

"You pulled me out because you knew you wouldn't sit down for a week when Dad found out you'd pushed me in."

Donna laughed. "Oh, yeah. I forgot that part."

"I miss having you here."

"We'll do it again—next summer. I promise. And if we can't get Alexis to go with us, we'll find a way to make her come to the beach house."

It was a dream they would talk about through the winter and, if nothing else, have the pleasure of planning.

"I've got to get to bed before it's too late to

bother," Donna said. "But first promise me something."

"What."

"You won't stay up all night waiting for Ray to call."

She wasn't expecting something this easy. "I promise."

"And, I want you to promise—"

"One is all you get."

"Can't blame a girl for trying."

"Go to bed, Donna."

"I love you."

"Love you, too." Kelly's hand lingered on the receiver when she returned it to the cradle. In a way she was glad Ray hadn't called. She'd had a wonderful day, too wonderful to end with a fight.

The thought brought her up short. How had she let this happen to her? When had she become captive to Ray's moods? Why had she made excuses for him when Donna told her about his wandering eye?

What if the situation had been reversed, and she was the one who had made the call and Ray hadn't answered? She simply would have called later, no questions, no pouting, no problem. The answer was like a flash of light in a dark room forcing her to see something she hadn't wanted to see. Rather than work though the revelation and face something she didn't want to face, she went to bed.

3

KELLY WOKE THE NEXT MORNING TO THE sounds of a bird singing outside her bedroom window. She listened, fascinated by the series of warbles that ended in a high *zeee* repeated over and over again. She went to the window and studied the eucalyptus tree beside the deck, but couldn't spot the bird.

Stretching, she considered crawling back into bed but decided tea on the deck with the bird held more appeal. She slipped into the red silk bathrobe Alexis had given her for her twenty-fifth birthday and went into the kitchen, automatically glancing at the clock and then the telephone as she passed. Six-thirty, Ray should be leaving his apartment about now. Obviously he'd decided to call her on his cell phone rather than risk leaving late.

She made her tea in an enormous earthenware mug and took it outside with her, careful to leave the sliding door open far enough to be able to hear the phone when it rang.

When Ray still hadn't called by eight, Kelly decided she'd waited long enough and picked up the phone to call him. She tried his cell phone first and then his office.

"Hi, Phyllis," she said to his assistant. "Is Ray available?"

Phyllis only paused a fraction of a second longer than usual before answering, but it was enough to let Kelly know that what was coming next wasn't the truth. "He hasn't come in yet, Ms. Anderson. Would you like to leave a message?"

She hated being lied to, but hated even more that Ray had Phyllis doing the lying. It was embarrassing—for both of them. "No, there's no message." She started to hang up, then changed her mind. "Wait—" Phyllis was still on the line. "Tell him I'm not going to be available for several days and not to bother trying to reach me."

"Are you sure there's no number?" She seemed astounded, as if it were impossible for anyone to go anywhere they would be out of touch.

"Tell Ray I'll call when I get back."

"Can you hold for a moment?"

"Certainly."

A canned message came on the line reminding her that quarterly taxes were due on the fifteenth and that it wasn't too early to start planning tax strategies for the end of the year.

"Kelly—," Ray said, stopping as if to catch his breath, "I was afraid I might have missed you."

When added to her personal revelation of the night before, she realized she was overwhelmingly weary of the pretense that went on between them. Nothing was happening that hadn't happened before or wouldn't happen again. And that was the problem. She simply didn't have the energy or desire any longer to trade her pride when all she received in exchange was the comfort of knowing she always had a convenient companion.

"You have," she told him, feeling an unexpected, heady rush.

"I don't understand."

Quickly, before she could change her mind, she said, "I'm done, Ray." Shouldn't she be feeling a sense of sorrow? What was this feeling of freedom? "It's over. We're over. It was fun for a while, but it isn't fun anymore."

"You're dumping me?"

Had he not been taken by surprise, he would have never used a demeaning term like "dumping." Five minutes after they hung up he would become the one who'd broken it off.

"Just like that?" he added.

"Just like that," she repeated.

"What about—"

"Yes?"

"I thought we had something going, some-thing that was eventually supposed to lead us somewhere."

Donna's words came back to her. "We did have something going, Ray. You had a woman willing to cater to your needs, and I had a man willing to let me. I don't want to do that anymore. The game stopped being fun a long time ago. I just didn't want to admit it. Now, I'm packing up my toys and going home."

"But—"

"Yes?"

"You can't call it off just like that," he sputtered.

"Why not?"

"I'm not ready."

"What are you trying to say, Ray? That you love me too much to let me go, that you'll miss me when I'm gone, or that your life won't be the same without me?"

"All I'm saying is that I'm not ready for it to be over."

"Give it a couple of hours, you'll be fine."

"You can be a real bitch, Kelly."

"I suppose it's too much to think we could still be friends?"

He hung up on her.

She waited. She should have felt bad, maybe even a little sad. Anger would have been appro-priate. But all she felt was relief. How long had she subconsciously known that they were in a dead-end relationship? A better question was how had she talked herself into tolerating the situation as long as she had?

She'd listened to women who'd spent years swimming in the murky waters of the dating pool claim a bad relationship was better than no relationship. She wasn't there yet. She might have come close with Ray, but as her grandfather used to say, close only counted in horseshoes. Whatever that meant.

KELLY CELEBRATED HER NEWLY WON INDEpendence by going to Monterey and joining a walking tour of the downtown historical district. Eleven Spanish adobe-and-stucco buildings and one blister later, she wandered into a bakery and ordered a slice of carrot cake that turned out to be three layers tall with a half inch of cream cheese frosting. She told herself she would only eat half and save the rest for the next day. Ten minutes later, the only thing left on her plate was the fork.

Satisfaction overrode guilt, but not to the point she gave in to the temptation to buy a second piece to take with her. Back in her car, she considered her options. Time was a rare commodity in her ordered life, something she rarely had in excess, and never for indulgence.

She tried to imagine what Donna would do in her place and decided she really didn't want another man in her life, even a temporary one. Instead she found a spa with an opening for a facial and massage.

On the way home she stopped at a roadside stand that proclaimed Castroville the artichoke capital of the world and bought a bag of the glorified thistles. That night's dinner consisted of artichokes dipped in melted butter and a half bottle of Merlot, a combination so good she put it on her list of all-time favorite meals.

After the dishes were done, she halfheartedly picked up Matt Landry's book and settled down to go to work. Three hours later she winced as she untucked and stretched her legs, stunned that she'd been so caught up in what she'd thought would be a series of dry statistics that she had barely moved.

She took a mental step back and thought about what she'd read. Employing fiction techniques, Landry had made the nonfiction work read like a novel, telling with relentless unfolding the catastrophic effects of man's disregard for his home. He'd ended the first section with the race to find cures for viruses that turned human organs into unfunctioning, gelatinous incubators ready to infect the next unprotected and unwary passerby, viruses unleashed by man's disregard for the balance of nature.

The man could write. She would give him that. And she was beginning to understand why and how his arguments worked with a jury. The key to winning a case where he was called to testify would be in the jury selection. *And in her ability to find reason in her opposing argument*, something that grew more difficult the more she read.

She went outside to walk around and work out the kinks while thinking about and absorbing the ideas Landry had presented. The waves carried a gentle breeze, heavy with moisture and smelling of brine. At the top of the stairs, with her hands at the small of her back, she leaned to one side and then the other, her gaze sweeping the moonlit beach. Joe and Maggie's house, her house for the month, sat in the exact middle of the cove, with twelve houses on each side. Most were cottages, some had small additions, and a couple bordered on ostentatious, filling their lots like size eight pants on a size twelve body. The pine and eucalyptus trees growing on, behind, and around the lots gave shelter to perching birds and squirrels and the occasional chipmunk.

The residents accommodated the wildlife, studiously obeying the posted twenty-five-mile speed limit, even stopping traffic to scoot fledgling birds or a slow-moving raccoon out of the way.

The community wasn't gated, but dead-end streets discouraged all but the most intrepidly curious, giving a sense of security she knew better than to accept but still enjoyed. At home she would not venture out alone at night the way she was now. Just walking on the beach by herself would have friends questioning her sanity. If small-town America survived, it was in places like this, where neighbors knew and looked out for each other. Kelly had yet to see half the residents on her floor at her high-rise apartment building, let alone know them by name.

She was back at the house, sitting on the deck, when a rustling noise beside the house startled her. She waited, not moving, barely breathing, hoping it was the cat and not wanting to frighten it.

It wasn't the cat, it was Andrew. "I thought I saw you out here." He came down the abandoned path that ran in front of the deck. "Beautiful night, huh?"

"Breathtaking. I keep expecting the dreaded fog that everyone warned me about, but every day has been prettier than the last."

"Well, you've done it now. The fog's sure to roll in tomorrow." He stopped but didn't open the gate to the waist-high railing that surrounded the deck. "If you want people to think you're a native, never talk about the fog unless it's all around you."

She smiled. "Thanks for the tip. I'll be more careful about what I say from now on." She went to the gate to open it for him. "Would you like to come in for a drink? I found a local Merlot that's wonderful."

"I wish I could, but the security company that makes rounds at the nursery just called. There's a broken pipe in one of the greenhouses. I'm hoping it's something simple, but if it isn't, I'm liable to be out there all night. In which case, I was wondering if you could do me a favor?"

"Sure."

"Matt Landry's coming over in the morning to borrow my surfboard. If I'm not here, would you mind letting him in the garage?"

Her brief fling with feeling special ended with the realization he'd asked her because she was the only one around in the morning. "Of course."

He dug a key out of his pocket and handed it to her. "I'll leave a note on the door telling Matt to come here."

"What time should I expect him?"

"Somewhere around six—a little before or after. He likes to hit the waves early." He turned to leave.

"I hope everything is okay at the nursery," she called after him.

"Thanks—me too."

Kelly went inside and put the key on the table by the front door. She wasn't crazy about the thought of seeing Matt again, but it was probably better to get past the initial awkwardness sooner rather than later. Somehow, somewhere she would get back at Donna for her clumsy attempts to hook her up with Andrew and Matt.

The phone rang. For a fraction of a second her heart soared with the thought it could be Ray. Acutely disappointed at her reaction, she answered with an impatient, "Hello."

"Bad time?" her father asked.

"No, it's a good time. I was just thinking about something that put me in a bad mood."

"You want to tell me about it?"

"Not particularly."

"Okay, then I'll get to why I called. I have a feeling they could be connected. Ray seems to think there's something wrong up there."

She was speechless. Never, not if it had been written in stone and passed down from on high, would she have believed Ray would call her father to intercede for him.

"Is he right?"

"No, he's not right. I'm fine. Better than fine, I'm terrific. I'm having a wonderful time. The house is beautiful, the beach is beautiful, I've made a new friend."

"Male or female?"

"Male."

"So that's it. I assume you told Ray?"

"What I told Ray was that I was through waiting for him to grow up." She wished she could see the look on her father's face. She had a feeling he was smiling.

"Meaning he'd better grow up fast or that it didn't make any difference whether he did or not, you were through?" he asked carefully.

"Meaning it's over—regardless."

"Good for you." His voice was a verbal high five. After several seconds, he added, "Of course, if you should change your mind, I don't want you to think I'm passing judgment on Ray. It's just that—"

"Don't worry. It's not going to happen. The

only thing that could make me change my mind would be if I were stuck on a desert island with him."

"I'll do what I can to make sure that doesn't happen."

Kelly laughed. "Take care, Dad."

"You too. And let me know what you think of this Matt Landry guy when you meet him."

"I've already met him. He's everything we've heard. We better hope we don't have to come up against him too often."

"You can handle him."

While it was wonderful having someone believe in her the way her father did, at times it was a burden. "Right now I'm basing everything on first impressions and what I've read in his book. Maybe I'll find a weakness or two when I get into the class."

"Everyone is vulnerable."

"So you've always told me."

"You just have to look hard enough."

"Yes, Dad."

"Okay, so you've heard it all before. That doesn't make it any less true. Keep me posted."

It was her father's way of saying good-bye. "I'll do that—as soon as I have something worth reporting."

"It's all right if you just want to call to check in," he added unexpectedly.

The warmth in his voice brought a smile. "I'm doing fine. Stop worrying about me."

"It goes with the territory. I worry about all three of you girls."

Telling him it was long past the time when worry would do any good wasn't what he wanted to hear. "One more thing," she said instead. "I recommended John Murdock to a friend of Donna's in case he mentions something to you."

"He did, and it's being taken care of."

"Thanks. Now go to bed, Dad. It's late."

"As soon as I finish going over this brief."

He worked harder and with more dedication than anyone else she knew. Someday she hoped to feel some of whatever it was that drove him. Right now it was everything she could do to impress the other partners with her skill and ambition and still have a little time left over for a life outside the office.

She said good-bye. And then, feeling guilty that her father was still working and she wasn't, she picked up Landry's book and took it to bed with her.

4

KELLY WAS ON HER SECOND CUP OF COFFEE, mentally cursing Matt Landry for keeping her up until three-thirty in the morning reading his book when he knocked on her door.

"We meet again," he announced, plainly pleasantly surprised. He gave her a smile bright enough for sunglasses. "Kelly with a 'y,' right?"

"I was hoping you'd forgotten." She reached for the key.

"No need," he said. "I do a lot of crazy things, but I don't surf in the fog. I just came over so you wouldn't hang around waiting for me." He backed off the brick porch. "When you see Andrew tell him I came by and that I'll catch up with him later."

She looked past him to the thick, gray fog hugging the ground like a down blanket. "Oh, my

God . . . I'm going to have to be more careful from now on."

He tossed her a questioning look.

"The fog," she said. "It's my fault—according to Andrew, that is. No one told me I wasn't supposed to talk about it."

Matt laughed. "Don't take it too hard. This isn't as bad as it looks. It'll burn off by noon, and you'll be back in everyone's good graces."

It could have been his casual thoughtfulness or his easy laugh or the fact that his book had made her aware of the brilliant mind inside the amazing package, or it could even have been her need for company the morning after ending her relationship with Ray. The reason didn't matter, the impulse did. "Would you like to come in for a cup of coffee?" she asked, surprising herself as much as him.

He considered the invitation. "As a matter of fact, I would. I could use a good cup of coffee."

She winced as she moved out of the doorway to let him enter. "Remember the 'good' part was yours, not mine."

He followed her into the kitchen. "I'll drink anything. I've had coffee where the grounds were tossed in a pot of water and boiled for three days and gone back for a second cup."

"I should be safe then." She took a mug from the cupboard. "How do you take it?"

"Black."

She poured, he took a sip. After several excruciatingly long seconds, he put the cup on the counter. "You win. Grab your coat."

"Where are we going?" she asked suspiciously.

"To this place I know that has the best coffee in Santa Cruz County."

"Thanks, but I've already had two cups and—"

"Did I mention they make cinnamon rolls the size of a dinner plate?" He looked at his watch. "If we hurry, we can get them right out of the oven."

She had no business going with him. It was one thing to have a friend as opposing counsel, another when he was a potential witness for that opposing counsel. Not that there was any law against it: more that her life was complicated enough without adding Matt Landry to the mix.

"Kelly?"

"What?"

"Did I mention it's a nonfat cinnamon roll?"

That made her laugh. "And sugar-free, too, no doubt."

"And loaded with beta carotene and an entire day's worth of fiber."

Even on the odd chance she and Landry did become friends, he was far too sophisticated to expect anything but her best if or when they faced each other in a courtroom. "Okay, you convinced me."

What was she thinking? Before she could change her mind, she took her purse and a windbreaker out of the closet by the front door.

"Was it the fiber that convinced you?" Matt asked.

"If you must know, it was the dinner plate size." She locked the house and followed him to Andrew's driveway, where he'd parked his car. "The artichoke I had for dinner last night is a distant memory."

He stopped to open her door before going around to the driver's side. Settling behind the wheel, he looked as if he were going through a mental checklist before starting the car. "Bear with me. I just got this thing yesterday, and I'm not used to all the bells and whistles."

Only then did she realize there was something different about the car. "What kind is it?"

"A prototype electric I'm testing for Karol Motors. It's the first one I've driven that I think has a real chance of succeeding in the marketplace. From the reports I've read, it handles freeway speeds and the around-town stuff as well as a traditional car."

She waited for him to go on. "But?" she finally prompted.

"There's always one of those, isn't there? Right now it's the cost. Assembly line models would still come in at half again what you'd pay for a gas-powered model."

"Even with fuel costs factored in?"

"People who can afford forty-thousand-dollar cars usually don't keep them long enough for something like that to matter."

The closest she'd come to an electric car before today was her father's golf cart. Having lived in Los Angeles the entire time she was in college, she had seen the need for cleaner cars firsthand. She just wasn't convinced electricity was the answer. "How long is it down for recharging?"

"It isn't. Or I should say rarely. The entire shell is a solar collector. It feeds the batteries whether the car is moving or standing still."

"What happens on a day like today?"

"The reserve kicks in." He glanced at her and grinned. "If not, we walk."

He started the car and backed out of the driveway. Kelly had trouble orienting without the traditional engine noise, and fought the feeling that they were floating over the road and not actually on it. "Weird."

"It took me a while to get used to it, too. This is the third car I've tested for them. They keep getting better, but they're not there yet."

"What do you usually drive?" She was curious if he practiced what he preached.

"I have a truck that's been converted to run on natural gas, but most of the time I ride my bike." They came to the state park road. Matt made a left and then another that led to Highway 1.

"As good as electric cars sound, I've always wondered if it isn't a wash as far as pollution goes. Don't most electric plants run on fossil fuel? If everyone converted their cars to electricity, wouldn't that lead to more dams and power plants and fossil fuel consumption?"

"You're right. The cars have to be made solar dependent."

"But doesn't that mean they'll only work in the Sun Belt?" she countered.

Matt pulled up to a stop sign and turned to look at Kelly. "Not that I don't find this stuff fascinating, but would you mind if we save it for class? I spin these arguments all day every day, and once in a while it's nice to take a break and talk about something else."

Only then did she realize how aggressively she'd been questioning him.

"Let's talk about you," Matt said. "Where are you from and what do you do for a living?"

"San Diego." There was no way out of telling the rest of it. "I'm a lawyer."

He chuckled. "Now I understand." He took off again, went through an underpass, and then north on Highway 1.

"Sorry you invited me for coffee?" she asked.

He surprised her with a grin and a wink. "Sorry you agreed to come?"

"No." And she wasn't.

"Me either."

⟋THE COFFEE SHOP WAS IN A SMALL CON-verted house that overlooked Soquel Creek. It was painted blue and white both inside and out, with polished hardwood floors, chintz curtains on the mullioned windows, and real flowers on the tables. The smell of cinnamon and fresh-baked bread filled the air with mouth-watering promise.

The owner knew Matt and responded to a called greeting by bounding out of the kitchen. Dressed completely in white except for a dark green apron with a picture of cartoon kids sitting around a campfire with a bear dressed like a firefighter, he looked more like a mechanic than a chef. "I heard you were back in town you old SOB. What in the hell took you so long to get over here to see me?"

He took Matt's hand and pulled him into an enthusiastic hug. "What's it been? Two years?"

"Closer to three. I came by on Sunday, but you were at some wine-tasting thing."

"No one told me." He peered over Matt's shoulder. "And who's this you've brought with you?"

The implication was impossible to miss. Kelly would have protested if the idea weren't so preposterous that it would take care of itself.

"Kelly—" Stumped, he looked at Kelly.

"Anderson," she supplied.

"Kelly Anderson, Oscar Stevens." To Oscar he said, "She's Andrew's friend."

His eyes widened in surprise before a frown drew his bushy eyebrows back together. "No kidding? I thought—" He shook his head and tried to cover his confusion with a smile.

"Something wrong?" Matt asked.

"I must've heard wrong," he said. "I thought Andrew was working on seeing Cheryl again." He gave Kelly a sheepish look. "My mistake."

Kelly waved him off. "I'm a friend of Andrew's," she said. "Not Andrew's *friend*."

Matt shrugged. "I don't see the difference."

The bell over the door rang, announcing another customer. Oscar led Kelly and Matt to a table. "What can I get you?"

"Two coffees, two cinnamon rolls," Matt said.

"Coming up."

When he was gone Kelly zeroed in on Matt. He hadn't fooled her with his innocent act. "Why did you want him to think Andrew and I were a couple?"

"It was either that or let him think you and I were a couple and have it all over Santa Cruz by noon. The last woman I brought here was my wife."

"You're married?" She was as disappointed as she was surprised, and neither made sense.

"I was. We've been divorced almost two years now. We're still friends—as much as people who live different lives a continent apart can be."

"Kids?"

"Luckily, no. We wanted them, but it just didn't happen." He leaned back to make room for the waiter to deliver the coffee and rolls. "What about you?"

"No kids and never been married. Came close once—to getting married—but that was when I was in college. We decided if we were going to make it work, we should stop going to parties and spend more time with each other. We did and real- ized parties and friends were what we had in common." She cut the roll, took a bite, closed her eyes, and made a low *mmmmmm* sound. "Oh, I can see this was a mistake."

"Don't like it?"

"Are you kidding? This is the stuff dreams are made of."

"Try the coffee."

She did. It was as good as the cinnamon roll. "I wonder how well coffee freezes," she thought out loud.

"I think we could talk Oscar into selling you some beans. Then all you'd need is a grinder."

"Won't make any difference." She took another bite. "I've tried every brand on the market—Fol- gers, Starbucks, Gevalia. I even managed to ruin some Kona that cost me thirty-five dollars a pound."

"Well, I can see I have my work cut out for me."

That sounded suspiciously like a plan to stick around, something her conscience told her she should discourage. *Easy enough,* a second inner voice countered. *Just remind him who you are and why you're here.* But she didn't. She was enjoying herself and didn't want the morning to be over. "It's hopeless. I'd feel guilty wasting your time."

He gave her a look that told her he knew exactly what she was doing. And then, as if testing her, added, "I don't mind."

She headed him off by switching subjects. "How do you know Andrew?"

"We used to sail and free climb together back in our wild and crazy days. Lately we've both gotten so busy the best we seem able to do is get together a couple of times a year and talk about what we can't seem to find time to do anymore."

"I'm surprised you don't make fun and games a higher priority." Ray insisted on it. Evenings and weekends with his male friends took precedence over everything but work.

"We both knew we had to grow up sometime."

Kelly guessed Matt and Ray to be near the same age—thirty-three. Ray, however, was a decade behind emotionally and showed no signs of maturing. "You mean you never sail or climb anymore?"

"I go every chance I get. I just don't make it the priority it once was. And I don't feel cheated if it doesn't happen."

He'd actually finished his cinnamon roll and was eyeing the half she'd left on her plate. "Are you through with that?"

"Help yourself." She thought he was kidding, no one could pack away that much sugar and look the way he did. He wasn't. He finished her roll with as much gusto as he'd eaten his own.

Satisfied, he sat back, ran a hand over his stomach, and glanced at his watch. "Ready?"

She nodded.

Matt left a twenty on the table and stopped by the kitchen to tell Oscar he hadn't lost his touch. Kelly waved and added she would be back, soon and often.

Outside again, Kelly stood on the sidewalk and looked down Riverview Avenue. "I think the fog is lifting."

Matt lightly touched her arm as they crossed the street to the car. "Do you have plans for the rest of the day?"

Tell him yes, her increasingly irritating inner voice demanded. "Nothing firm. Andrew suggested several places he thought I should see while I'm here. I checked the map and Mission San Juan Bautista and Fremont Peak were close enough that it looks as if I could do them both in a day, so I'll probably head inland."

They were in the car before he said, "I've been invited to join some friends on a research vessel that's leaving from Moss Landing in about an hour. You can't see as much of the country from the bay as you would from Fremont Peak, but I guarantee what you do see will be spectacular. Want to come?"

All the reasons she'd had for not going to breakfast with him were still in place and still valid. He couldn't be her friend, at least not a good friend. It wouldn't be fair to either of them. Her father would be furious. Donna would never let her hear the end of it. But then the only way they would know was if she told them. "I'd love to."

Again the voice. *You are out of your mind. The salt air has corroded your good sense. You're acting like a starstruck teenager, not the ambitious, focused woman who graduated with honors from law school.*

She'd spent her whole life listening to the voice of reason and looking back with nagging feelings of regret. Not today.

Matt traveled Highway 1 south for several miles before taking an off-ramp and backtracking. "I forgot I'd promised Ed I'd return the research material I borrowed from him on Friday." He made a right onto a road that led into the hills. "It will just take a minute."

After several more turns onto narrower and narrower roads, he pulled up to a small, rustic bungalow surrounded by redwoods and pines.

"This is where you live?" Aware from her own research how many boards he sat on, how often he was paid to testify, and how much he was paid as CEO of H.O.M.E., she'd expected something a little grander.

"I needed a place to live after the divorce and stumbled across this house." He chuckled. "I couldn't believe my luck when it turned out I could actually afford it." He climbed out of the car, then leaned down to ask, "You want to come in?"

She was relieved to discover she did have her limits and knew where to draw the line. "Thanks, but I'll wait out here."

He was back in less than a minute, a folder in one hand, a coat in the other. He put both in the backseat. "I thought you might need something more substantial than that windbreaker. It can get cold on the bay."

An hour later she was standing on the deck of the *Western Flyer*, wrapped in Matt's coat, her head pulled into the collar turtle fashion, trying unsuccessfully to decide the last time she'd been as cold. Matt stood next to her in his shirtsleeves talking to the crew as they prepared to leave the berth and maneuver through the harbor to open ocean.

The *Western Flyer* was a twin-hull research vessel operated by the Monterey Bay Aquarium Research Institute. Ed had explained that they were on their way to measure the rise rate of carbon dioxide droplets in the upper ocean. Why anyone would care, she didn't know, but intended to ask when they reached their destination.

Another half hour and she was standing at the railing, the wind to her back, focused on the five-hundred-foot towers at the electrical plant at Moss Landing. They emitted steam into the fog-laden air like the nostrils of a fire-breathing dragon. The ship's crew had confidently predicted the fog would be gone by noon, but it didn't matter whether it was or not. Their work was conducted underwater by a remote-operated vehicle, and transmitted to television monitors in a heated cabin by a high-resolution HDTV camera.

She loved being a part of anything that was behind the scenes. Always had, from the time she was five and her father had taken her into the pits at a NASCAR race where she'd watched a crew frantically try to fix a wrecked car to get it back on the track to finish the race. When she'd visited a movie studio, the actors weren't what caught her attention. It was the director and cameraman and lighting people. The summer she'd worked for the state legislators' office she'd paid more attention to the mechanics that brought a bill to the floor than its actual introduction.

Matt came over and leaned against the railing, his back to the shore, his gaze locked on her face. He had a disconcerting way of looking directly in her eyes, as if, at that moment, she were the most important person in his life.

"Do you want to go inside? You look a little cold."

"I am, but I don't want to miss anything. I overheard someone at the institute say a pod of killer whales was spotted in the bay this morning."

"You've never seen them in the wild?"

"I've never even seen one in a tank. But then I don't like seeing caged animals of any kind. When I was eight my sister won a canary in a raffle. I couldn't stand seeing it confined, so while she was at a friend's house I turned it loose. I never admitted what I'd done, but my father sat me down and gave me a lecture about how hard it is for an animal raised as a pet to survive in the wild."

"I have a friend doing research on the familial ties and social structure in killer whale pods. She's downright militant about closing any park that uses marine life for entertainment."

"Every cause has its extremists." His eyes captivated her. They were a deep-sea blue and surrounded by lashes as thick and black as his hair. In the short time they'd been together she'd instinctively realized Matt Landry was exactly what he purported to be. There were no hidden meanings to what he said, no guarded aspects to his personality, no playing her for what she knew or believed.

Without saying a word he'd let her know he understood who and what she was and that it was okay with him. It was the kind of acceptance she'd only experienced with her family and, even then, with qualifications. Donna wanted her to be more social, Alexis more aggressive, her father more focused. Not that Matt wouldn't have his own opinions if he knew her better. She was miles from perfect, a work in progress, a lump of clay spinning on a potter's wheel ripe with possibilities.

"I believe in extremists. I don't think anything would ever get accomplished without them."

"You can't be serious." She believed true

change came from reasonable people willing to compromise.

"Without someone to set the pendulum's swing, we wouldn't know where to find the middle. None of us in the business of making changes gets everything we want, the extremists allow us to look like moderates and to go after changes that will make a difference."

"I understand how you might feel this way about those on the left, but what about the right?"

He laughed. "You're quick, Kelly. And you're not afraid of me. I can't tell you how refreshing that is."

"I imagine it can get lonely up there on the pedestal," she teased, enjoying herself with him more than she had any man in a long time.

Suddenly serious, he said, "You have no idea."

The words stuck a chord of response that melted another layer of reserve. *Oh, no you don't,* her obnoxious inner voice warned. *No matter how tempting, no matter how intriguing, you will not go where this man could lead you.*

This time she listened . . . reluctantly.

⌁ AS PREDICTED, BY NOON THE SUN HAD WON its battle with the fog, thinning the drops of water like a five-year-old with a stickpin in a room full of balloons. The *Western Flyer* had reached its destination and launched the remote-operated vehicle.

Everything was in place to begin the experiment.

Matt provided a running commentary, only a fraction of which Kelly understood. She did, however, manage to grasp the overall picture and ask questions a step above rudimentary.

They were there to measure how fast carbon dioxide would rise to the surface when released at different depths. The depth today was eight hundred meters, the release made in a plastic box that protected the droplets from lateral water movement but without a top or bottom to impede its upward motion.

Kelly watched the progress on the bank of monitors. After several minutes she leaned closer to Matt, and said softly, "I understand what's going on, but I'm a long way from understanding why."

"The oceans act as a clearinghouse for the earth's carbon dioxide, but it's a painfully slow process. Until the last century there was no need for it to occur any faster. Now there's compelling evidence that the carbon dioxide—which is primarily a by-product of modern industry, our love of the automobile, and the destruction of the rain forests—is responsible for the disappearance of the ozone layer."

"Resulting in what is commonly called the greenhouse effect," Kelly added.

"You've done your homework."

"I've read your book." According to a note on the dust jacket, all profits from the sale of the book went to environmental groups, including one she actually recognized, The Nature Conservancy. She was usually skeptical about such things, having seen too many balance sheets come through the office with travel, entertainment, equipment, and questionable miscellaneous items listed as expenses that were charged against profit. Now that she'd been to Matt's house, seen his bicycle, and his on-loan car, knowing he borrowed a surfboard instead of owning one, she was willing to bet that unless he had a secret bank account in the Cayman Islands, there were, indeed, donations being made to the charities designated.

"But I don't understand what releasing bubbles—" And then it hit her. "Oh, I get it. You're testing to see if you can get the ocean to absorb the carbon dioxide faster."

"Without creating a bigger mess than we already have. We don't want to jump into a 'cure' that turns out to be worse than the problem."

"This seems more a business solution than something an environmentalist would come up with. I thought you guys were focused on stopping the pollution, not finding a way to live with it."

"Us guys?" Matt repeated.

"Sorry, it just came out." Even while sparring with him, she was aware of him physically. She wasn't a toucher. She never put her hand on someone's arm during a conversation to make a point or intimate closeness. Yet she found it was almost all she could think about with Matt. At one point she'd actually reached up to adjust his collar before she realized what she was doing and stuffed her hands in her pockets. Then it was as much as she could do to keep from brushing his hair back from his forehead when they went inside to watch the monitors.

"Those of us who have done the research and come up with the facts and figures are in a race for answers. We've recognized we're not going to win the cooperation of enough countries in time to stop what's happening, so we're looking for a backup plan."

Spoken in a careful, even tone that belied the importance of the message, the words were too devastating to absorb all at once. Either she believed Matt and his friends were wrong, or she believed the planet was dying. On that, there was no middle ground. "There are a lot of people—good people—who disagree with you."

"If I hadn't seen the evidence for myself, I would look for a way to disagree with me, too. It's a damn big pill to swallow."

"What evidence?"

A slow smile formed. "If we do this now, you're going to fall asleep in class."

There was something about the way he said it that made Kelly hesitate. "How do you do it?"

"How do I do what?"

"Live like this. How can you get up in the morning knowing—believing—what you do?"

Instead of answering, he took her hand and led

her outside. "Look," he said and pointed to the sea.

She did. "I don't see anything."

"Look closer."

Off the bow, gleaming black cormorants rode the swells, there one second, gone the next, then silently surfacing again with a silver flash of fish that disappeared in a quick swallow. A sea lion surfaced behind them and rolled to his side, his flipper stuck in the air as if waving.

"They do that for temperature control," Matt said. "The way elephants use their ears."

He moved behind her, put his hands on her shoulders, gently turned her to the left, then leaned forward and grabbed the rail on either side of her. "Do you see the white fishing boat out there?"

She nodded, acutely aware of his body pressing against hers. She glanced at his hands, at the way they held the railing, at the way the muscles moved on his forearms. For an insane instant she imagined his hands touching her, felt their power as he cupped her face and gazed into her eyes.

"Look just to the right and keep watching."

"What am I—"

"Don't talk, just look."

She did, afraid to blink for fear of missing something. And then she saw what Matt had seen before her. It took her breath away. A blue whale surfaced to exhale, just once, leaving a spout of warmed mist in the air, before diving again. They were too far away to see the animal distinctly, but that didn't matter. Just knowing a whale was near, swimming in the same water that held their boat, filled her with awe. She was speechless with a yearning she didn't understand.

"I do what I do," he said softly and as a simple matter of fact, "because I see these things, and I don't know how to stop working to protect them."

5

ON THEIR WAY BACK FROM MOSS LAND-
ing the traffic on Highway 1 slowed to a
crawl, then stopped for minutes at a time. Kelly
glanced at the dashboard clock. It was going to be
seven or later by the time Matt dropped her off. "I
don't know about you, but I'm getting hungry."

"Did you want to stop somewhere?"

Knowing it was a mistake, she said, "I was
thinking more along the lines of a home cooked
meal—to thank you for today," she quickly
added.

"If you did that, then I would just have to take
you out again tomorrow to thank you for the
home-cooked meal and you would feel you had to
cook again and the next day . . ." He looked at her
and grinned. "Who knows where it would end?"

"You can't take me out tomorrow, you're teaching a class."

"Well, I guess we're safe then. I have to warn you, though, I'm a vegetarian."

"Why doesn't that surprise me?"

"Think you can handle it?"

"You are looking at a woman knee deep in vegetables. Since I've been here, I can't seem to drive past a fruit-and-vegetable stand. I don't think there's one I've spotted that I haven't stopped and bought something."

"Then all we're missing is bread and wine."

"Got 'em."

"Where have you been all my life?"

"San Diego."

He laughed. "Are all lawyers so literal?"

"I would think you'd have a pretty good idea of what lawyers are and aren't by now."

"I'm constantly being surprised." The cars in front of them started moving again. "That's another thing that gets me out of bed in the morning."

They traveled the next mile without either of them saying anything. Finally, Kelly broke the silence. "You aren't what I expected."

"You came with preconceived ideas?" he gently chided.

"I'd heard a lot about you."

"From?"

"Other lawyers."

"And you expected a frothing-at-the-mouth, hard-nosed, humorless, son-of-a-bitch fanatic."

She looked at him out of the corner of her eye. "Well, maybe not frothing at the mouth." He laughed again, and she realized it was what she'd been after. When he smiled, one corner of his mouth rose higher than the other, his eyes crinkled, and a single dimple appeared high on his left cheek. She found it almost impossible not to smile in return.

As soon as they cleared the forest and turned onto the beach road, Kelly spotted a strange car in her driveway, a candy apple red Mustang, the kind lusted after by men who believed in beer commercials.

"Looks like you have company," Matt said.

"It's probably a neighbor using the driveway. You and Andrew are the only people I know here."

"Or someone using the beach who didn't know the house has been rented and was afraid to get caught parking on the road."

The road was posted with "NO PARKING" signs from the public parking lot at the state park to the last house on the beach. While the promised fines protected the homeowners from being overwhelmed by cars, most had been forced to widen their driveways to accommodate visitors. According to Andrew, cars frequently spilled over to neighbors' houses when someone was having a party.

The question was answered as soon as Matt pulled into Andrew's driveway and Ray looked out from behind Kelly's house to investigate.

"Oh, no," she groaned.

"You know this guy, I take it?" Matt said.

"Regrettably." She opened her car door.

Matt got out and joined her.

Ray stood his ground and waited for her to come to him. "I thought I would surprise you," he said. "I can see that I have."

"Ray Sperling—Matt Landry," she said.

They shook hands, Matt with good humor, Ray with a scowl.

"What are you doing here, Ray?" Kelly asked.

He looked at Matt before turning his attention to her. "Could we talk about this inside? In private?"

"I've invited Matt to dinner."

"This is important, Kelly," Ray said.

"Why don't we make it another night?" Matt offered.

He wasn't backing away, he was simply making it easier for her, letting her make the decision. "Thank you."

He looked into her eyes and smiled. "Anytime."

"I'll walk you to your car." She left Ray standing in the middle of the road, his hands on his hips, his posture possessive.

Matt opened the car door and paused before getting inside. "Old boyfriend?"

"Yes . . . but not so old. I broke up with him two days ago. Obviously he didn't believe I was serious."

"Are you okay with this? Do you want me to stick around?"

She looked at his mouth, at the soft shadow of a beard on his chin and above his top lip, and without stopping to consider the consequences, told him exactly what she wanted. "Kiss me."

He only hesitated a second before he put his hand on the back of her neck and brought her forward for what must have looked like a searingly deep kiss to Ray. When she realized he had no intention of giving her the kiss she wanted, she opened her mouth and touched her tongue to his. He responded immediately, taking the lead, tasting, testing, sending a shot of liquid fire from her lips to her toes.

It was more than she'd bargained for, more than she expected, and less than she wanted.

"Will that do it?" Matt asked.

"For now," she said.

He glanced over her shoulder. "I think you got what you were after."

She started to turn and look, then thought better of it. "What do you mean?"

"Once he gets past the strutting jealousy part, he'll be putty in your hands."

She frowned, confused. And then it hit her, she hadn't kissed Matt to make Ray jealous, she'd done it to show him that she'd moved on. But that wasn't the way Matt had seen it. He had no way of knowing that with Ray actions spoke louder than words. Embarrassed beyond words of explanation, she mumbled, "I'm sorry. I shouldn't have involved you in this."

He lowered his head and tucked his hand under her chin to force her to look at him. "Hey, what are friends for?"

"Not this." She'd used him, and she didn't like people who used people. She was losing control of everything—her life, her beliefs, her honor. "I'm glad Ray saw us together—but I kissed you because I wanted to."

"Good luck." He got in the car and rolled down the window. "I'll see you in class."

He didn't believe her. She nodded and watched him drive away, feeling as if she'd lost something it would be impossible to regain.

"That was quite a show." Ray jammed his hands in his pockets. "I didn't know you had it in you."

"Why are you here?" She was suddenly, overwhelmingly tired, her lack of sleep and the emotional roller coaster ride she was on putting her near the edge of civility.

"Can we go inside?"

She walked past him, cutting through the garden instead of taking the brick pathway that ran in front of the house. He backtracked the way he had come and met her at the front door.

As soon as she rounded the corner she understood Ray's insistence on going inside. He wanted her to see the flowers and Godiva chocolate that were sitting on the porch, believing they would do most of his work for him. She unlocked the door and stepped over the elaborate presentation bouquet as if it were a nuisance.

Obviously annoyed at her casual dismissal of his gifts, Ray brought them inside and tried to hand her the candy. "They're your favorites," he said accusingly.

"Not anymore."

"Since when?"

"I've switched—" For the life of her she couldn't come up with another brand of chocolates. "To cinnamon rolls."

He tossed the box on a chair, looked at the flowers, and tossed them there, too. "All right, I'll give you this one. Just tell me what it's going to take to make things right between us, and I'll do it."

"It's not going to happen."

"Don't you think you're carrying this a little too far? I said I was sorry, why can't you—"

She held up her hand. "Hold on just a minute. I must have missed something. Exactly when was it that you said you were sorry?"

He motioned toward the candy and flowers. "What do you call this?"

"A bribe."

He flushed an unattractive red that left splotches on his cheeks. Before saying anything, he made an elaborate bow. "I'm sorry." Upright again, he glared at her. "Is that what you want?"

"What I want is to be left alone." She kicked off her shoes, sat in the corner of the sofa, and pulled her legs up against her chest. "I don't understand why you're doing this, Ray. You don't love me. You never really did. We had fun for a while, then it stopped being fun. Once word gets out that you're free again, you'll have women crawling over each other to get to you."

"I don't want other women. I want you."

If he'd shown half this much passion when they were together, it would have been twice as hard to leave. "You've always said you thought Dara was—"

Stunned, he looked as if she'd slapped him. "How do you know about Dara? Who told you? It was Donna, wasn't it? She's always butting into things that aren't any of her business."

How could she have been so stupid? All the signs were there, she'd just refused to see them. "I wasn't accusing you of anything," she said evenly. "I was about to suggest you might want to go out with Dara now that you're free."

"Nothing happened between us. We went out a couple of times, but that was it."

"I don't care." Amazingly, she didn't. "Now you can do whatever you want, whenever you want, and not worry about who might see you. It's called freedom, Ray. And I'm giving it to you. Now be grateful and get out of here and leave me alone."

For what seemed an eternity, he stood in the middle of the room and stared at her, his eyes betraying his inner conflict. Finally, he moved toward her and went down on bended knee. "I wanted to save this for later, but you've forced my hand."

Ray dug in his pocket and brought out a small velvet box. Before she could say anything, he opened the box, and presented it to her. "You win, Kelly. I knew this was what you were after, but I didn't think I was ready. I do now."

Kelly looked at the diamond solitaire ring, the stone large enough to be noticed but within the bounds of good taste. Knowing that only days ago she probably would have accepted his insulting proposal horrified her. She tried to give the ring back to him. "I can't take this."

He held his hands up and backed away. "This is getting a little old, Kelly. I understand you're angry and that you were trying to get back at me for some wrong you think I've done, but this has gone on long enough. I made a mistake. You've made more than your share since we started going together, and I've always forgiven you. Is it so wrong to expect the same in return?"

Finally she understood. In his own way, Ray really did love her. Did she have the right to blame him if it wasn't the way she wanted to be loved? She unfolded her legs and reached out to take his hand. "Timing really is everything, Ray. From the beginning we've been off step with each other. When I wanted you to make a commitment, Dara got in the way. And now—"

"Don't tell me you feel something for that guy

you were with. You can't have known him more than a couple of days."

"Sometimes that's all it takes." She didn't care that she was letting him believe something that wasn't true. Ray needed sound reasons for their breakup and nothing was more sound than her finding someone new. "My mother and father knew from the moment they met that they were destined to be together."

"Give me a break, Kelly. Love doesn't happen like that. Not real love. Odds are if your mother had lived, she and your father would be divorced and they would be with other people today."

"You're wrong."

"Oh, grow up." He flung her hand away. "Look at the statistics. Forever is a greeting card fantasy."

"Then what is it you're asking me? You want us to be married—for a while? Until you get bored or someone better comes along?"

"No, of course not. I'm just being realistic. If we go into this without illusions, and it works out better than we thought, think what a coup that will be. We've put too much time into this relationship to just toss it away now."

A sadness enveloped her. "Better now than later, Ray. When I finally do get married—if I ever get married—I want to believe with all my heart that it will last a lifetime. Without that I'd rather be alone."

"Even if it's an illusion?"

"Yes, even then."

"I can't give you that," he said. "I can't even pretend it's possible."

He gave Kelly a lopsided grin filled with irony and mischief, reminding her what had drawn her to him in the first place. "My guess is you wouldn't have gone for the prenuptial agreement I was going to have drawn up either."

He walked over to the chair and picked up the flowers. "These need to be put in water. No sense letting them go to waste."

"I'll take care of them."

"About the chocolate . . ."

She exchanged the box for the flowers. "Take it. I know Godiva's your favorite."

She walked him out to the car. "Do you have something going with that Matt guy?"

"No," she answered truthfully. Whether she wanted to have something going with him was another matter.

"He's not your type, you know. You don't want to rebound from us and end up with someone like him. It will never work." He leaned over to give her a kiss good-bye. Their lips touched and it was over. "Take care of yourself."

"I will." For one brief moment she felt a twinkling of hope that they might find a way to be friends.

He paused as he started to get into the car. "God, Kelly, I feel so sorry for you. Someday you're going to look back on this and know it was the biggest mistake you ever made. What I offered might not have lasted, but it was the best chance you're going to get. Ask your girlfriends. There aren't a whole lot of men like me out there."

"Thanks, Ray. You will never know how much it means to me to hear you say that."

He nodded, missing the point entirely.

She watched him drive away, noting that he waited until he reached the end of the road to stop and open the box of chocolates.

She was free. No guilt, no regrets, no sorrow. Maybe a little numb, but nothing that wouldn't be gone by morning.

6

KELLY LEFT AN HOUR EARLY FOR HER FIRST class. She'd been warned that parking was at a premium on the University of California Santa Cruz campus and that walking a half mile or more to class was the norm rather than the exception.

Located on two thousand acres, the university's eight colleges were patterned after the Cambridge system. Each was a self-contained and independent unit that shared library and laboratory facilities. Incorporated into a densely forested hillside with spectacular ocean views, the university's buildings were architectural masterpieces blended into the landscape.

The student body was noted for its freethinking and acceptance of alternate lifestyles. Vegan and vegetarian meals were the standards in the cafeterias and local politics as important as national to the students.

The path leading from the parking lot where Kelly finally found an empty space to the classroom where Matt was lecturing had a posted warning to be on the lookout for mountain lions. She took the warning seriously and chanced being late by taking the road to class instead of the shorter route through the trees.

She found a seat on the top row just as Matt entered the room and crossed the stage to the blackboard. He wrote his name and the title of the class in bold block letters.

"Good morning," he said, dusting his hands as he walked to the podium. Low murmurs of response rolled toward the front of the room. Matt's gaze skimmed the crowd and when he reached Kelly he hesitated just long enough to let her know he'd found her.

Dressed in jeans and a collared knit shirt, he looked slim and hard and incredibly sexy. Kelly's heart quickened at seeing him again. Unbidden, memories of her response to his kiss surfaced, and she felt her heart quicken.

"How many of you have seen a passenger pigeon?" Matt began. As anticipated, no one raised their hand. "None, of course. A species of bird that once numbered in the billions—" He paused. "Yes, I said *billions*." He paused again, giving the number emphasis with his silence. "A bird that made up forty percent of all birds on this continent, a bird that flew sixty miles an hour in flocks that took three days to pass—this personally witnessed by James Audubon and noted in his journal—is *gone*. Every last one of them. The last official sighting in the wild, a lone female, was shot for stealing corn. Another female lived out her life in a zoo, which made it possible, for those who care about such things, to achieve the dubious distinction of knowing the exact day the species became extinct."

He walked to the edge of the stage and focused on a young man sitting in the front row. "Now, I'd like you to tell me how this has affected you personally? Is your life different somehow? Have you suffered an economic loss? Physical? Mental?" The target of Matt's intense questioning appeared upset, but shook his head and shrugged in response to the questions. Matt shifted his focus to a girl on the second row. "On a larger scale, has it changed the world in any way?" She, too, shook her head.

"I'll go along with that," Matt said, moving to the opposite side of the room and looking at a woman with braids hanging over her shoulders. "So why should you care?" His gaze traveled up several rows, stopping to make eye contact with many of the now uncomfortable students. "Why should any of us care?

"This country is spending enormous time, effort, and money to save species that a mere generation or two before us were considered vermin.

In some cases, these efforts are directed toward animals our government once paid bounties to eradicate.

"Other than a sometimes obnoxious and vocal fraction of the population who have chosen to champion the black-footed ferret, the wolf, the prairie dog, the spotted owl—" He stopped for dramatic effect. "—*who the hell cares*?" Slowly, he moved from one side of the stage to the other. "Certainly not the inner-city kids whose daily routine includes hiding under their beds to dodge bullets. Or the homeless mother who is forced to stand outside a shelter every night hoping there will be room for her and her children."

She recognized his brilliant use of reverse psychology; that alone should have made her immune to its effects. But not this time. Intellectually, she could remain aloof, emotionally she found herself being drawn into the issue—on the wrong side. He'd surprised her and made her care that a billion birds, an entire species, had been wiped off the face of the earth in less than a half century. More important was the subtext—nothing had changed. It could happen again. It was happening again.

Did she care? In the grand scheme of things, did it matter? The world would go on without frogs and whales and elephants. It had gone on without dinosaurs. For that matter, it could go on without humans.

As it stood now, the powerful few were deciding these things for the voiceless many. It wasn't right. And she did care.

She'd read about defining moments in people's lives, moments that changed them forever. Until then she'd considered herself too ordinary to have something like that happen to her. And yet there she was, experiencing her own revelation, not quite sure how she'd gotten there, a little scared, a lot excited, not knowing where she would go from where she was, only knowing her life would never be the same.

"I mentioned the spotted owl," Matt said. "Depending on your political leanings, either the most beloved or hated symbol of the last decade." He meandered back to the center of the stage. "Don't worry, I'm not going to go over that well-trod territory again, except to say that 90 percent of the old growth forest in California, forest where the spotted owl and a long list of other endangered species and plants live, has already been cut. When we talk about preserving a home for the owl and the other plants and animals on the list, we're talking about setting aside a percentage of a percentage."

Kelly felt as if he'd been speaking directly to her. She was just as sure everyone else in the room felt the same way. Matt Landry was mesmerizing, his beliefs compelling, his integrity unquestioned. She understood the power he would bring to a courtroom and the fear he engendered in opposing counsel. And she understood her father's insistence that she come here to discover for herself what she would be up against when she faced Matt as a witness.

Matt's voice softened. "But even with 90 percent of the old growth forest gone, there's no denying we're all still here. So what's the big deal?"

People began to shift uncomfortably in their seats. This was not what they'd come to hear.

"What has the activism of the twentieth century gained us? Government regulations forced through Congress by left-wing environmentalists have sent businesses fleeing the United States to set up shop in friendlier countries. Thousands of people with generations-old skills are without jobs.

"People without jobs can't afford the products that are now produced elsewhere. A company that can't sell what it makes can't stay in business. Eventually, inevitably, the marketplace will collapse and a global depression will hit that will make the last depression look like good times."

Kelly held her breath in anticipation of what would come next. A fire burned in her mind fueled by hope and possibilities. She had a cause, something to believe in. And something she was smart enough to realize would break her heart as often as it would feed her soul.

Matt looked into her eyes, and, for an electric instant, they connected. It was as if he knew what had just happened to her, as if he'd been waiting for it—as if he'd been waiting for her. And as if she'd come all this way to find him.

Was this how it had happened with her mother and father? Were they drawn to each other with intellectual as well as physical passion? Was that what it was like to find a soul mate?

The thought left her reeling. She'd spent one day with Matt Landry. No one fell in love in a day. No one. She was attracted to him. Easily understood. He was handsome and had a smile that made it impossible not to smile back. His kiss had been like a promissory note that she couldn't get out of her mind. And on top of everything else, he smelled good, like the air after a summer rain.

And he challenged her. He made her think, and question, and believe in new things. It was hardly a mystery why she was drawn to him. But love?

Matt took several seconds to let what he'd said sink in. "There are people who sincerely believe what I just told you and there are people who don't, but who are very good at using it to persuade others. I'm not here to point fingers or to dwell on what has been destroyed in the past, and I hope you aren't either. If you take anything away from this class, I want it to be the belief that cooperative, mutually beneficial change is still possible between big business and environmental interests. Let's not be the engineers sitting in a lifeboat watching the *Titanic* go under saying we knew it was impossible to build a ship that wouldn't sink.

"Those of us on the environmental side have tried scare headlines. We've learned that no matter how dramatic or terrifying, they don't work. Confrontation may succeed on the open seas between a whaler and a lifeboat, but it doesn't work in Congress or in a courtroom. We've learned the hard way that nothing is accomplished when people face each other shouting words that neither hear.

"When two sides to an issue become adversaries, cooperation is lost. The result is gridlock. Time and effort and energy are consumed that are desperately needed elsewhere.

"We have to find a way to break these patterns." He stopped to look at the row of students directly in front of him, taking time to make eye contact with each of them. "That's why I'm here. And that's what we're going to be talking about for the next four weeks. You are the hope and the promise for change. Without you, not only can't we accomplish what needs to be done, we will lose everything we have gained."

As she watched and listened to Matt, a thought hovered just outside Kelly's reach, caught like a piece of paper in a breeze, dancing away without direction or reason when she tried to grab hold. There was something about her father sending her there that had bothered her from the beginning. No matter how he presented the idea, there were holes in the reasoning. She'd gone along because the new direction he'd envisioned for her in the firm seemed so important to him.

Almost too important.

Almost too well thought out—with too much subtext.

Damn. He'd done it again. He'd manipulated her. Realizing that made all the loose ends come together, answered all the questions. Well, not all of them. What she didn't know was why.

Vacillating between anger and curiosity, Kelly glanced at the clock. Twenty minutes before the scheduled fifteen-minute break. Settling in for the wait, she focused on Matt, looking past the idealist to the man. Had he figured in her father's equation? And, if so, how?

Could her father, without ever meeting him, have known she would find it impossible not to be drawn to Matt intellectually? Had he guessed how compelling she would find his arguments and commitment and drive?

⁓KELLY SLIPPED OUT OF CLASS AT THE BREAK and found a public phone. Turning to the airline page of the directory, she found a carrier flying out of San Jose that could get her to San Diego that afternoon.

Four hours later she was sitting in her father's office waiting for him to return from the courthouse. She paced and sat and got up to pace again. Stopping to stare out the window at the expanse of ocean visible from her father's corner office, she thought how only a week ago her driving goal had been to one day have a corner office, too.

She heard the door open and turned to see her father looking at her, a mixture of concern and delight on his face. Before he said anything, he opened his arms for a hug. Kelly stepped into his embrace. She loved her father, but there were times he made it almost impossible for her to like him.

"Sheila told me you were here." He leaned back to look at her. "What happened? I thought your class started today."

"We have to talk."

"Sounds serious."

"It is."

He took her hand and led her to one of the leather chairs beside the desk. Before joining her he buzzed Sheila to tell her to hold his calls. He looked at Kelly. "Do you want anything? Coffee? Coke? A drink?"

She shook her head.

"That's it, Sheila," he said. He sat opposite Kelly. "I'm all yours."

She pulled in a deep breath. "I want to know why you sent me to Santa Cruz. The real reason."

"I tried the direct approach to get you to look at who you are and what you really want to do with your life, Kelly. It didn't work. You left me no choice but to put you in the path of change."

"You manipulated me—*again*. Why?"

He leaned forward and took her hand. "All your life you have been so hell-bent on pleasing me, you've talked yourself into doing things you really didn't want to do—like working in this office. I knew I was right when I offered to let you head the new division, and you accepted. That's not who you are, Kelly. Why would you even consider taking on a job like that if it weren't to please me?"

She thought about all the work he'd put in arranging to send her to Santa Cruz, how he'd found the beach house and even registered her in the class. "You obviously had something in mind when you sent me off on this voyage of self-discovery. What was it?"

"I know what you're thinking, but never once did it occur to me that by sending you up there it would mean the end of your relationship with Ray."

"Or, I suppose, you would have done it a long time ago."

"That's not fair."

"Maybe, but it's the truth."

He gave her that much. "Perhaps."

"You know if I go into environmental law it won't be here. I'll have to leave the firm."

He nodded. "I was afraid that might be how you'd feel."

It hurt that he wasn't willing to fight to keep her a part of his life when she'd fought so hard to be there. "And you still went ahead?"

"Actions speak louder than words, Kelly," he said softly. "This is my way of telling you how much I love you."

"By driving me away?"

"By letting you find your own way, by letting you discover your own passion. You can't live your life to please me. I thought I was doing what was best for you and your sisters when you were sitting on my knee and I preached ambition instead of reading you fairy tales. I came to the realization too late for Alexis and Donna; they look at me as if I'm out of my mind when I try to tell them what they are missing in their single-minded drive for success. They have ambition but no passion. They go from one relationship to another without regret when it ends or hope that they've found their life's partner when another one begins."

"That's the way things are now, Dad. No one believes in ever after anymore. Alexis and Donna—and me, too—are simply trying to make the best of what we've got."

He was suddenly, pointedly angry. "If you're willing to settle, then that's what you'll get. Expect better. Demand better. You and your sisters deserve the best."

"What you want for us isn't out there." How could she explain that she'd never dated a man, that she'd never met a man who didn't flinch at the mention of marriage and children. If pressed, they would talk about settling down someday but not until they'd experienced all that life had to offer. Their goals were to live in an upscale apartment, own a status car, and at forty-five marry a trophy wife who was twenty years younger than they.

"All I want for you is what your mother and I had."

Her gaze locked on his. "You, of all people, should know how rare that is. How long has it been since Mom died? Has anyone come close to replacing her?"

She had him. He sighed and patted her hand. "We were destined for each other. I knew it the minute we met."

"How?" Her question went far deeper than simple curiosity.

"I had never been so comfortable around anyone. Right from the beginning, we talked and laughed as if we'd known each other forever. She felt it, too, and we knew we had to find a way to be together."

"And you were married two and a half months later." Growing up, she'd asked to be told the story so many times she had the words memorized and would say them with him. She never felt closer to her father than when he talked about her mother.

"How did you know what would happen if I went to this class?" she asked.

He grinned. "Because you have the heart and soul of an environmentalist. I never did understand how you managed to bury it under all that commercialism that took hold of you in college."

"You're going to have to explain yourself better than that."

"Think back to when you used to help me in the garden. Do you remember the time you accidentally cut that worm in half?"

"Yes . . . and I bawled my head off until you told me that God liked worms so well that he made them special."

"When you cut them in half . . ."

She smiled. "You had two."

"I found you in the garden the next day digging up worms and cutting them in half so we would have twice as many." He chuckled. "I often wondered how many of them lived."

"I loved the time we spent in Mom's garden."

"You loved the garden, too, Kelly. How could you not grow up to care about this great big garden we all live on?"

"I should be mad at you."

"But you understand why I had to do what I did."

"You're going to miss me," she warned.

"Don't think I didn't consider that." He reached for her other hand and held it between his own. "Now, tell me about Matt Landry. He seems an interesting sort."

She smiled. "I have a feeling you know a lot more about him than I do."

"Indulge me."

"He's everything I didn't know I wanted in a man."

One of Harold's eyebrows rose in surprise. "Is that good?"

Kelly laughed. "Better than good. Now I have to find out if he feels the same way about me."

"How could he not?"

"From your lips to God's ear."

7

MATT STOOD AT THE TOP OF THE STAIRS and scanned the beach, looking for Kelly. He'd been there five times over the past two days, and had decided that if he didn't find her this time, he would start making phone calls.

He spotted her halfway to the southern promontory, standing at the shoreline, talking to a fisherman. His heart took off, thumping his ribs with all the subtlety of a drummer in a garage band. Like it or not, convenient or not, rational or not, something had happened to him where Kelly Anderson was concerned. He'd known her all of three days—five if he counted that first day on the beach—and all he could think about was seeing her again.

She couldn't have come into his life at a more

inconvenient time. He was too busy for a courtship longer than the four weeks he'd be there for the class, and then it was off for months of nonstop conferences, legislative meetings in Washington, and three court cases that were scheduled to come to trial before the end of the year. No woman would put up with that. No man had the right to ask.

On top of everything else, there was the boyfriend to consider. Undoubtedly they'd patched things up by now and were back together. There was no reason Kelly should know, or even suspect, the doors she'd opened in his mind the day they'd spent together, or how she'd turned his world upside down with that kiss. He'd tried to mentally compartmentalize her, to slide her into the category of friend—special friend, maybe, but no more than that. But he couldn't get past the kiss, how it had made him feel, and how thinking about it took him back to the boat and triggered memories of her laugh and her smile and her quick intellect. She'd made him think of possibilities instead of roadblocks to a new relationship.

There wasn't a major city in the world that he couldn't pick up the phone and contact a friend. Until now that had been enough. After his divorce he'd accepted that from then on his work would be his passion, his mistress, his wife, his lifelong companion. He refused to acknowledge the loneliness because it didn't matter, it couldn't. He

believed his work was important, more important than personal sacrifice or happiness.

And then he'd met Kelly.

⁓KELLY WAVED GOOD-BYE TO THE FISHERMAN
and turned to watch a pelican skim past the foam
on an incoming wave. The salt-laden breeze
caught her hair and filled her open windbreaker
like a kite straining to be airborne. A flash of
brown caught her eye, a sleek curving movement
in the aquamarine of a swell. She waited for it to
appear again and when it did, saw that it was a
sea lion shopping for a late-afternoon snack.

Growing up in San Diego she'd always loved the
ocean in a fun-and-sun way. Here she'd come to see
it differently, in the life that called the rolling water
home and in the fragile forgiveness she'd always
taken for granted. When the beaches at home were
closed because of pollution it was an inconven-
ience, no more. Whatever party she or her friends
had planned was moved poolside, the food cooked
on backyard barbecues instead of portable grills.

There was never a thought given to the fish or
seals or passing whales or even to the men and
women who caught fish to supplement the food
they put on their tables.

She'd thought and believed what she had because it was what her friends and their friends
thought and believed. To be or think any differ-

ently would put her on the outside. She didn't know how to be an outsider. She'd always played by the unspoken, but understood rules in her comfortable society.

As much as she didn't know how to be an outsider, she didn't know how to be an environmentalist either. She didn't understand the people in small inflatable boats who put themselves between whales and whalers risking their lives in what was too often a fruitless gesture. And then the memory of what she'd felt when she saw the whale spout came back to her. Had she known that whale was about to die, would she have put herself in danger to save it?

Out of the corner of her eye she saw someone approaching and decided to ignore them in the hope they wouldn't stop. She wanted to be alone to think, to plan. The person came closer and she could see that it was a man. Finally, he came so close she couldn't ignore him and looked up—directly into Matt Landry's eyes. She caught her breath in surprise at his unguarded happiness to see her.

He stopped inches away, just short of touching her. "You're back."

"I had some things I had to do."

"I was worried."

They weren't just words, he meant them. "I'm sorry. I shouldn't have left without saying something."

"Are you all right?"

"Yes." How strange that they were acting so polite with each other, like casual acquaintances, when in her mind they were so much more.

He nodded. "Coming back to class on Monday?"

She smiled. "Yes."

"Good." He shoved his hands in the back pockets of his jeans and for a moment looked as if he were going to leave. "Was it something I said?"

The easy answer, the one that wouldn't leave her vulnerable if she'd completely misread his feelings, was on the tip of her tongue when she decided she didn't want to play it safe with him. If he couldn't handle knowing how she felt, he wasn't who she believed him to be.

"It's who you are," she told him. The tide was coming in. She should either back up or let the waves claim her. Drawn by the symbolism, she stayed where she was. "I've never known anyone like you."

"It's the trappings. When you know me better you'll see how unextraordinary I am."

The extraordinary thing was that he was sincere. He saved his ego for his work. "I can't be like you, Matt. I'm a detail person. I build cases methodically and relentlessly and even when I know it's a necessary means to an end, I don't bend well. I'm an oak, not a willow."

He looked at her long and hard. "Where's Ray?"

"Home."

"Is he coming back?"

"No."

A piece of fishing line rolled in with a wave. Matt stooped to pick it up and put it in his pocket. "I take it the kiss didn't work?"

He was protecting himself. She would have done the same. "Oh, it worked all right. Just not the way I expected."

He eyed her. "How so?"

"Ray asked me to marry him." She hesitated telling him the rest, fearing it was too much too soon. Then her ever-present inner voice intruded and insisted she take the chance. "The whole time he was trying to convince me I should say yes, I was thinking about you—and the way you kissed me."

A slow smile tugged at the corners of his mouth. "Well, that pretty much settles it."

"Settles what?" she asked carefully.

"The story we're going to tell our kids when they ask how we met."

She should have protested, at the very least she should have told him he was moving a little fast. Instead she said, "Don't you think we should get the second kiss out of the way before we start planning a family?"

He put his hand at the back of her neck and brought her to him. With their lips almost touching, he murmured, "To show you how good I am at compromising, I'm even willing to wait for the third and forth."

He covered her mouth with his, sparking a liquid fire that enveloped her. She came up on her toes and wrapped her arms around his neck, pressing her body close, unable to get close enough. She'd been kissed in passion by a dozen men, but never like this. The yearning she felt left her breathless.

Stunned, she moved out of his arms and looked at him, finding her own thoughts and emotions mirrored in his eyes. "Okay, so the first kiss wasn't a fluke. Where do we go from here?"

He brought her back into his arms, holding her as he looked at her. A wave washed over their feet. "I don't think we should try to rush anything. We have another three and a half weeks to work things out."

"Bad timing, huh?"

"I'm going on the road as soon as the class ends. But I'll find a way to get back as often as I can."

"What if I went with you?" she said impulsively.

"What about your job?"

"I quit."

"You didn't have to do that. I would never expect you—"

"I know." And she did. It was one of the things she liked about him. She tilted her head and kissed him, long and slow and inviting.

She was no longer afraid of loving him. From then on what they didn't know about each other they would exchange like beautifully wrapped presents. She thought about the "present" her father and sisters would make and smiled.

"There are some people I need to tell you about . . ." she began.

Matt took her hand and led her to a log, where they could sit and watch the sunset and mark the beginning of the rest of their lives.

July

1

"WELL? WHAT DO YOU THINK?" CRAIG Davis stopped on his way to the kitchen, bracing the box he was carrying against the back of a living room wing chair. "Is it what you expected?"

Ann turned from the window, a blank look in her eyes. "What did you say?" When he didn't immediately answer, she added, "I'm sorry. I was somewhere else."

It was a statement as common as the silence that had replaced their once eager sharing of the day's events. He shifted the box under his arm. "Never mind. It wasn't important."

"Please—" She held out her hand in a helpless gesture. "I wasn't ignoring you. I was just thinking about . . . about how much fun Jeremy is going to have here and how hard you worked to get the whole month off."

He knew what she'd been thinking, and it had nothing to do with him or Jeremy or the time they would be there. He hated that she lied to him and at the same time was grateful she spared him the truth. "I asked what you thought of the house."

She looked around as if just then noticing her surroundings. "It's lovely. Nicer than I expected." She struggled for something else. "Rentals usually look . . ." She shrugged. "Like rentals. But this is really . . . nice."

He'd found the house through a friend and had almost backed out when he learned it had to be rented for an entire month. He'd never taken a two-week vacation, let alone stayed away from the office for four. But desperate times demanded desperate measures. If this didn't work, at least he would know he'd given everything he had to give. "Where's Jeremy?"

She blinked and then frowned. "I don't know. I thought he was with you."

"Jesus, Ann. You were supposed to—"

Jeremy came into the room from the hallway. He moved protectively toward his mother. "It's okay, Dad."

With his light brown hair in need of cutting, wearing a Garth Brooks T-shirt passed down from his cousin and two-size-too-big pants held in place with a tightly cinched belt, he looked like a poster boy for neglected children. No one would ever pick him out of a line up as the nine-year-old son of a man who had his own CPA firm and a woman who, until a year ago, had managed conventions for the largest hotel in Reno, Nevada.

Jeremy took his mother's hand. "I told her I was going to unpack my stuff. She probably didn't hear me."

Ann gave Jeremy a grateful smile. "Would you like me to go to the beach with you later? You used to love the water. Remember the time I held you until a big wave came in, and then I'd let you go and Daddy would catch you?"

"He was only two when we took him to Hawaii," Craig said. "I doubt he even remembers what the ocean looks like."

"I do remember, Dad. And I was three. Bobby came with us because Uncle Carl and Aunt Marcia were getting divorced." As if obliged to convince his father, he added, "We went out to dinner and there were lizards in the restaurant and they scared Bobby."

With their son in Hawaii, Carl and Marcia had worked out their problems instead of working out the details of the divorce. Nine months later, Bobby had a brother and an intact family that grew more solid every year.

As convincing as Jeremy sounded, Craig wondered if his memories were real or ones that came from the photograph albums he took into his room and studied every night the way he'd once disappeared to absorb Harry Potter.

"Give me another half hour to get things put away, and I'll go down to the beach with you." Craig worked to make the statement appear casual. Jeremy didn't need to know how worried his father was about leaving him alone near the water with his mother.

"I can help," Ann said. "What else needs to be done?"

A futile flash of anger shot through Craig. All Ann had to do was look around and see what still needed doing. A woman who had once directed a staff of thirty, who'd thrived on challenge, who had an attention to detail to rival NASA's, had become like a second child in the family. For months now she'd refused to take responsibility without direction.

As always, Craig's sorrow overrode his frustration. "The suitcases are only half-unpacked and the kitchen stuff still needs to be put away."

She had tears in her eyes when she looked at Craig and silently mouthed, "Thank you."

He nodded and glanced at Jeremy, noting his obvious relief at the gentle ending to what too often in the past had led to confrontation between his parents. Jeremy's reaction was harder for Craig to deal with than Ann's. When he thought about the outgoing, happy kid his son had once been, Craig had a difficult time accepting the serious, taciturn child he was now.

"I'll help Mom," Jeremy said. They were words

spoken so often the past year they almost went unnoticed, like a period at the end of a sentence.

Knowing his presence would put some unintended pressure on Ann, making her question every decision no matter how simple until she was unable to make any decision at all, Craig went into the bedroom and filled the dresser drawers and closet with the clothes he'd packed the day before.

The sun was low on the horizon by the time they left the house for the beach. Jeremy walked between Craig and Ann, holding their hands, both an emotional conduit and insulator.

"Look at those clouds sitting on the water," Jeremy said.

"That's fog," Craig told him. "It will probably roll in tonight after we go to bed."

"Cool." He toed a broken shell without breaking stride. "Will it still be here when we get up?"

"Probably. And if not, there will be plenty of chances to see it the month we're here."

Jeremy didn't say anything for several seconds. "What will we do if it's foggy on my birthday?"

"I take it you'd prefer sunshine?" Craig wished Ann would say something. She was better at this kind of trapped-in-the-car conversation with Jeremy than he was.

"They might shut down the rides. If it's bad enough, they might even have to shut down the whole boardwalk. Then what would we do?"

"They won't."

"But what if they do?"

"They won't, Jeremy," Craig insisted. "These people are used to fog. It's as much a part of their summer as sunshine every day is part of ours."

"How do you know that?"

"My grandmother lived here when I was your age, and I used to visit her."

That seemed to satisfy him. Jeremy looked at Ann. "Where did your grandmother used to live when you were my age?"

She didn't answer him.

"Ann?" Craig prompted.

She turned to look at him. "What?"

"Jeremy's talking to you."

"I'm sorry, sweetheart. I was thinking about something. What did you say?"

"I was just wondering where your grandmother lived when you were my age."

"Why would you want to know that?"

Craig looked away. She hadn't heard a thing they'd been talking about. It wasn't going to work. He'd been a fool to believe her promise to try harder if he took time off and they went away together. Nothing had changed. Nothing was going to change.

"It's okay, Mom. You don't have to tell me. Me and Dad were just talking about stuff."

"Shouldn't you be looking for driftwood?" Craig asked Jeremy. They'd stopped for dinner that night at a restaurant selling wind chimes made out of driftwood and seashells. At first Jeremy had asked to buy one to hang outside his bedroom window, and then, unable to decide which one he wanted, announced he would make his own.

Jeremy seemed torn between going and staying.

"Go ahead," Ann urged. "We'll be right behind you."

He let go of their hands and took off to explore the already picked-over treasures left behind by the last high tide. Craig pointed to a bleached log sitting well back from the shoreline. Too large to have been rolled there by kids, the log's size and location were silent witness to the fierce storms that occasionally hit the area.

"We can see the whole beach from here," he said.

"And Jeremy can see us," she added.

Craig sat on one end, giving her room to take the middle where the wood had been worn smooth. Instead she sat at the other end.

"It's not like Hawaii," she said after several minutes. "But it's nice," she quickly added. "Just like you said it would be."

"What would you like to do tomorrow?"

She gave him a blank stare. "I don't know what there is to do."

"I take it you didn't read any of the books I brought home?" Hoping to get her involved in planning the trip, he'd picked up several travel books on the Monterey area and asked her to look through them for ideas.

"I meant to . . ."

"Did you at least bring them?" He worked to keep the frustration out of his voice, but the look she gave him let him know he'd failed.

Ann crossed her arms over her chest and looked down at her feet. "You know, it's hard for me to remember the last time we talked, and I wasn't apologizing to you for something. Everything I do, everything I say, is wrong somehow." She glanced up to him. "Are you as tired of it as I am?"

"What do you want me to do? I'm willing to try anything to have our old life back."

She lashed out at him. "Our old life is gone, Craig. We *can't* go back. Why am I the only one who can see that?"

"Are you saying that we should just give up?" How could he pray that she would say no and hope that she said yes at the same time? "Is that what you want?"

"If I could really have what I want, we wouldn't be here." Tears filled her eyes and spilled over to her cheeks. "We'd be home playing with our baby, sending out invitations for her first birthday party, and writing the letters for her time capsule. I'd be decorating the house and . . ." Her voice caught in a hiccupped sob. "And . . . and instead I'm here. How could you not know what being away from her on her birthday would do to me?"

"You should have told me you didn't want to come."

"I ordered pink roses for her." She went on as if

she hadn't heard him. "Barbara is going to put them on her grave for me." Doubling over, she put her hands to her face and sobbed. "I'm her mother, Craig. *I should be the one giving them to her.*"

Craig knelt in front of her and took her into his arms. "She was my daughter, too, Ann," he said. "We gave her everything we had to give when she was with us. She's somewhere that she doesn't need us now. Jeremy does."

She held herself rigid, unable to accept the comfort he offered. Even when they were touching, they were apart.

2

ANN WAITED FOR CRAIG'S BREATHING PATtern to change from light to heavy sleep before she slipped out of bed and took her robe off the chair by the dresser. Instead of curling up on the sofa the way she normally did at home, she carefully unlocked the sliding glass door and went out onto the deck.

A full moon rode the crest of the night sky, laying a shimmering path across the water. For a moment she imagined herself on that path and that the path led to Angela. She would go there even if told there might be no way home—no hesitation, no doubts, no looking back. She couldn't bear the thought that her baby had no one to hold her when she cried or sing to her when she was sleepy or tell her how much she was loved when she awoke in the morning.

Ann's arms ached to hold her little girl. Her daughter's feel was imprinted in her memory. She had only to close her eyes and have Angela there again. Only more and more the baby who came to her wasn't the smiling one with the sparkling happy eyes. She was the fragile, unresponsive little girl the nurses and doctor had told her was beyond their help. They unhooked her from an array of leads and monitors to wrap her in a soft pink blanket and put her in Ann's arms.

Ann knew without being told that she had only moments left with her daughter. She struggled to find the words to tell her how much she was loved, words with the power to bring solace and comfort in the loneliness of a world without her mother and father and brother.

Then for a brief heart-stopping moment Angela did what no one believed she would ever do again. She opened her eyes and looked directly into Ann's. It was as if she could feel her mother's heart breaking and with incredible effort had gathered the delicate threads of strength left in her tiny body to rally and say good-bye.

Ann didn't need the nurse to tell her when Angela was gone. She'd known the moment the light left her daughter's eyes. She hadn't understood until later that a part of her had died, too, the part that found joy in spring mornings and believed each day was a small miracle.

She'd held Angela and rocked her and sung to her until Craig arrived from the airport two hours later. Angela grew cold inside the pink blanket despite being held in her mother's arms and Ann still fought releasing her, even to Craig.

Finally, Jeremy convinced her to let go. Craig had called the woman taking care of him and asked her to bring him to the hospital. He came into the room and silently put his arm around his mother. After several seconds he reached down and gently ran his hand over Angela's downy head, the way he did when he left for school in the morning. Only this time he kissed her, too.

Tears spilling from his eyes, he pressed his cheek to his mother's and asked to hold his sister one last time. Ann made him sit in a chair, then carefully placed Angela in his arms, reminding him by rote to hold her with both hands and support her head.

Jeremy huddled over his sister, his back curved, his head bent as if it were still possible for him to protect her. His voice barely above a whisper, he recited from memory "The Three Little Kittens," the poem he'd read to Angela every day for three and a half months. It was from a book his grandmother had read to him as a baby. Finally, he said he would take care of her toys, then he kissed her good-bye. The parting over, he turned to his father. The bond between them was unmistakable.

Craig took Angela and walked to the window that overlooked the Sierra Nevada Mountains. He stood motionless for a long time, his back to Ann and Jeremy, softly talking to his daughter. He told her how the green leaves on the trees outside the window were beginning to change to gold and red and orange and how snow would follow to coat the branches in white and how those bare branches would come alive again in the spring. Unheeded tears spotted the pink blanket as he promised that from then on he would look closer and longer at the world he had come to take for granted because he would be looking for her, too.

Every moment of that day remained in Ann's memory as if it had been etched in the window to her soul. She'd never prayed as hard or long as she had the three days following Angela's death—not for her return, but for a way to go with her. Only knowing what her leaving would do to Craig and Jeremy kept her from finding her own way. At the time, the division of her love and loyalty between Angela and Craig and Jeremy had nearly destroyed her. Now, after eight and a half months, she was numb from the battle, unable to give the smallest piece of herself to anyone or anything.

The fog that had lain offshore all day began its journey inland, consuming the moon's silver path. The damp breeze caught Ann's cotton robe, rippling the hem around her legs. She brought her chin up and closed her eyes and focused on the sound of the waves.

Tomorrow she would try harder to be the wife

Craig wanted and the mother Jeremy needed. She would dig deeper and find the woman she used to be so they could be a family again.

If only she could remember who that woman was.

⟶THE NEXT MORNING, HIS APPETITE CONSUMED by the escalating argument between his mother and father, Jeremy ignored the orange juice his father put in front of him. In response to the half-hearted order to finish his breakfast, he poked at the scrambled eggs, moving them to the other side of his plate and tucking a forkful under a slice of toast.

"Can I go outside now?" he asked.

Craig looked at his plate and sighed. "Drink your juice."

Jeremy managed half the glass. "Now?"

"Stick close to the house. I don't want you going down to the beach without me or your mom."

Ann put her hand up to stop Jeremy. "Wait a minute." She took a piece of toast and scooped the scrambled eggs into the middle, then folded it over to make a sandwich. "Take this with you."

He looked to his father for confirmation.

"Do it," Craig said. "And I better not find it in the bushes later."

It was on the tip of Jeremy's tongue to ask where his dad wanted to find it, but that would only get him sent to his room. Then he really would have to eat the gross-looking thing.

He opened the front door, saw the fog, and went back inside to get his sweatshirt. When he was outside, he stood on the porch for several seconds and looked around, hoping to see some other kids. Even though the fog wasn't thick or even very cold, there wasn't anyone outside, not even a grown-up. Thinking they might be on the beach, he went around the house to the old pathway that ran in front of the deck. He followed a brick sidewalk through some flowers and was almost to the back when he heard something in the bushes that scared him so bad he let out a scream—just like a girl.

He waited for it to happen again, his back pressed against the side of the house. The second time it was clear enough for him to make out what it was. An animal was hiding in the flowers. A big animal, judging by its fierce growl. Probably something that lived in the forest they drove through to get to the house. Probably wild.

His dad had told him he should never run from wild animals no matter how scared he was, something that sounded easy enough when they were hiking in the mountains and nothing was around. But it was hard when it actually happened. So hard Jeremy was afraid he might wet his pants if the thing growled again. And then he would just have to let the thing eat him because there was no way he was going to let anyone see him with a big wet spot in the front of his pants.

He should yell for his dad, but it was like his throat had closed and nothing would come out. He could throw something, but all he had was that stupid sandwich.

The flowers moved. He threw the sandwich. It bounced off the yellow rosebush and landed on the bricks not two inches from the toe of his tennis shoe. A high moan squeaked through his closed throat. Seconds later something big and gray and brown and ugly poked its head out. It looked around and cautiously moved toward him.

It was a *cat*.

All that screaming and squealing for a dumb old cat. He felt so stupid his first thought was to walk by and pretend it wasn't there. But he liked cats, at least he liked his grandmother's, and since no one had seen how dumb he'd acted, it was just as easy to drop to his haunches and put out his hand as it was to walk away.

The cat moved away, arched its back, and let out a hiss with all its teeth showing. When it stopped hissing, its eyes started shifting from Jeremy to the sandwich.

"You hungry? Is that what's wrong with you?" He retrieved a piece of egg that had fallen on the ground and held it out toward the cat.

The cat stood its ground but stopped hissing.

"It's okay. I'm not going to hurt you."

Something in Jeremy's voice triggered a response. Slowly, hesitantly, the cat came forward. When it was inches away from his outstretched fingers, it lunged, incredibly snatching the egg without biting Jeremy. It backed away and swallowed what it had taken in one big gulp, then looked up to see if there was more.

Jeremy fed the cat another chunk of egg. With each morsel, the cat became more trusting. Soon all that was left was the toast. Jeremy showed the cat his empty hand. "All gone," he added.

The cat sniffed every finger. Detecting something unseen, it licked his fingertips, tops, bottoms, and sides. Jeremy tore off a corner of toast. The cat took it without hesitation.

Settling into a cross-legged position, Jeremy fed the cat pieces of the toast until it, too, was gone. After licking his fingers a second time, the cat sat on the walkway in front of Jeremy and ritually began cleaning himself.

"Well, would you look at that."

Startled to discover he was no longer alone, Jeremy glanced up to see an old man watching him, his white hair covered with a baseball cap. He was standing beside the tall wooden gate that had roses growing over the top and had a beach bag in one hand and an umbrella under the arm of the other hand. Obviously the fog didn't bother him either.

The smile he gave Jeremy crinkled his eyes. "That cat has been wandering around here look-

ing for someone to take care of him for over a
month. Not one of us has been able to get near it."

Jeremy wasn't supposed to talk to strangers.
Everyone said so, even his teachers. But the man
didn't look anything like the strangers he'd been
warned about. And not only was he all the way on
the other side of the garden, there was no way he
could catch Jeremy if he decided to run. "He was
hungry."

"For more than food from the looks of it. I think
he needs a friend every bit as much as he needed a
meal."

Jeremy stared at the cat. He was right. The cat
didn't seem afraid anymore. "I could be his
friend. Just for a while though. Then I have to
leave because this isn't where I live."

"Sometimes 'a while' is enough."

"Do you have a cat?" He seemed to know a lot
about them.

"I used to."

He looked kind of sad when he said it, so Jeremy didn't ask what happened. He didn't think
he wanted to know anyway. He didn't like hearing sad things. "I had a snake once, but it wasn't
really mine. I just got to keep it over the summer
because it couldn't stay at school all that time by
itself. Timmy got to take the rat. He really wanted
the snake, but his mom wouldn't let him bring it
home."

"Jeremy—"

"That's my mom," he said, unfolding his legs and standing. "I better go see what she wants."

"It was nice talking to you, Jeremy."

"Thanks. I liked talking to you, too."

He smiled. "Take good care of your new friend."

"I will."

Ann called again, louder. "*Jeremy—*"

"Coming," he called back.

He found her standing on the front step, still in her bathrobe. "Where were you?"

He pointed toward the way he'd come. "Over there."

She moved out of the doorway to let him pass. She used to make him hug her before she let him in the house. It was a game she liked to play and he kind of liked, too, but he never told her. Now she hardly ever touched him at all. She'd let him hold her hand, but he could tell she didn't like it because she let go as soon as she could.

"What were you doing over there?" Ann asked.

"Stuff."

"If I went there and looked, would I find your sandwich hidden someplace?"

"Huh-uh." He liked telling her the truth even if it wasn't the right truth.

She believed him and rewarded him with a smile that he wished he deserved.

3

JEREMY PUT HIS PILLOW OVER HIS HEAD TO muffle the sounds of the birds outside his window. It helped some, but he could still hear them and knew there was no way he was going to go back to sleep. He'd looked to see if the fog was still hanging around when he got up to go to the bathroom and check on his mom. The sky was clear, and she was sleeping on the sofa. He saw that his dad had been there first and covered her with a blanket, so he went back to bed.

Today was July 4. His birthday. He'd liked it when he was little because there were fireworks at the end of the day and he'd believed everybody when they told him the fireworks were for him. Now he knew better. He knew a lot of things weren't what people said they were.

Sharing a day with a whole country that was

supposed to be special just for him was hard. He could never have his party on the actual day because his friends were always busy doing something with their families.

Then his sister was born on his birthday and it had made him a little mad that he would have to share the day with her, too. He never said anything to anyone and even changed his mind when Angela came home and he saw how cool it could be to have a little sister grab his finger and hold on like she knew what she was doing. Then she started smiling at him whenever she saw him and acting like she was listening when he read "The Three Little Kittens" and he figured sharing his birthday with her wouldn't be such a bad thing after all.

But he never got a chance. Now, he wasn't even sure he wanted to have a birthday anymore.

He pulled the pillow off his head and tossed it on the floor. Lying spread-eagled on the bed, he stared at the ceiling and discovered a spider doing a zigzag dance toward the light in the middle of the room. Seconds later another spider came shooting out from the light, heading straight for the first. It stopped inches away. For a long time neither of them moved, then the zigzag guy started to zig and the straight-running one charged and the first one dropped like a brick onto Jeremy's bed.

Wide-eyed, Jeremy bolted up and hit the floor before the spider had time to get its eight legs headed in the same direction. Almost by accident Jeremy caught a glimpse of the glistening thread that ran from the ceiling to the bed. His first impulse—to pick up something and smash the spider—disappeared on a wave of wonder. All of a sudden *Spiderman*, his favorite cartoon, made a brilliant kind of sense. Peter Parker did what real spiders did, escaping danger the same way. It wasn't something someone just made up.

Wanting to share his discovery, Jeremy hiked up his pajamas to keep from tripping on the too-long legs and left to find his father. At the same time he glanced into his mother and father's bedroom he heard their voices in the kitchen—not happy, conspiring voices planning a birthday surprise for their son, but cold, tired ones saying the same old things they said to each other almost every day at home.

Jeremy didn't stick around to see if the voices would change. There was no reason to believe being in a new place would make any difference.

When he got back to his room, the spider was gone.

⌐ "HE WON'T EVEN KNOW I'M NOT THERE," Ann insisted. "All those rides only take two people at a time anyway. I'd just be standing around all day waiting while you two were going from the Ferris wheel to the roller coaster to the tilt-a-wheel."

"You don't have to stand around. You can go on the rides with him."

"You know I don't like that stuff. I never have." Ann opened the egg carton and began cracking eggs into a bowl for French toast, Jeremy's favorite breakfast. "And Jeremy knows how much I hate crowds. You two can spend the day together and then we'll all go to Monterey tonight to watch the fireworks."

"How can you do this to him, Ann?"

She turned on him. "How can you do this to me?" She sucked in her bottom lip and bit down hard. She might not be able to give Jeremy what he really wanted or needed on this day, but she was determined she wasn't going to let him see her cry on his birthday.

"I'm hanging on by my fingertips, Craig. And you keep pulling on my ankles."

"It's his *birthday*, Ann. Can't you get it together just this one day?"

Her throat hurt from trying to hold back tears. "It isn't just Jeremy's birthday—it's Angela's, too. I don't understand how you can put that aside so easily."

"And I don't understand why you pick days to focus on her loss. Why was it more important to think about what she missed by never experiencing a Christmas or Valentine's Day or Easter than it is to know she missed knowing what a terrific big brother she had every single day of the year? Who the hell cares about a box of candy shaped like a heart when there are snowflakes and rainbows and butterflies to see and feel?"

"You can't know what it's like to carry a baby all that time and—"

"But I do know what it's like to cut the cord that attached her to you. And I know what it felt like to be the first one to hold her and welcome her into the world."

"You welcomed her . . . I told her good-bye." Ann couldn't look at him anymore. She turned away and picked up another egg, balancing it on the edge of the bowl as the tears she could no longer control began to fall.

"Please," Craig said. "This will be a birthday Jeremy remembers the rest of his life."

"Don't you think I know that?"

"If you know," he said, anger thick in his voice. "Why don't you care?"

She caught her breath in surprise and in pain at his cutting remark. She turned to face him. "How could you say that to me? What gives you the right?"

He stared at her a long time before answering. "How long is this going to go on, Ann? Months? Years? Give me something to shoot for. If nothing else, dangle a carrot in front of me to keep me going. I need something to hang on to." Looking away and then purposely looking back again as if making the point that what he wanted to say was more important than mere words, he told her, "I can't go on without it."

"What are you saying?"

"You know exactly what I'm saying."

"You want a divorce?" How could she not have known? Craig didn't make quick decisions. He thought things through from every angle, looked at every option, planned for every possibility. He must have been thinking about this for a long time. And yet she hadn't seen it, hadn't even guessed.

"You need help, Ann. *We* need help. Our lives are falling apart. Jeremy is—"

"You think us getting a divorce is what's best for Jeremy? You would leave him?"

"No," he said softly.

She gasped. "There's no way I would let you take him from me."

"You left him months ago," he countered.

"That's not true." But it was, and she didn't know how to find her way back.

"When was the last time you talked to him?"

"We talk all the time."

"*Really* talked to him. His first day of fifth grade you were so wrapped up in Angela you didn't notice when he left the house and then on his last day of school you were still so wrapped up in losing her you forgot to pick him up."

"I didn't forget; I overslept," she protested weakly.

"Because you won't sleep at night."

"Because I can't."

Craig didn't immediately answer. In the

strained silence they heard the soft click of the front door closing. He ran his hand through his hair in a frustrated gesture. "Jeremy heard us arguing." He picked up the towel from the counter and threw it across the room. "Some birthday. Maybe we could arrange for it to rain and really screw it up for him."

⌐ AS SOON AS JEREMY ROUNDED THE HOUSE HE stopped to pull out the toilet paper he'd wadded up and shoved in his ears. He used to listen to the things his mother and father said to each other when they were fighting, but he didn't anymore. Most of the time it was like some stupid contest to see who missed his sister the most. His mother always won because she would cry and his dad would get up and leave. Jeremy would wait to come out of his room until his dad was back and he and his mom pretended everything was all right again.

No one ever asked him how he felt about Angela being gone. It didn't seem to matter that he missed her, too, or that he secretly read her "The Three Little Kittens" every night before he went to bed.

He talked to Timmy about it sometimes when they were alone in his fort in his backyard. Not a lot. Just once in a while when they'd run out of other things to talk about. Timmy didn't think he'd miss his sister as much as Jeremy missed Angela, but then Timmy's sister was older and always thumping him on the head when their mom wasn't around.

Jeremy came to the place he and the cat had met the past three mornings and sat down on the brick pathway to wait. He'd gathered stuff from the refrigerator the night before, not taking too much of any one thing so his mom and dad wouldn't notice. He didn't want them to know about the cat because they might make him stop feeding it, and he didn't want to stop.

He took the paper towel off the plastic bowl he'd found in the bottom cupboard, and softly called, "Hey, kitty, kitty, kitty." It was the way the lady next door at home called her cats when they were outside.

The cat didn't come. Jeremy called again. When he still didn't come, Jeremy checked the daisy bush and then the one next to it with the pink flowers. He could see where the cat had been lying, the stems were pushed aside making a kind of cave, but it wasn't there.

He stood and called again, his voice a notch above a whisper but low enough not to be heard inside. He was at the end of the walkway when he saw the cat running up the path toward him.

Instead of immediately going to the bowl, the cat stopped to rub himself against Jeremy's legs, moving back and forth and purring like he'd turned on a motor inside his chest. Jeremy smiled.

"It's my birthday," he said, bending down to scratch the cat's ears.

The cat let out a soft meow.

The old man in the straw hat appeared at the garden gate again dressed for another morning on the beach. "I'm pretty sure that means happy birthday in cat language." He smiled. "How old are you today?"

"Ten."

"Ten . . ." He got a faraway look on his face. "You're going to have such a good time being ten. It's a wonderful age to be."

"Nine wasn't very good."

"I'm sorry to hear that. Usually nine is a very good year, too. But not always. Mine wasn't either."

The cat left Jeremy and walked toward the bowl. He stopped and looked back, as if waiting for Jeremy to follow. He did and could see it was clearly what the cat had wanted. He stood nearby while the cat ate. "What happened when you were nine?"

"My father lost his job and didn't have the money to feed us, so my brother and I were sent to live with cousins. They didn't like us much and weren't happy to have us there."

Jeremy wouldn't like living with his cousin either but he wouldn't mind living with Timmy for a year or so, even if his sister thumped him on the head once in a while, too. "Did your dad get a job again?"

He nodded. "When I was eleven. That was a very good year for the whole family."

Maybe eleven would be a good year for him, too. Ten wasn't starting out too well. "I'm going to the boardwalk for my birthday. Then we're going to come back here for cake and ice cream. Would you like to come for cake?" he asked on impulse. "You don't have to bring a present."

"Oh, but I already bought you a present."

"You did? How did you know it was my birthday?"

"As it turns out, it was just one of those fortuitous things." He put his umbrella on the ground and reached inside his beach bag.

Jeremy had no idea what fortuitous meant, but went along. "My grandma sent something in the mail last week, but my dad said I couldn't open it until tonight."

"Well, you don't have to wait to open this." He held out a small, brightly wrapped package.

Jeremy stepped over the cat to reach him. "Thanks."

"As you'll soon discover, the present is actually for both of you." At Jeremy's confused look, he added, "You and your cat."

Now he really was curious. "I can open it now?"

"Please do."

He turned it over and popped the tape. Inside was a funny-looking comb, a bag of cat treats, and a collar with a tag that read, *Francis—friend of Jeremy.* "His name is Francis?"

"I don't know for sure, but I thought he looked like a Francis. And I liked the way it went with Jeremy. Give him a treat when you want to comb him, and he'll get the idea that being combed is a good thing. I have a feeling there's a beautiful cat just waiting to be found under all that matted fur and that you're just the young man to find it."

Jeremy smiled and turned to look at the cat, who had finished his breakfast and was licking his paws and wiping his cheeks in front of the empty bowl. "I never knew a Francis before."

"And I never knew a Jeremy." He picked up his umbrella and beach bag. "Time to go."

"Thank you for the present. I like it a lot."

"You're welcome."

He went back to the cat—to Francis—and when he looked up again, the man was gone. Sitting on the ground with his legs out in front of him, he opened the treats and offered one to Francis. He stretched his neck forward, working his nose. He stood to move in for a closer smell, decided it was something worth pursuing, and gently plucked the treat from Jeremy's palm.

Tomorrow they would try the comb. He liked thinking about having something to do. The man's present was a good one.

4

ANN WORKED SUNSCREEN ACROSS HER FORE-
head and over her nose as she waited for
Jeremy to join her on the deck. She was incredibly
grateful for the phone call from Craig's office that
had sent him searching for a fax machine that
morning. The tension from the blowup between
them on Jeremy's birthday had continued for four
stressful days. They'd been civil for Jeremy's sake,
but then it was easy to be civil when they stayed
in separate parts of the house.

Amazingly, Jeremy didn't seem to notice. Or if
he did, he'd chosen not to get involved. How
many times could you try to bring your parents
together and fail and not give up trying? Surely
Jeremy had reached his limit months ago.

Craig was convinced she didn't see what was
happening to Jeremy. Of course she saw how he'd

changed, but it wasn't the dramatic change Craig
insisted had taken place. They'd all changed.
How could they not? What would it say about
them if they'd simply resumed their lives after
Angela died? She couldn't go back to the life
they'd once had. She couldn't even remember
what that life had been like.

For all the protesting that she would be missed
if she stayed home while Craig and Jeremy went
to the boardwalk for his birthday, they'd gotten
along fine without her. While they were gone
she'd baked the cake she'd promised, yellow with
chocolate frosting, and even made Jeremy's favorite dinner, spaghetti with meat sauce and a
green salad with Ranch dressing.

She'd cried when he blew out his candles and
said it was because she was sad to see him growing up so fast. Craig gave her a look that said he
didn't believe her; Jeremy didn't look at her at all.

The sound of the screen door moving in its
track alerted her that she was no longer alone.

"I'm ready," Jeremy announced.

She worked up an imitation of a smile before
she turned to greet him. He was wearing last
year's swimming suit, the red, white and blue one
she'd bought at Macy's preseason sale and worried he would grow out of before the end of summer. Now it hung so loose the first wave would
have it at his ankles if he didn't hold on to it.
When had he gotten so thin? How could she not
have noticed?

"You forgot your towel."

He looked at the bag at her side. "I thought you—" Turning to go back in, he added, "Never mind."

He'd assumed she would bring his towel. Why not? Wasn't looking out for her family her job, something she did automatically, something they had every right to expect?

Guilt might be a five-letter word, but in her mind it had more power than any four-letter word ever conceived. She was consumed by it, every breath carried its odor, every spark of hope was dulled by its tarnish.

Jeremy appeared at the back door again, towel in one hand, the bag full of beach toys his grandparents had given him for his birthday in the other. "Did you want to bring the camera? Dad left it on the table."

"No." The last picture she'd taken had been of Angela with her nose red from her first cold—the minor upper respiratory infection none of them had taken seriously, the one that had killed her three days later. Ann hadn't been able to pick up the camera since.

Jeremy closed the door and followed Ann down the path to the stairs. She shifted her canvas chair to the left when he moved to that side. He was a hand holder and it was the only way she knew to discourage him without hurting his feelings.

Something terrible had happened to her when Angela died, something she still didn't understand. She recoiled at being touched. It was everything she could do to hold still instead of pushing friends and family away when they came at her with consoling hugs. At night she clung to her side of the bed until Craig was asleep and she could slip into the other room without being questioned.

Ann stopped halfway to the water. "Where do you want to go?"

Jeremy surveyed the uncrowded beach. He pointed toward an elderly couple sitting in canvas chairs under an umbrella. "Over there."

Ann didn't question his choice. She followed him until it seemed he would throw out his towel right next to them. She motioned him to a spot several yards away. "How about here?"

He joined her without comment, spreading his towel and toeing one foot and then the other out of his tennis shoes. He'd grabbed his bucket and shovel and was headed for the wet sand when Ann called him back and handed him sunscreen.

He squirted a small amount in his hand, rubbed his hands together, and swiped it on his arms and chest. "You need more than that," Ann said. "At least twice that much."

"It makes the sand stick to me," he protested. She looked at him without saying anything. "All right. But I can't do my back."

She put out her hand for the bottle and motioned for him to turn around. Three quick swipes and the lotion was distributed. "Now you can go."

This time, instead of heading for the waves, he cut to his left and went up to the couple under the umbrella. Ann frowned. Jeremy knew better than to approach strangers. But then she could see by the welcoming look on the man's face, he and Jeremy weren't strangers. They talked for several minutes before the man rose from his chair and accompanied Jeremy to the shoreline. They sat down together and began digging in the wet sand, the man with his hands, Jeremy with his shovel.

Debating what to do, Ann did nothing. After several minutes the woman turned to Ann and motioned to the empty chair beside her. Her mouth formed words that were lost on the breeze the way Ann was sure hers would be, too, if she tried to reply. Trapped by a lifetime of abiding by social mores, Ann stood and brushed herself off, then reluctantly joined the woman.

"I apologize if Jeremy disturbed you." Ann took the man's vacated seat, not intending to stay but reluctant to stand over the woman for their moment of polite conversation.

"Not at all. He's a delightful young man."

"You know each other?" Ann asked carefully.

"I've seen him in the flower garden when I walk by in the mornings on my way to watch the otters forage for their breakfast."

"Do you live around here?"

"We're summer residents—like you. Only we've been coming so long it seems like home."

"It's beautiful here," Ann said. "I can see why you would want to come back."

"Is it just you and Jeremy?"

"No, my husband came, too. He had some business he had to take care of this morning, or he would be here with us." Already she was sensitive to being alone. What would it be like if she and Craig really did go their separate ways?

"Men never seem to be completely free of their responsibilities." She glanced at the man happily playing in the sand with the boy and smiled. "It's such a shame and yet so much of who they are, don't you think?"

Ann had never thought about it before, but Craig was without question the most responsible person she'd ever known. It was something she both relied on and took for granted. "It does seem to be something ingrained in the best of them."

The old woman smiled, and Ann felt as if she'd been given a gift. "Do you come to the beach to watch the otters every morning?"

"It's become a bit of a habit for us. We like to come when we can have the beach to ourselves. It's something we've been doing for years." She reached over and put her hand on Ann's arm. "Not that we wouldn't like company. You're most welcome to join us when you're up and don't have anything else to do."

Strangely, Ann felt no sense of intrusion or violation at the woman's touch. Instead she was filled with a powerful feeling of empathy, as if

Ann could tell her anything and she would understand. "Sometimes I have trouble sleeping—or going back to sleep after I wake up. It would be good to have something to do besides lie there and think."

"I know what that's like. And you're right about having too much time to think." She gently patted Ann's arm and gave her a wistful smile. "There isn't a problem that can't be made bigger or more important by spending too much energy trying to solve it. I've found most things work themselves out eventually. You just need to give them enough time."

"How much is enough?" Ann asked, not really expecting an answer.

"The trick is to pay attention to the clues. Most of us don't. We seem to get so caught up in feeling bad, we forget what it is to feel good. Or we feel guilty when we do, as if we don't deserve it." She shook her head. "Guilt is such a useless emotion, and rarely singular. Even when we treat it as a closely guarded secret, we can't help but involve those around us."

"Sometimes guilt is deserved," Ann stated flatly.

The old woman eyed her. "Something terrible must have happened to make you believe that."

Ann couldn't say the words out loud, not even to someone she would likely never see again. "It's been a difficult year for me . . . and my husband."

"And Jeremy?" the woman asked gently.

"Yes, I suppose. But you know how kids are. It doesn't seem to matter how hard they fall, they bounce right back."

The woman didn't say anything for a long time, plainly thinking about what Ann had told her. "Forgive me for intruding in something that is none of my business, but you seem upset with Jeremy."

The suggestion caught her off guard. "That's ridiculous. How can anyone blame a kid for being a kid?"

"I'm sorry. Now I've upset you. It's just that I see such sadness in Jeremy, I assumed—"

Jeremy interrupted the conversation when he let out a loud, raucous laugh. Startled, Ann swung around to see what had happened. Like a door thrown open, it hit her that she hadn't heard Jeremy laugh that way in so long she almost hadn't recognized it for what it was.

Glistening with a fresh dousing of water, it was obvious an errant wave had caught Jeremy and the old man by surprise as they were filling their bucket with wet sand. Jeremy sat in the retreating surf holding his sides and squealing in delight while, laughing almost as loudly, the old man took off to reclaim their bucket.

The contrast between this child and the child Jeremy was at home was too stark to ignore. He went to school and played with his friends and celebrated his birthday a couple of hundred miles from home without protest. He was a normal ten-year-old boy. Or so she'd convinced herself. Could it be she saw what she wanted to see—or what she *needed* to see?

What she wanted, what she needed right then, was to be alone. A smile in place, with more effort than she wanted to reveal, she said, "I've enjoyed talking to you, but I've taken up way too much of your time. Perhaps we'll run into each other again."

"Six-thirty tomorrow morning—if you'd still like to join me."

It took a second for the invitation to register. "Oh—you mean to watch the otters."

"If you're up and not doing anything, it truly is a special way to start your morning."

"I'll certainly keep it in mind." She could hardly claim six-thirty was too early when she'd already admitted she had trouble sleeping. "But please don't look for me. I would hate to think you were outside waiting while I was still curled up in bed."

The woman nodded and smiled tolerantly. Ann couldn't decide if she'd accepted the polite brush-off or discounted it. Either way she left with the feeling she had been maneuvered into something. She just didn't know what it was.

5

CAUGHT UP IN THE PROSPECT OF A FIELD audit by the IRS for his biggest client, Craig almost missed his beach house neighbor waving to him as he pulled into the driveway. They'd spoken in passing but nothing beyond a casual good morning or evening so he was mildly surprised when he glanced out the rearview mirror and saw Andrew Wells approaching.

"Do you have a minute?" Andrew asked.

"Sure." Craig tucked the faxes he'd picked up at the copy shop under his arm. "What can I do for you?"

"The woman who rented your house last month just discovered she was missing an earring. It's only sentimentally valuable, but she's going nuts looking for it and was hoping she might have left it here."

"Miniature sand dollar on a silver hook?"

Andrew smiled. "That's it. The guy she's engaged to gave it to her, and she wants to wear it at their wedding."

"Come on in. I'll get it for you."

Andrew followed him in the house and waited in the living room while Craig went into the bedroom. He was back seconds later and handed Andrew the earring. "I'm always amazed how this place changes with the people who rent it," Andrew commented. "Same house, same furniture, but somehow different. It's almost as if it takes on the personality of the people who are staying in it."

"Have there been a lot?"

"Not as many as you'd think considering how old this place is."

"Whoever owns the house obviously loves it. I was surprised to see how well cared for it is. If there was any way I could manage it, I'd stay another month. But like I told the rental agent, one month away from business was a challenge, two is downright impossible. I have a feeling she's not going to be able to find anyone at this late date, at least not anyone who can take it the whole four weeks."

"I was under the impression the house had been rented for August."

"It was, but I guess the people backed out."

"When did you find out?"

"Yesterday. The agent said we were the first people she called because she wanted to give us first refusal. I have a feeling it had a lot more to do with us being the only prospects."

"I think I might know someone who would be interested," Andrew said.

Craig decided it had to be someone Andrew was involved with. No man lit up like that at the prospect of friends moving in next door. Even with the darkness of the past year clouding his thoughts, he could clearly remember the anticipation he'd felt at his and Ann's first weekend away together. Looking back he saw himself as impossibly young and carefree.

"I'd call right away—just in case I'm wrong about the agent's motives for getting in touch with us first."

Andrew grinned. "My thoughts exactly."

Craig saw him to the door. "If you're not doing anything tonight, why don't you come over. I picked up a bottle of Merlot that I've been wanting to try, and Ann isn't much of a red wine drinker."

"Thanks. What time?"

"Seven?"

"I'll be here."

Andrew checked his watch as he crossed to his house. He had another half hour before he had to be back at the nursery for a meeting with a new distributor. He could try to run down Cheryl and chance losing the house, which would make her saying yes a moot point. Or he could call the agent and take the house and worry about convincing

Cheryl later. Logic told him it was too late for her to get that much time off. He didn't even know if she had vacation coming.

But she had weekends. Even if that was all she had, it would be worth taking the house no matter what the cost.

The decision made, Andrew called the agent and was told the house was still available, although she had a couple coming to look at the photographs that afternoon. Andrew told her to call and cancel, that he would be there with the deposit in ten minutes.

Putting himself in a bind for time provided the perfect excuse for delaying his call to Cheryl. Sometimes things just fell into place.

CRAIG CHANGED INTO SHORTS AND SANDALS, took a towel out of the linen cupboard, and headed for the beach. He'd promised Jeremy a day of sand castles and shell hunting and had already spent half of it on work. He had the right to expect at least one of them would keep their promises.

Standing at the top of the stairs, he spotted Ann immediately. She was sitting in the blue-and-white canvas chair they'd brought from home. It took a second to find Jeremy. When Craig did, his jaw literally dropped in surprise.

Jeremy was working on a sculpture of a castle at least six feet long and half as tall. Even from this distance, Craig could see turrets and windows and a flag fluttering in the breeze.

There was no way Jeremy could have built that structure by himself. At just the possibility that Ann had been the one helping him, Craig's heart did a tap dance that would give Savion Glover a run for his money.

It had to be Ann. No one else was around. At least no kids Jeremy's age. Hope was like a red carpet of welcome that led him across the sand to his wife and his son.

"That's amazing," Craig said, stopping to drop his towel beside Ann and giving her what had passed for a kiss between them the past few months. "How long did it take you?"

She flinched at the obvious happiness in his voice. "I can't take any credit. I didn't have anything to do with it."

He didn't bother to try to hide his disappointment. "Jeremy did that all by himself?"

She came forward in her chair and shielded her eyes from the sun with her hand. "A man helped him."

Craig looked around. "What man?"

"He and his wife left about fifteen minutes ago."

"No kids?"

Ann smiled and shook her head. "Not unless they're one of those medical miracle couples. I'd put them near eighty, if not over."

Craig stared at Ann's mouth. Her smile was different. She didn't have the pinched look she did when she was trying too hard. "He just moved in and started building that thing with Jeremy?"

"If you want to know something, ask. Don't beat around the bush."

"I'm trying to understand what an eighty-year-old man is doing playing in the sand with a ten-year-old kid."

She sent him a piercing look. "Don't you dare mess up this morning for Jeremy with stupid questions. For every child molester in this world there are a hundred thousand terrific normal people. We were lucky enough to meet a couple of them today, and I hope we get to see a lot more of them while we're here."

Her reaction wasn't what Craig had expected, but he'd take it. Anything was better than apathy. Still, he'd feel more comfortable when he'd met these people himself. While he disliked the idea that he and his peers were raising a generation of paranoid children, he adamantly believed it was better to be safe than sorry.

"I'll watch what I say," he told her.

Jeremy spotted him. "Dad—" he shouted. "Come see my fort."

Craig kicked off his sandals and joined Jeremy, patiently listening as he told him how he and his friend had put everything together. His final statement put an unanticipated lump in Craig's throat.

"Mom was the one who said there should be windows. She found all the shells and helped me put them in. They look great, don't they?"

Craig backed up to take it all in. A wave washed over his feet, and he realized the tide was coming in. In an hour the incredible castle would be a memory.

As if reading his mind, Jeremy said, "It's okay, Dad. We're going to build another one tomorrow. You can help."

"Not tomorrow, Jeremy. I have to go home for a couple of days."

The spark left his eyes.

"I'm sorry. If there was any way I could get out of it, I would." Jeremy had heard the words too many times for them to carry the meaning Craig wanted to convey. There were things he'd missed in the past when he could have put work off to his partners and didn't. This time it was just too important. "I promise I'll be back as soon as I can."

"It's all right."

"I'll make it up to you."

"I don't want you to," Jeremy insisted.

Craig scooped Jeremy up in his arms and swung him around. "Are you telling me I'm going to have to go to the aquarium all by myself when I get back?"

Jeremy wrapped his arms around Craig's neck and held on tight. "What if me and Mom go while you're gone?"

"What is this? Are you trying to threaten me, young man?"

Jeremy giggled.

"Do you know what happens to little boys who threaten their fathers?" he asked menacingly, walking backward toward the water.

Jeremy wrapped his legs around Craig's waist and let out a loud, piercing squeal of delight. "Nooooooo—"

"Too late," Craig told him, stumbling into a wave. "Hold your nose."

They went under in a tangle of legs. When they popped up again they were laughing. A memory as warm as a fireplace after a day of skiing worked its way into Craig's consciousness. This was what it felt like to be happy.

6

A NN WAS UP AND DRESSED IN SWEATS AND running shoes before the sun rose the next morning. She wrote a note for Craig telling him where she was and that she would be back before he had to leave and left it taped to the bathroom mirror.

She was looking forward to time alone—just her and seagulls and sanderlings, and if she were lucky, an otter or two. While it would have been nice to have a guide to the wildlife, she didn't expect the old woman to be up this early, and Ann couldn't wait around for her and still get back before Craig had to leave.

Quietly unfastening the lock on the front door, Ann stepped outside and looked at the eastern sky. In minutes, the clouds hugging the mountains had gone from deep purple to lavender. Like sprinters, mornings seemed in a rush to get started while nightfall moved at the slower, more even pace of a marathoner.

She missed running. It was something everyone assumed she did to keep in shape, but they were wrong. She ran because she liked the way it made her feel. Alone on a course with only her thoughts for company, she experienced an intoxicating freedom that made whatever she had to face that day possible. Craig had understood this need in her and for her birthday—which was a month after Angela and Jeremy's—had given her a high-tech baby stroller so they could go together when he wasn't there to baby-sit.

When her six-week leave from work neared an end, she asked Craig what he thought of her staying home until Angela started school. He'd given his enthusiastic support, immediately refiguring their budget to accommodate the lost income.

Their lives had been perfect. For three and a half months they had known unbridled happiness and had been lured into believing it would always be that way. How naive they'd been. How foolish.

By the time Ann reached the beach, the sky belonged to the day. She stretched, then headed toward the rocky outcropping at the southern end of the cove at a brisk walk, obeying all the training rules that said to start slow after a long layoff. Despite the good intentions, she was soon at a gentle, loping run, her feet hitting the hard wet sand in long strides, digging in and moving on.

The lope became a trot and the trot a run. Pumping her arms, she ran faster and faster, feeling the salty air on her face, the wind in her hair, and the treasures of the night's high tide at her feet. She ran to escape, to find, to forget, and to remember. She ran until the muscles in her legs burned and her heart pounded in her ears so loudly it was the only sound she heard. She ran until her toe caught a piece of driftwood and she was sent tumbling head over heels through the cream-colored bubbles at the edge of the surf to land on the compacted sand.

Struggling to catch her breath, she rolled to her back and stared at a lone cloud drifting toward the mountains. Tears ran from the corners of her eyes into the curve of her ears and onto the sand to mix with the salt water from the ocean. Deep wrenching sobs tore from her throat and were lost in the roar of the waves as she rolled to her side and curled into a fetal position.

A desperate need rose in her, one she'd refused to acknowledge until then. She wanted to be well, to feel joy again, to be a whole person, a mother, a wife. But she didn't know how to move forward with her life without leaving her beautiful little baby girl behind.

CRAIG PULLED ANN'S NOTE FROM THE BATH-room mirror and frowned. Two years ago he would have showered and shaved without giving her absence a second thought, unless it was to check the time and day to see if they were free to take a shower together when she returned. Some of the most exciting and adventurous lovemaking of their marriage had taken place in their oversize shower at home.

The memory of those mornings triggered an ache deep in his loins. He missed sex with Ann. But more than the sex, he missed the closeness they had shared, the feel of her head on his shoulder, her insistence on sharing bits and pieces of the morning paper over his accompanying groans, the way she would come up behind him unexpectedly and put her arms around his waist. He missed the deep kisses and the playful ones and being told that he was loved.

Ann talked about the heartbreak of seeing the light leave Angela's eyes. For nine months he'd lived with the memory of walking into the hospital room and seeing the light gone from her eyes. His cross to bear, the one he would carry the rest of his life, was not being with her when she needed him the most and not knowing if it would have made a difference if he'd found a way to get there sooner.

His recurring nightmares all centered around his frantic attempt to get home after Ann's phone call telling him Angela was in the hospital. The hardest were the times he dreamed he'd made it to the hospital and then woke up to the truth.

He shouldn't have gone. The trip easily could

have been handled by someone else in the office. It was his ego that got in the way, his chance to be wined and dined by power brokers in Washington, D.C., who believed he was important enough for them to spend valuable time getting to know. The freak snowstorm caught everyone by surprise, closing the roads and airports, making it impossible to get out of the city. Desperate, he'd hired a taxi to take him to the closest city with a functioning airport. He'd pleaded and bargained with three airlines telling them he was willing to take anything going west. Thirty-two hours, three airports, and a favor from a client later, he landed in Reno.

Jeremy had colds when he was a baby. Lots of them. How could they have known Angela's would be different? Where were the articles in the Sunday newspaper supplements that told how fast a baby's cold could turn into a deadly infection. It wasn't until your child died that someone told you more infants died of respiratory infections every year than died of SIDS. Where were the warning pamphlets in the doctors' offices, the parents on talk-show circuits, the banner headlines in women's magazines?

If he'd known . . . if only he'd known. He would have been there for his little girl, if not to save her, to tell her good-bye. She wouldn't have died looking for her father, wondering why he wasn't there. She would have known how much he loved her, how he would grieve, and how she would always own a piece of his heart. She was Daddy's little girl. A bond formed the moment she was placed in his arms. He'd given her a T-shirt that said so. He'd promised he would break down any door closed to her because she was a girl and bought her a pink dress with ruffles.

Craig turned from the mirror, unable to look at his reflection, at the agony in his eyes over the unfulfilled promises and possibilities that would haunt him for the rest of his life.

"Dad?" Jeremy called.

Craig wiped his eyes with the edge of his fingers and found a smile that almost looked real. "In here."

He came to the door. "I can't find Mom."

"She left a note saying she was going for a walk."

"By herself?"

"She didn't say." He reached for the shaving cream. "But since she doesn't know anyone here, I'd say it's a pretty safe bet that she went alone."

"Are you going to go find her?"

Craig leaned against the sink and looked at Jeremy. "Do you think I need to?"

He shrugged. "Maybe."

"Why don't we give her another fifteen minutes before we start looking? At least until I'm out of the shower."

Jeremy hiked up his drooping pajama bottoms. "When are you leaving?"

"After breakfast."

"Tell me again when you're coming back?"

"As soon as I can."

"How long is that?" he persisted.

"Two days. Maybe three."

"I thought . . ." He turned to go. "Never mind."

Craig grabbed the tail of Jeremy's shirt, pulled him back into the room, and turned him around. He sat on the edge of the tub and looked directly into his eyes. "I know I'm breaking a promise to you and your mom, and I'm sorry. But there's no way I could have known this would come up while we were here. I wouldn't do this for just anyone. The man I have to go back and help is the one who sent his plane to pick me up in Dallas when your sister was in the hospital. I owe him this, Jeremy."

He waited for Jeremy to say something and when he didn't, added, "Would it be better if I took you and your mom home with me?"

"Would we come back?"

"Yes, of course."

He thought about it for several seconds. "You don't have to do that. We can stay here."

"Are you sure?"

"Yeah."

He took hold of Jeremy's ears and brought him forward for a kiss on the forehead. "Then get out of here so I can finish getting ready."

Jeremy surprised them both when he threw his arms around Craig and gave him a fierce hug. "Hurry back."

"I'll be in the car the first minute I can get away, and I won't stop for anything."

"You can get a hamburger if you want." He grinned. "And go to the bathroom. But nothing else."

"It's a deal."

Jeremy left and headed for his bedroom thinking he would wait under the covers where it was warm while his father finished his shower. And then he thought about Francis and figured he was probably waiting for him and went into the kitchen to find something to give him for breakfast. He'd tried leftover pizza the day before and had to sneak back in the house to find something else because Francis didn't go for the mushrooms and olives.

There wasn't anything in the refrigerator or the cupboards. Except a can of salmon his dad put on crackers. He listened for the shower before using the can opener, then buried the lid deep in the trash.

As Jeremy had expected, Francis was sitting in the middle of the walkway waiting for him. As soon as he saw Jeremy, he let out a meow and came to greet him, wrapping himself around his legs, making it impossible for him to walk. Jeremy dropped the can and picked up the cat. He put his face down to let Francis head butt him a couple of times and push against his nose. All the while he was purring so hard he had to stop and swallow every once in a while or he would choke. After several swipes along Jeremy's chin, he was ready to get down and eat.

The salmon was gone before Jeremy had a chance to settle his back against the house and take out the comb. Francis wasn't crazy about being combed but would put up with it for a few minutes before he made a point of standing up and lying back down on his other side.

"Maybe if you let me get those knots out of you and you didn't look so dirty, I might be able to talk my mom into letting you come home with us." Francis settled deeper into Jeremy's lap, kneading the front of his shirt, his purr a steady rumble.

"You wouldn't have to sleep outside anymore. You could sleep in my bed with me. I'd even let you have one of my pillows."

Francis tucked his head under his paws and let out a contented sigh.

"I live in a big house with a big backyard, so you would have lots of room to play. And if you came home with me, we could get you your own food and you wouldn't have to eat leftover pizza anymore."

Watching him fall asleep was the best part, the part that made Jeremy feel good all over. In a funny way it was a little like holding his sister again.

⌒ANN SAT ON THE SAND WITH HER BACK TO the log she and Craig had sat on their first day at the ocean. She should get back, Craig was undoubtedly waiting for her so he could take off. But she wasn't ready yet. She just needed a few more minutes to get herself together.

"Good morning," a female voice offered.

Ann turned to see the old woman approaching. Only then did she realize she'd been waiting for her. She got up and brushed herself off. "Good morning."

"Did you find them?"

"I assume you mean the otters?"

"Yes." She rounded the log and took a minute to tuck a strand of gray hair under her hat.

"I didn't know where to look."

"Come with me." She started to take off. "I'll show you."

"I can't this morning," she said with sincere regret. "I have to get back to Jeremy. Perhaps we can both come with you tomorrow."

"I'd like that." She sat on the log, her legs straight out in front of her. "I think Jeremy will, too."

Ann sat next to the woman. "We're going to be on our own for a couple of days. I'd like to do something special with Jeremy. Do you have any suggestions?"

"Goodness, I'm going to have to think about that one. Of course, just about anything you did with that young man would be special. Parents try so hard to create moments their children will remember when they're grown, and it rarely works out the way they expected. From what I've seen, it's the walks on a beach and the little discoveries and the dinner that burned because mom was caught up in a game that kids carry with them into adulthood." She chuckled. "It's also been my experience that most often it's the very things we don't want them or expect them to remember that they do."

"So what you're saying is that you don't know about anything special," Ann gently teased.

"On the contrary. If I were you and had the opportunity to spend the day with Jeremy, I know exactly where I would take him."

Ann listened to the woman's ideas and decided they were exactly what she wanted to do. She thanked her and got up to leave.

The woman reached out to take Ann's arm. "Before you go . . ."

"Yes?"

"Would you like to talk about why you were crying?"

Ann looked at her long and hard. There was something about this woman she couldn't explain and didn't understand. Something special, something she was afraid would disappear if she looked too hard. "I don't know how or why, but I think you already know."

The woman smiled gently. "I don't have magical powers, I simply see the sorrow in your eyes."

"My baby girl died eight and a half months

ago. I thought she had a cold and that she would get over it in a couple of days. I didn't even call the doctor until her fever was over a hundred and two. By then it was too late to save her." They were words as familiar as the sound of her own breath, words she'd carried with her for months, words she'd never spoken aloud. "She counted on me to take care of her. She had every right to believe I would."

"Did Jeremy ever have a high fever?"

"Yes."

"Then how could you have known this would be any different?"

"I've tried that argument. It doesn't work."

"Could it be because you don't want it to?" she asked without accusation.

"What do you mean?"

"It isn't in our nature to accept that sometimes things just happen, and there isn't anything we can do about it. We want answers. We want to blame something or someone. It gives us some kind of perverse comfort to be able point a finger because we think it will keep us safe."

"My mother keeps telling me God wanted Angela."

"But you don't believe her?"

"Why would God do something like that? There are lots and lots of babies in heaven. He didn't need another one." She looked into the woman's eyes and silently pleaded with her to understand. "Every part of me—my mind, my

body, my soul—knows that God didn't have anything to do with Angela dying. It was my fault. It
had to be my fault. She would be alive today if I
had taken her to the doctor sooner."

"If you could, would you exchange your life for
hers?"

"Yes." She would do so in a heartbeat, without
a second thought.

"But you can't," she added reasonably. "You
know that it's impossible."

Ann nodded.

"Then why do you keep trying?"

"I don't understand."

The woman looked up and saw Craig headed
toward them. "Think about it," she said softly. "I
have to go now, but we'll talk again."

Ann watched her husband move across the
sand toward her. She saw love and concern in his
eyes and a tenderness she didn't deserve. As always, she wondered how those feelings would
change if he knew the truth.

7

"Hurry up," Ann told Jeremy, scooting him toward the shower. "I want you ready to leave as soon as the rental car gets here."

"Where are we going?"

"It's a surprise."

He stood where he was and stared at her.

"*What?*"

"A surprise . . . ?" He looked utterly confused. "What does that mean?"

"It means I know something that you don't, and I'm not going to tell you what it is until you get there."

Along with the confusion came a slow smile. "It better be good."

"Or?" she challenged.

"Or I'm not gonna act surprised."

The perverse logic brought a return smile. "Oh yeah? Well, I happen to know this is so good you're not going to stop talking about it for a whole week."

"Oh yeah? Well, I betcha I could—"

"Jeremy?"

"Yes?"

"Get in the shower."

"Okay." He didn't walk down the hall, he ran.

As soon as she heard the bathroom door close, Ann went back to cleaning the kitchen.

The rental car—a dark green, four-door Saturn—arrived forty-five minutes later. Still, it was pushing noon by the time they were on the road and headed south.

"I know where we're going," Jeremy announced.

"No, you don't."

"The aquarium."

"Didn't your dad say he wanted to take us there?"

"We could go twice."

Ann felt a little guilty over how much he was enjoying the guessing game. It used to take more to get him this involved in something. "Do you want me to just tell you?"

It was obvious he didn't, but he said, "If you want to."

"We're going to a really cool vegetable stand your friend told me about. She said they have the best green beans and turnips in California." She glanced over to see his reaction. He was so unaccustomed to being teased, he actually believed her. She managed to keep a straight face. "So, what do you think?"

"Maybe we should wait so Dad could come, too."

Ann laughed. It felt as if a weight had been lifted off her chest allowing her this freedom.

"Are you all right, Mom?" Jeremy asked carefully.

"I'm better than that, Jeremy. Or at least I want to be." She reached over and ran her hand over his hair. "But I need you to help me remember how to have fun. Do you think you could do that for me?"

Instead of the enthusiastic response she'd expected, he grew quiet. "Sometimes I forget, too."

The small part of her heart that was healing broke a little. "Then I guess we're going to have to help each other and practice a lot until we get it right."

"I know something we could do."

"What?"

"We could go to a movie."

"And then we'll go to a video store and rent ten more and watch them until we're so sick of movies we run outside and jump in the ocean."

"We can have popcorn." His voice rose the way she remembered it used to when he was excited.

"And Junior Mints."

"And Coke," he squeaked.

"And chocolate milk," she added.

"And hot dogs."

"With catsup and mustard and relish."

"And *no* turnips or green beans."

Again she laughed. How could she have forgotten how quick and clever her son could be? "But lots of potato chips."

They added items to their gastronomical feast for the next ten miles. Finally, Jeremy's curiosity about the landscape got the best of him.

He pointed to rows of boarded-up, single-story buildings painted tan. "How come no one lives there anymore?"

"It used to be a military base. Fort Ord was where your Uncle Shawn went for basic training before he left for Vietnam." Shawn was Craig's oldest brother and Jeremy's favorite uncle.

She pointed to their right. "See those sand dunes? That's where they used to practice shooting their guns."

"Didn't it scare the birds?"

She had given birth to a lover, not a fighter. "I'm sure it did. It probably scared a lot of things, including people."

"I don't like guns."

"Me either."

"Mom?"

"What?"

He hesitated. "Could we talk like this again?"

It took her a second to figure out what he was asking. And then it hit her. He thought they were having a good day, one that might not happen again. *Oh, Jeremy, what have I done to you?*

"I know I've been sad for a long time now," she said. "And I wish I could tell you that it's over and that I'm going to be okay from now on, but I know I still have a long way to go. The one thing I can promise you is that I'm going to try every day to make that day less sad than the one before."

"How come you're better now?"

She could hear the wariness in his voice. As much as he wanted to believe her, he was afraid to. "I think it's because I finally want to be, Jeremy. For a long time I thought that in order to get better I had to stop loving Angela. I know now that isn't true."

He didn't need to know about the guilt she would carry the rest of her life. That was her problem, not his.

"I asked God to let her come back," he said softly, plainly telling her something he had told no one else. "But He didn't. I don't think He was listening."

"I asked, too, Jeremy. And so did your dad. Because Angela didn't come back doesn't mean God wasn't listening. Sometimes we're so intent on getting exactly what we ask for that we miss the fact our prayers have been answered in another way."

He looked deeply, hopefully into her eyes. "How?"

"I don't know yet. I'm still trying to figure it out myself."

They slipped into an easy silence that was with them all the way into Monterey. They were at the waterfront when Ann asked, "Have you studied the California missions in school?"

"A little. Our teacher said the priests were really mean to the Indians."

"They were by our standards today. Back then whoever was stronger and more powerful didn't try to understand or respect anyone who was different than they were. It was the way people treated each other."

"Timmy's sister treats us that way sometimes."

"I think we should visit a couple of the missions while we're here and see what it was like back then."

His eyes grew wide. "You're going to make me do history things for my surprise?"

"No, not for your surprise. That's something different. I'm going to make you do history things for fun."

"It wasn't very much fun in class."

Until fifth grade Ann had made the effort to know all of Jeremy's teachers, the good and the bad. Luckily, he'd had mostly good. She had no idea what his teacher had been like this year. "It's going to be fun here—I guarantee it."

She turned at the sign that said PACIFIC GROVE. "While you were in the shower I was looking in a

book I found at the house that had a hundred fun
things for us to do around here."

"School things?"

She laughed. "Not all of them."

"Good."

Ann turned onto Lighthouse Avenue, and told
Jeremy, "Look for Seventeenth Street." He pointed
it out several blocks later. She turned right and as
soon as they came to the end, pulled into a parking spot.

Jeremy looked around. "This is the surprise? I
don't get it."

"You will."

She got out and came around the car, slipping
her arm across his shoulders to guide him toward
a landscaped park sitting on a rocky promontory
overlooking the bay. Wind-sculpted cypress provided shade on sunny days, grass a place to lay
blankets, and below the cliffs, sandy beaches a
place to play in the surf.

Jeremy immediately spotted divers in face
masks and scuba gear, then farther out, a bright
red kayak skimming across the calm water. Ann
took him to the railing and let him explore on his
own for several minutes. "Look closer," she finally
said.

"Where?"

She pointed to the kelp beds. "Down there."

"You mean at the wood—" He sucked in his
breath in surprise. "Wow. Is that—It *is*," he

squealed. "Otters. Tons of 'em. Wow. Look over there, Mom. That one's got a baby on his stomach. And look at that one, the one rolling over and over. Why is he doing that? Look, there's another one with a baby."

He climbed on the bottom rail to get a better look. Ann grabbed the back of his shirt, biting back the warning to be careful. She pointed to a spot another fifty yards offshore. "Look over there."

"What is it?"

"A harbor seal."

"He's looking right at us. This is soooo cool."

A man who looked to be in his early fifties, wearing shorts and a 49ers cap turned to look at Jeremy. "I take it this is your first time to Lover's Point?"

Jeremy nodded. "My mom's, too."

"I come every day. It's never the same."

"The desert can be that way, too," Ann said.

He smiled. "I guess home is where the heart is."

It was such an unusual thing for him to say she didn't know how to answer.

"We live in Reno," Jeremy said.

"An interesting city." He bowed his head slightly and moved to leave. "I hope you have a wonderful vacation."

"Thank you," Ann said.

She looked at Jeremy, at the color in his cheeks, the unconscious grin, the light in his eyes. *Home is where the heart is.* A timeworn cliché, the kind stitched and framed and sold at craft fairs. One she'd never given more than a passing thought.

Her heart had been divided between a beautiful little girl who no longer needed her and a husband and son who desperately did. A part of her heart would always be with Angela, but it was time Ann returned to the home where she was cherished and loved and complete.

"Come on," she said to Jeremy, reaching for his hand. "We have one more place to go today."

8

"How did you know?" Jeremy asked, as Ann pulled into the parking lot of a grocery store in Capitola. They were there to buy cat food.

Ann was tempted to make up a story about mothers having second sight, but settled for the truth. "Dad told me."

"How did Dad know?"

"He saw the cat sleeping on the side of the house near the empty can of salmon and figured it out."

"He doesn't belong to anyone," Jeremy said defensively. "He was really skinny before I started feeding him."

She waited for what she was sure would come next, the plea to take him home, but Jeremy didn't say anything. "He must have belonged to someone once. Dad said he was wearing a collar that had a tag."

"I put that collar on him. And the tag has my name on it. It says, Francis, friend of Jeremy's."

Ann frowned. "How did—"

"It was a birthday present. From my friend who helped me build the sand castle. He gave me a comb and some cat treats, too."

She found a parking place near the front door, pulled in, and turned off the car. "How long has this been going on?"

"Since the day after we got here."

"Why didn't you say anything?"

"Because you and Dad would have said he had rabies or something, and you would have made me stop feeding him."

He was right. It was exactly what she and Craig would have said and done. "I'll make you a deal."

He eyed her suspiciously. "What kind of deal?"

"We'll take him to a vet tomorrow and have him checked over. If he's all right, you can take care of him while we're here."

"I don't want to take him to a vet. If he's sick, they'll put him to sleep. That's what they did to Timmy's dog." Dejected, his chin dropped to his chest.

"A vet only puts an animal to sleep if it can't be made well. I just want to make sure your cat is okay, that he doesn't have worms or anything like that. If he is sick, we'll get him medicine."

He looked up at her through long, golden

lashes. "You said *my* cat. Does that mean I get to keep him?"

She and Craig had agreed that as long as they were both working they wouldn't have pets. It wasn't fair to keep an animal locked up and alone all day. But she wasn't working anymore and didn't know if she would ever go back. "You can keep him—"

"I can? Really?" In his excitement his voice rose to a high-pitched squeak. A second later the smile faded. "Forever or just while we're here?"

What she'd meant to say was that Jeremy could take care of him while they were there and that they would make sure there was someone to take over when they left. She should have known they couldn't just stop and pick up cat food. What could she have been thinking? It wasn't fair to make this kind of decision without Craig. He didn't like cats.

She looked at Jeremy and decided she owed him this one. "Forever." He started to get excited again, and she held up her hand to stop him. "But—and this is a big one, Jeremy—first we have to check with the animal shelter and the newspaper to see if someone is trying to find him."

She could see the battle taking place in his mind. Jeremy had a sense of fair play that went beyond self-interest. No matter how much it hurt, he would do what was right.

"Okay," Jeremy said. He opened the car door.

"But I won't give him back if he ran away because the people are mean to him."

"That's fair." She met him at the front of the car and put her arm across his shoulders. "Let's get this over with. I want to meet this cat of yours."

"He only comes in the morning, so you have to wait until then. And he's not very good-looking right now. He has all these big clumps of hair that I can't get out with the comb even when he lets me try."

"We'll ask the vet to recommend a groomer and let them get the mats out." This was turning into a project.

They stopped in the pet food aisle in front of shelves and shelves of different brands and varieties. "If we make him look good again, the people might want him back," Jeremy said.

Ann stopped reading labels to stare at him. "When did you turn into such a worrier?" She wished she could take the words back the moment they were out. She knew, they both knew, when and why Jeremy had changed.

⌒ THE NEXT MORNING ANN STOOD BY THE COR-ner of the house as Jeremy called Francis. When he didn't come, Jeremy went around to the back to check the deck. Minutes later he returned, looking scared. "He's not here. Something happened to him."

"Maybe he's late."

"He's always here when I come out." He looked down at the dish of food he was carrying. "Always."

"Maybe my being here scared him off." The possibility something could have happened to the cat made Ann sick with fear. "He's not used to seeing me with you."

A glimmer of hope shone from Jeremy's eyes. "You think he's hiding?"

"Could be. Why don't I go back inside and give him a chance to see you out here alone."

Jeremy sat in his usual place and called, "Francis . . . hey, kitty, kitty, kitty. I brought your breakfast, Francis. It's real food this time. Come and see."

Ann went inside and stood by the kitchen window. She listened to Jeremy call Francis for a half hour before she went outside again. "I don't think he's coming," she said gently.

Jeremy looked up at her with eyes red and swollen from crying. "What if he got run over by a car and needs me to help him?"

"Come on. We'll ask the neighbors if anyone has seen him."

He put the dish in the middle of the walkway, just in case. "I wish Dad was here to help us."

"Me too." She started back to the house to pick up her key, then stopped to wait for him to catch up. When he did, she brought him into her arms for a long, tight hug.

"We'll find him, Jeremy." She had no right telling him something she didn't know to be true, but a few more hours of hope was all she had to give. "We won't stop until we do."

They knocked on doors and looked in bushes and climbed over fences and walked on the roads around the houses and in the park for three hours without success. They were on their way back to the house to check if the cat had sneaked back and eaten the food Jeremy left him when a green Honda pulled alongside them and stopped.

A young man who looked to be in his late teens stuck his head out the window. "Did you lose something?" he asked.

"A cat," Ann answered.

"What does it look like?"

Ann had no idea. She glanced at Jeremy.

"He's about this big—" He held his hands a foot apart. "And he's gray and brown and has long hair that's all stuck together."

"Sounds like the stray that's been hanging around here the past month. He's yours?"

"Not exactly," Ann said. "We want to adopt him."

"I saw animal control out here yesterday. You might check with them."

"What's animal control?" Jeremy asked.

A half-truth would do for now. "They pick up lost animals and take care of them until the owners can come and get them."

With natural ease, the young man in the car

reached out and put a comforting hand on Jeremy's shoulder. "You must be some special kid to make friends with that cat. I've been trying for weeks, and he wouldn't have anything to do with me."

"He knew I was coming," Jeremy said with conviction. "Only he got here too soon and had to wait for me."

Ann stared at Jeremy. He'd never made things up before. It was disconcerting to think he would start now. "How could he know you were coming?"

"I don't know. He just did. The man told me Francis was waiting for me because he needed me." Jeremy looked at her. "And I needed him."

Despite the warm day, a shiver raced through Ann, raising goose bumps on her arms. "We'd better get going. Thank you . . ."

"Paul," he said. "Paul Williams. I live in the house with the green shutters." To Jeremy, he said, "Let me know when you get your cat home, will you? All I've ever seen is a streak of gray running through the bushes."

"You can see him after my mom takes him to the groomer."

Paul smiled and shifted the Honda in gear. "Don't forget."

"I won't," Jeremy called after him.

⌒ANN AND JEREMY WENT FROM THE SHELTER, where they paid several fees to bail Francis out, to a walk-in veterinarian, and immediately afterward to a groomer. While Francis was being bathed and clipped and brushed and dried, they went to a pet store to pick up a litter pan, litter, a brush the groomer had recommended, toys, catnip, treats, hair ball medication, and a cat carrier. The entire time they were shopping Ann thought about the possibility of finding Francis's real owner. By the time they reached the checkout line, Ann had decided she would do whatever was necessary, pay whatever was asked, to allow Jeremy to keep his cat.

With three hours to wait, Ann took Jeremy to The Wharf House at the end of the pier in Capitola, hoping to distract him with a lunch of fish and chips and an ocean filled with surfers and sailboats. He looked and he listened, but his heart and mind were with Francis.

"Do you think Dad will like him?"

"I don't know," she said honestly. He'd seen Francis at his worst: maybe at his best Craig might weaken a little. Especially when he saw how much the cat meant to Jeremy.

"Do you like him?"

What she liked was the cat's reaction when he saw Jeremy at the shelter. He'd started meowing the minute he spotted Jeremy coming down the aisle, then reached between the bars with his paw as if waving to him. As soon as the cage was open, he jumped into Jeremy's arms and purred so loudly she could hear him from the other side of the room. When they rubbed noses it was every-thing Ann could do to keep from telling Jeremy not to get too close to the less-than-wonderful-smelling animal. Instead she busied herself with the papers for Francis's release and tried not to think what might be crawling around under the mats in the cat's fur.

"I do like him. And I think I'm going to like him even better when he's clean."

"What if Dad doesn't like him?"

He was looking for something she couldn't give him. No matter what she said, Jeremy would worry about his father's reaction until Craig him-self told him how he felt about having a cat. "If your dad doesn't like Francis, there's only one thing we can do."

"What?"

"Get another dad."

His jaw dropped, and his eyes grew wide in stunned surprise. It took several seconds before he realized she was teasing. "I'm going to tell Dad you said that."

Ann laughed. "Don't you dare."

He giggled and crawled across the bench seat to give her a hug. His face buried in her neck, he said, "You're the best, Mom. I love you."

She ran her hand through his silken hair. In her grief over the child she'd lost, she'd almost forgot-ten what a special child she still had. "I love you, too, Jeremy."

9

ANN FINISHED EMPTYING THE DISHWASHER
and went to check on Jeremy. He was
sleeping curled on his side, Francis tucked against
his stomach. The cat had shadowed Jeremy from
the moment they picked him up from the
groomers, following him from room to room,
even sitting outside the bathroom door to wait
while Jeremy was inside. Looking at the two of
them together she could almost believe there was
a special bond between them and that Francis *had*
known Jeremy was coming.

The bath and grooming had produced an animal she almost hadn't recognized. Once his hair
grew back from the clipping, he would be a strik-
ing cat. Now all they had to do was convince
Craig.

She'd left a message for him on the machine at

home and at the office and still hadn't heard back. If there was no return call by the time she went to bed, she would try him on the cell phone, something she rarely did when he was working.

On her way back to the kitchen to start pancake batter for breakfast, she stopped to pick up the newspaper Jeremy had left open on the coffee table. Dutifully, he'd checked the lost-and-found column, breathing a sigh of relief when none of the missing cats fit Francis's description. After a tense discussion over ice cream, she and Jeremy had settled on a plan of action to look for Francis's original family. In addition to phone calls to local vets and animal shelters, they were to go to a library in Santa Cruz to check back issues of the newspaper. She'd yielded on putting up signs saying they'd found Francis when Jeremy pointed out no signs had been put up saying he was lost.

She'd never been more sure she was right in what she was doing nor more afraid of the potential consequences. As important as it was to teach Jeremy a moral lesson, she desperately wanted it to go his way. Lost in the black hole of her grief, she'd left Jeremy to fight his own battles for too long.

How could she even think of trying to resume the life she had known before when nothing was the same? To put Angela aside was to deny her. Who would remember her little girl if she didn't?

Her legs gave out and she sank to the sofa. She'd been fooling herself to think two days of being Jeremy's mother again, of smiling and laughing and believing she'd found her way back, would lead to a third. Maybe Craig was right. Maybe they would be better off without her. It broke her heart to see what she'd done to her son, how she'd almost destroyed his self-confidence and his belief that being loved wasn't a privilege but a right.

She covered her face with her hands to stifle her sobs and rocked forward, her elbows on her knees. The hope she'd seen in Jeremy's eyes made failing him again unbearable. Why was it impossible to love Jeremy and Angela at the same time?

The weight of this new depression sat on her chest like a concrete monolith. She couldn't move, she couldn't reason, she could barely breathe.

She wasn't aware Francis had come into the room until he started insinuating himself onto her lap. Her first instinct was to push him away, but he made it clear he would not leave. He forced her to sit up and then crawled onto her legs and looked up into her eyes.

He didn't meow or purr, he just sat there with an enigmatic expression on his face. Slowly, with conviction, she realized something she would have thought insane a day ago. A strange peace came over her. *He knew what she was thinking. He understood what she was feeling.*

She didn't know how she knew this, she just did. No one, no matter what argument they used, could talk her into believing any different. The connection she felt wasn't magic or mystic or supernatural, it was a gift. She didn't need to know from where or whom, it was enough that she'd been told it was all right to move on. Angela wasn't alone anymore.

Francis settled into her lap. Ann ran her hand over his downy fur. Her fear that they would find someone who had been looking for Francis disappeared. They would never find out where he had come from, but it was clear why he was there.

CRAIG MADE THE FINAL TURN OUT OF THE forest and onto the beach road. He was surprised to see the living room lights still on in the house and glanced at the dashboard clock. One-thirty. Ann must be having another rough night.

He parked the car in the driveway, got out, and rolled his shoulders. After the long day he'd put in at the office wrapping things up so he could leave, the six-hour drive from Reno had seemed more like twelve.

After unlocking the door, he carefully turned the handle, making as little noise as possible in case Ann had managed to fall asleep on the sofa. If so, he'd cover her with a blanket and wait until morning to tell her about the thoughts that had been going through his mind and the conclusions he'd reached the past two days.

She was asleep, tucked into the corner of the couch, her head tilted back, a gray pillow on her lap. She looked peaceful, almost serene, words he hadn't used to describe her in a long time. While disappointed their talk would have to wait until morning, he was glad she wasn't sitting in the dark trying to hide her tear-swollen eyes from him.

Craig took the plaid blanket from the back of the chair beside the fireplace and unfolded it. He started toward Ann and did a double take when the gray pillow moved.

A head popped up and turned toward him. A mouth opened in a yawn and two legs extended in a stretch.

Craig smiled wryly. He leaned down to scratch the cat's chin. "I'm gone two days, and another guy moves in and takes over."

Ann stirred. Francis stood, stretched, hopped down, and headed for Jeremy's bedroom.

"Craig?" Ann frowned and sat up. "What are you doing here? I thought you were gone until the end of the week."

He sat next to her. "I couldn't stay away."

She put her hand on his knee and leaned into him. "I'm glad. There's been a lot going on here that I need to talk to you about."

Tentatively, he put his arm around her shoulders. Instead of resisting, she snuggled closer. He savored the moment. "I missed you," he said softly, his breath teasing her hair.

She looked up at him. "I missed you, too. But I'm so grateful I had this time alone with Jeremy."

"What I said before I left . . . about us . . . about

my not being able to take it anymore. I was
wrong, Ann. I'm sorry. I'm back, and I'm staying.
Whatever it takes, however long it takes, we'll get
through this."

She put her hand on his cheek. He turned his
head to press a kiss to her palm. There were tears
in her eyes when she said, "I love you, Craig
Davis."

He couldn't remember the last time she'd told
him she loved him, or the last time she'd let him
hold her this way. And he couldn't remember the
last time he'd kissed her, really kissed her, not the
perfunctory kind given in passing but the deep,
from the bottom of his soul kind filled with the
longing that at times threatened to consume him.

She tilted her chin to bring her lips up to meet
his. For a breathless moment he hesitated. He'd
traveled this road with Ann before, seeking the
comfort of her body in his own struggle to overcome the grief of losing Angela. She'd rejected
him, her own sorrow demanding isolation. The
two people whose lives were forever changed by
the loss could not give each other what the other
needed to survive.

What started as a tender exploration, a careful
dance with a potentially reluctant partner, soon
turned into an explosion of need. A deep moan of
pent-up desire came from the back of Ann's
throat. She moved to straddle Craig, locking her
arms around his neck.

She kissed him again, hard and deep, moving

her hips in unmistakable invitation. In seconds she'd become wild and primitive and insistent, and he responded in kind. There were no words to describe how profoundly he'd missed her or what it meant to have her back in his arms, wanting him, needing him, loving him.

Craig grasped her thighs and stood, carrying her into the bedroom. He carefully closed the door behind them with his foot. Ann reached down and turned the lock.

They undressed each other with hurried, practiced movements, dropping and tossing clothing from the floor to the dresser. Craig pulled back the bedspread and they tumbled onto the bed, rolling so that Ann was on top and then on bottom. Bracing himself over her, he kissed her neck and throat and the soft curve of her breast.

He loved his wife's body, the smell and feel of it, the way her nipples hardened at his touch, the soft flesh of her inner thigh when she pressed her legs against his waist, the sounds she wasn't aware she made when she was nearing climax. And he loved the way she loved him, the tenderness, the playfulness, the teasing, the stroking, the sexy nightgowns, waiting up for him after a late meeting. She was the only woman he had ever wanted.

And she wanted him again.

He hovered over her, looking into her eyes in the light of the full moon streaming in through the window. "I've been lost without you."

"I know . . . me, too."

He entered her in one long, slow stroke. She was wet and warm and tight with anticipation. Her hips rose to meet his thrusts. He tried to hold himself back, to make this first time together again the best Ann had ever known, but it was asking too much. He didn't have that kind of control, not now, not ever with her. He heard her soft cry of readiness and he was lost and found at the same time.

He was home.

10

ANN NESTLED INTO CRAIG'S SHOULDER AND listened to the sounds of the incoming tide. There was something reassuring and fundamental in the soft roar, a continuation that brought acceptance. Life went on, no matter how heartbreaking the journey.

Angela had been given three and a half months of life. She and Craig had been given thirty-five years—so far. What they did with the time remaining would mark their success or failure at the end.

Mourning would not bring Angela back. Neither would guilt.

She looked at Craig and saw that he, too, was deep in thought, his eyes staring unseeing at the shadows moving across the ceiling. She would never be rid of guilt or accept it until she shared her dark secret with him.

"I could have saved her," Ann said.

He turned to look at her. "What are you talking about?"

"Angela. If I had taken her to the doctor sooner, she wouldn't have died."

"Who told you that?"

"I overheard the intern talking to a nurse. She said antibiotics should have been started right away. But I didn't bring her in right away. I waited . . ." She caught her breath in a stifled sob. "I thought she had a cold . . ." Her throat tightened as she fought the tears. "I didn't want anyone to think I was a panicky new mother." She lost the battle. Tears filled her eyes and spilled onto Craig's shoulder. "I cared more about what people thought than I cared about Angela."

Craig brought her to him and held her tight against his chest. "You loved our little girl more than your own life. You would have traded places with her if you could." He pressed a kiss to her temple, and softly added, "I know that as well as I know you would do the same thing for Jeremy or for me."

"I can go on," she said. "I know that now. But I can never forgive myself."

"I'm going to tell you something." He leaned away from her so that she was forced to look at him. "And I want you to listen carefully."

She nodded.

"For a long time I beat myself up for not being with you when you and Angela needed me. I even convinced myself I could have done something if I had stayed home and not gone off looking to have my ego stroked at that conference."

She started to turn away. "There was nothing you could have done."

He caught her chin and turned her back to face him. "Listen to what you just said. Really listen. Why was there nothing I could have done, but something you should have done?"

She didn't have an answer.

"I went farther with my guilt. I wanted confirmation, so I made an appointment with the doctors and nurses who took care of Angela. By then they'd had a meeting to go over her treatment and what they could have done differently to try to save her."

She needed what would come next but couldn't bear hearing the words.

"*Nothing*," he said. "We've come to believe there's always an answer, always a cure, always a way. Sometimes there just isn't. There was nothing I could have done, nothing the doctors could have done—nothing *you* could have done that would have made a difference."

They were different words, but the same thoughts the old woman had expressed. Ann had carried her guilt for so long it was hard to let go. "How do they know?"

"We weren't the only ones devastated by Angela's death. The people who tried to save her at the hospital were, too. Only their way of dealing with it was to try to understand it while we were looking for a way to get from one day to the next."

"I can't bear to think of her all alone waiting for us."

"I know," Craig said. Tears pooled in his eyes, shimmering in the moonlight. "I let myself believe she would live a long and wonderful life. I imagined her growing up. I made all these crazy plans about things we would do together, places we would go. I was her father. The most beautiful little girl in the world would walk by my side and hold my hand and call me 'Daddy.' " A lone tear escaped his eye and slid down his cheek. "I allowed myself to dream, and those dreams are a part of me for the rest of my life."

Ann put her arms around Craig and held him. For the first time since the funeral they cried together instead of apart.

⌐THE NEXT THREE WEEKS WERE A TIME OF RE-newal, discovery, and healing. Craig and Francis worked out their territories, the basic tenent being ignoring each other as much as possible. Only Francis kept pushing the envelope, first sitting beside Craig's chair at breakfast, then next to him on the sofa while he was reading the newspaper, then boldly climbing onto his lap and curling up for a nap during a video movie.

Ann and Jeremy had dutifully searched old lost-and-found columns in the newspaper and called local veterinarians and a couple of outlying shelters. As Ann had predicted, no one had actively looked for Francis.

They finally made it to the aquarium the last week in July. Jeremy touched the bat rays and sea slugs and left his fingerprints on dozens of exhibits. On the way out he stopped by the gift shop to buy a present for Timmy—a plastic shark that shot water out of its mouth when you squeezed its stomach.

Ann and Craig held hands and exchanged smiles and made love without protection, believing it impossible to get pregnant without the help of the fertility specialist who had helped them get pregnant with Angela. On their last day she put off the queasy feeling that had come over her during breakfast to the clams she'd had the night before.

Every day she watched for the old man and woman as she went on her morning walk on the beach. She never saw them again.

As they were packing to leave, Ann spotted Andrew outside cutting back the nasturtiums that grew wild around his house. She went over to tell him good-bye.

He saw her walking toward him and came down the path to meet her. "Leaving a day early?"

"We thought we'd try to beat the traffic on I-80. It's awful going over the mountains on the weekends."

"I used to go that way to ski at Squaw Valley but haven't been up there in years."

"I wouldn't leave here either if I were you. I'd stay another month if we could arrange the time off for Craig."

"I'll pass that on to Julia."

She frowned.

"The woman who owns the house," he explained. "She'll like hearing you had a good time."

"There is one thing—the first week we were here, Jeremy and I met an old couple who said they'd been coming here for years. I was wondering if you knew them. What I'd really like is an address where I could write to them." She wanted to thank them for their kindness and wisdom and to let them know her and Jeremy's story had a happy ending.

"How old?"

"Eighties? Maybe a little younger."

He thought for several seconds, then shook his head. "What did they look like?"

She described them, the warm smiles and caring eyes given as much importance as their age and gray hair.

"They sound like the couple that used to own the house you've been staying in, but that's impossible. They've been dead for over three years."

She held out one of Craig's business cards. "If you should run into them, would you give them this and tell them we'd love to hear from them."

Andrew took the card and slipped it into his shirt pocket. "I'll keep an eye out."

She smiled her thanks. "We're going to try to come back next year. Hopefully we'll see you then."

"Have a safe trip home."

Ann went back in the house for one last walk through to make sure they hadn't forgotten anything. Jeremy was talking to Francis, who was stretched out on the mantel wisely steering clear of the packing.

Jeremy reached for the photograph on the mantel. He looked long and hard at the man and woman. A slow smile of recognition formed. They were his friends. Much younger, of course, about the age his mom and dad were now.

He and Francis had been alone on the deck one morning when they had stopped to say good-bye. Jeremy had wanted to tell his mom and dad where his friends had said they were going but decided it was better to wait until they were back home again. He didn't know whether it would make them happy or sad and selfishly didn't want to take the chance it might be sad.

Jeremy hoped the news would make his mother stop worrying about Angela being alone. After all, the man and woman weren't strangers anymore, they were friends. And friends took care of him sometimes when his mom and dad went places. Shouldn't it be all right if these new friends took care of Angela, even if they were kind of old?

His mother was at the door telling him it was time to leave. Jeremy put the picture back on the mantel, started toward her, and stopped to call Francis. He stood and stretched and took a minute to look at the photograph, as if he were saying good-bye, too. Then, without a backward glance, he jumped down and followed Jeremy to the car.

August

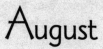

1

ANDREW LOOKED UP FROM THE ORCHID catalog he was reading and glanced out the window. Cheryl was late. She was supposed to leave Oakland at ten. Even taking morning traffic through the bay area into account and figuring a fender bender or two on Highway 17, she still should have been there an hour ago.

It had taken a week of phone calls and a weekend with her in Oakland to convince her to stay the month in Julia and Eric's house. She'd finally admitted she was afraid he would get the wrong signal if she agreed to come. She liked the way things were between them, slow and easy, and didn't want to mess things up by forcing the situation.

Then, for some unfathomable reason, at least to Andrew, she'd changed her mind. He'd almost asked her about it a couple of times, but decided to leave well enough alone.

He'd turned to go back to his catalog when out of the corner of his eye he spotted a blue van on the forest road. Cheryl drove a red Subaru; it couldn't be her. Still, he stayed where he was and watched as the van cleared the forest and came toward the houses. He watched right up to the minute the van pulled into the driveway of the Chapman house and the driver's door opened and Cheryl stepped out.

He moved to go outside to greet her when he saw two more doors open and three teenage girls get out.

Cheryl looked at Andrew's house, saw him standing at the window, and waved. Instead of waving back, he came outside. He stuck his hands in the back pockets of his jeans and crossed the path, stopping at the end of the driveway.

"Heavy traffic?" he said by way of greeting.

"Late start." She came forward but left a telling distance between them. Their planned month together would not start with a kiss. "I should have called, but was so grateful finally to get on the road that I didn't want to take any more time."

Cheryl didn't have a car phone and didn't want one. He couldn't imagine being out of touch with the office when he was away from the nursery. Somewhere they'd switched places, he'd become the button-down businessman and she'd insisted on her freedom.

The girls stood behind Cheryl expectantly. She motioned to bring them forward. "Andrew, I'd like you to meet some friends of mine."

A young woman with ebony hair, bronze skin, and the blackest eyes and thickest lashes Andrew had ever seen held out her hand. "Maria Ramos," she said, beating Cheryl to the introduction. "I understand you have a nursery and might be looking for help."

"I do—and I'm always looking for good help," he told her, wondering what the hell was going on.

"Thanks for letting me work into it gradually, Maria," Cheryl said.

"I couldn't see no sense in putting it off," she said. "I told you, I don't mind being here, but I can't be sitting around on my butt all day."

Cheryl reached back and brought a second girl forward. "This is Karen Devlin, and—" She glanced around and spotted the third girl still at the van. "And Deanna Riparetti."

Andrew shook each of the girl's hands. Karen had blond hair bleached almost white, with half an inch of dark roots showing. One ear was lined in gold hoops from the lobe to around the arched top, the other had a single diamond stud. A small gold ball sat on the side of her nose. A tatoo of a protruding tongue, Mick Jagger style, was on one shoulder, Tweety Bird on the other.

Deanna had fire engine red hair, earrings circling both ears, a barbed wire tatoo around one arm, and a cobweb without a spider on the side of her neck.

"Pleased to meet you," Andrew said. The unspoken question—*what are you doing here*—hung heavy in the air.

"Hold on a minute while I let them in," Cheryl said to Andrew. She opened the front door to the house and the back door of the van. The girls unloaded their suitcases and disappeared inside.

Cheryl gave Andrew a sheepish smile and put her hands up in surrender. "Surprise."

He waited.

"Aren't you going to say anything?"

Where to begin? "Friends of yours, I take it?"

"Yes, in a way."

"And they'll be staying how long?"

"August."

"The entire month?"

She nodded.

"I see . . ."

"No, I don't think you do. Well, maybe you see, but I doubt you understand." She came forward and touched his arm. "Believe it or not, this is a good thing, Andrew. I'm letting you know that I'm ready to take the next step. These kids are part of who I am. This is what I do. I want you to see me the way I am, what's important to me, what I could never give up."

He couldn't tell whether he was more annoyed

with Cheryl for not telling him the girls were coming or curious about what she would say next. "So it's 'love me, love my friends'?"

"You don't have to love them—but you do have to understand. I've found something to do with my life that makes a difference. For the most part, these girls have never been outside their neighborhoods. They've grown up believing what they have is all they can ever have, all they have a right to expect. Maria even thinks it's all she deserves. I want to show them they have options. I couldn't let this opportunity pass."

"What options does a girl with a spiderweb tatoo have?"

Cheryl instantly went on the defensive. "A turtleneck sweater. If that's what it takes to get past someone blinded by prejudice."

"Okay, I can see I'm on dangerous ground here. Why don't I let you get settled, and we can talk later?"

"You're angry."

He thought about it. "Disappointed."

For two weeks Cheryl had fought a mental battle over telling him about the girls. The coward in her won every time. If Andrew insisted she come alone, she couldn't face a battle where they would both come away losers. "I can handle that. If I were in your position, I'd be disappointed, too."

"Is that supposed to make me feel better?"

He'd undoubtedly made plans, lots of them—plans that didn't include three eighteen-year-old girls. "Remember when you told me you would do whatever was necessary to prove that we could make it this time?"

Despite an obvious effort to keep a smile from forming, one did. "I had a feeling that might come back to haunt me."

"I can promise these girls are not your worst nightmare. You're going to like them, a lot, when you get to know them." Especially when he came to see how much they had in common with him. Deanna had lived in almost as many foster homes as Andrew, and Karen had the same hunger to see the world. Maria had his dreams and drive to succeed, but was held back by a sense of obligation to her family. She was determined to keep her younger brother and three younger sisters in school and away from the gang influence that had put her older brother in prison for being in the car during a drive-by shooting.

"Was Maria serious about coming to work for me?"

"Regrettably, yes. Promising her a job here was the only way I could get her to leave the one she had in Oakland. Her mother can't make it through the month without Maria's paycheck."

"I don't pay unskilled beginners much above minimum wage," he warned. "But I guess I could make an exception."

"You don't have to do that. Maria isn't expecting it."

"I'll see how she does."

Deanna came to the door. "What do you want us to do with your stuff?"

"I'll take care of it. You can unpack the groceries."

When Deanna was back in the house, Andrew said, "So you're here officially, I take it? Taking care of these girls is part of your job."

"Not exactly," she equivocated. "The agency is watching to see how our month turns out, and if it's successful, they'll come on board next year. They did request that I only bring girls who were eighteen or older, and I agreed."

"Seems to me you're taking quite a chance."

"They're worth it."

He shoved his hands in his back pockets again. "Okay—what can I do to help?"

She wasn't surprised, this was the Andrew she'd expected, the man she'd loved in flesh and memory. Still, her heart skipped a beat as hope nudged the wariness of whether they could make their way back to each other.

~~"HE'S GOING TO KISS HER," MARIA SAID, peering through the blinds of the living room window.

"How do you know?" Deanna countered, looking over her shoulder.

"See that look on his face? He's got it bad." Maria tucked a long strand of black hair behind her ear. She recognized what was going through

Andrew's mind because she'd seen the same expression on Carlos's face when he was trying to talk her into doing it with him in the backseat of his brother's car. After weeks of trying, he'd grown impatient, decided blondes were more fun, and taken off with one.

"What are you two doing?" Karen asked, coming into the room from the hallway, scratching the tattooed tongue on her shoulder.

"Spying," Deanna said.

"Get a life—there ain't nothin' those two are going to do out there that's worth gettin' caught watching." Still, Karen joined them at the window.

"He's kinda cute," Deanna said.

"For someone old," Karen added. She continued moving her fingernails over the protruding tongue on her shoulder. "Damn this thing. I think I'm getting allergic or something."

Maria moved to make room for Karen. "How old do you think he is?"

"Forty," Karen guessed.

Deanna shook her head. "Thirty-five tops. Look how flat his stomach is. No forty-year-old guy has a gut like that."

"The ass ain't bad, either." Karen made an exaggerated show of licking her lips. "Yum."

Maria studied Andrew. Cheryl had told them she had a friend who lived next door to the house where they would be staying, but she'd figured anyone who grew orchids for a living wasn't boyfriend material. At least not the girlfriend/boyfriend kind. Plainly she'd been wrong. "How old do you think Cheryl is?"

Deanna answered. "Same age."

"What—thirty-five or forty?" Karen asked.

"Didn't she just go to her twenty-year high school reunion?" Maria asked. "That would make her thirty-eight, maybe thirty-nine."

Karen looked closer. "You really think she's *that* old?"

"Unless she graduated early like that weirdo, Sandy." Bored, Deanna turned away. "I'm gonna see what there is to eat."

"What's with you lately?" Karen asked. "You're always stuffing something in your mouth."

Maria prepared for the explosion. Deanna had always been on the heavy side of normal, but she'd really been packing it on lately.

Ignoring Karen, Deanna went into the kitchen and came out a few minutes later with a bag of chips and a Coke and headed for her bedroom.

Karen ran her hand through her hair, then glanced down at the blond strands that had broken off. She brushed them onto the floor. "We gotta find a way to keep her out of the food, or we're going to need a trailer to haul her home."

Karen was obsessed about her weight and could recite the calorie content of everything on the menu at every fast-food restaurant in the city. Maria couldn't remember ever seeing her eat more than a few bites of anything. Push her, and she'd tell you she'd eaten earlier or had plans for later.

Push too hard, and she'd tell you to fuck off, that what she did or didn't eat was no one's business.

Maria figured if Karen was lucky, she would wake up hungry one morning and realize that no matter how long she starved herself, she would never look like the women in the magazines she was always reading. If she was unlucky, she'd wind up anorexic and in a hospital somewhere. If talking made any difference to her or Deanna, Karen would be eating and Deanna wouldn't.

Deanna's appetite forgotten for the moment, Karen sat sideways in the overstuffed chair beside the fireplace. "You really going to get a job while we're here?"

Maria sat on the sofa and propped her feet up on the coffee table. "Sitting around doing nothing drives me nuts."

"Yeah? Just wait till you've been lyin' under the sun a couple of days with me and Deanna. You'll come around."

"I'm already as brown as I want to be. I don't need that skin cancer shit to look good the way you white people do." She sat up and looked around. "You see a CD player around here? Or a radio? It's too quiet."

"Deanna said she was gonna bring hers."

"You think she'd mind if I borrowed it?" Maria asked.

"Toss her a candy bar and you could take everything she owns and she wouldn't care."

"That's mean."

"Am I wrong?" Karen countered.

Cheryl interrupted the conversation when she came inside. "Everything put away?"

Maria nodded.

"Which bedroom did you leave for me?"

Maria and Karen exchanged glances. "We thought we each got our own," Karen said. "Isn't that why we're here—to see how the rich kids live?"

"Actually, you're here to wait on me hand and foot and be on call at all hours of the day and night."

Maria laughed. "For minimum wage, no doubt."

"Who said anything about getting paid? Now, which room did you leave me?"

"The first one on the right," Karen said. "Me and Deanna took the one in the back. We let Maria have a room by herself 'cause we didn't want her waking us up in the morning getting ready for work. This is our va-cay-shun and we're sleepin' in."

"Not tomorrow," Cheryl said. "We're going to get on the road early before we lose Maria to her job."

"When do I start," Maria asked. "And how do I get there?"

"Andrew said he would talk to Paul about giving you a ride."

"Who's Paul?"

"I don't know anything about him except that

he's one of the guys who works at the nursery and he lives around here."

Maria got up and went into the kitchen to get a bottled water. She came back and leaned a shoulder into the doorframe. "Am I going to be the only woman working there?"

"I wouldn't think so, but I don't know for sure." The question puzzled Cheryl. It had never occurred to her that the employee mix would make a difference.

"I thought you were checking out this job for me." She opened the water and took a long drink.

"If you don't think you'll like working at the nursery, we can look somewhere else."

She twisted the top off the water and rolled the cap in her hand. "I just don't want to put up with a lot of guys hittin' on me. I get enough of that at home."

"Yeah," Karen chimed in. "I see them followin' you home from the Taco Bell every night. The line's gotta be half a mile long."

"Shut up, Karen," Maria said flatly.

"Are the groceries put away?" Cheryl asked.

Maria took a drink of water before she answered. "Deanna took care of it."

"Probably sampled everything before she did," Karen added.

"Cut it out, Karen." Cheryl was as concerned about Deanna as they were, but determined to let whatever was going on with her come out when she was ready. She'd learned a long time ago that when pushed for information, girls this age only dug their heels in harder.

Karen dropped her voice to a whisper. "Someone's got to say something. Those pants she has on are so tight someone could get killed if she sneezes and they let go."

"Criticizing her isn't going to help. She gets enough of that from Jake. We're going to make sure she knows she's liked no matter what size she is." Cheryl looked from Karen to Maria. "Aren't we?"

Maria shrugged. "I ain't gonna say nothin'."

"You mean you expect us to watch her stuff herself and not say anything about it?" Karen's tone made her feelings clear. Given the opportunity, she would parcel out Deanna's food. "What kind of friend wouldn't say nothin'?"

"The kind of friend who cares more for what's inside a person than what's outside." Cheryl was used to the magazine-fed culture of the teens she worked with. Although they didn't have the resources to have plastic surgeons correct their perceived imperfections the way their counterparts in the suburbs did, they had remarkable skills with cheap drugstore-brand makeup, could starve themselves with frightening ease, and could put together outfits from thrift shop racks that left designers scrambling to catch up.

"You have some really strange ideas, Miz Walden," Karen said. "There ain't nobody I know who thinks the way you do."

Deanna came down the hall. She'd put on her swimming suit with her flannel bathrobe as a cover-up. "I'm going to the beach. Anyone want to come with me?"

"Yeah," Karen said. "Give me a minute to get in my suit." She started down the hall. "Wait till you see it. I got it on sale at that new place that opened up next to Rico's, and it's *hot*."

"What about you, Maria?" Deanna asked.

"I might come down later."

"Do you have a towel?" Cheryl asked Deanna. "I brought extras in case someone forgot."

"I was gonna use my bathrobe to sit on, but maybe a towel would be better."

Cheryl went into the bedroom and dug through her duffel bag for the oversize towels she'd picked up at Walmart, knowing the girls were unlikely to have their own. Normally she refrained from buying them things. Her job was to be their friend and mentor, not their fairy godmother.

Money wasn't something she talked about with them. They had no idea whether she had any or was living from paycheck to paycheck the way their parents did.

As far as they knew, the beach house had been an unexpected, last-minute gift from a friend who'd encouraged her to share the month with them. That was stretching the truth a bit, but it created only a small pang of guilt. The girls being there provided an opportunity to see a world outside their neighborhood, something Cheryl would have compromised more than the truth to attain. For her and Andrew, the month would pull them out of the emotional cloud their reunion had put them in and solidly ground them in the reality of her day-to-day life. If they could survive the abrupt change, they just might have a chance, something she found herself wanting more and fearing less.

She found the towels and the gift Maria's mother, Juanita, had quietly slipped to her the day before she and the girls left Oakland. She'd asked Cheryl to keep it a secret until they were settled and then to give it to Maria when they were alone.

Cheryl slipped the small package under the bed pillow and crossed mental fingers that whatever Maria's mother had sent would encourage her daughter to spend at least part of one summer being a real kid.

2

MARIA STOOD ON THE BED TO SEE HER-self in the mirror that hung over her dresser. She turned sideways and then to the back, twisting to see how much of her rear end hung out of the bright red suit. Just enough.

She couldn't believe her ultraconservative mother had taken a suit like this from the rack, let alone paid for it. The legs were cut almost to the waist and her breasts clearly outlined, her nipples straining the fabric. At first she'd been upset at the gift. They couldn't afford things like new swimming suits for her when school was starting in a couple of weeks and they still hadn't bought Enrique, Alma, and Rosa their new uniforms.

But the suit was so beautiful and she looked so good in it she couldn't stay mad and be excited at the same time. She understood why her mother

had given the present to Cheryl and told her to
wait until they arrived to give it to her. She never
would have even tried it on at home. It would
have gone straight back to the store.

There was a knock on the door. "Ready?"
Cheryl asked.

"Coming." Maria stepped off the bed and
smoothed the spread before opening the door.

"Wow," Cheryl said appreciatively. "That's
some suit." She motioned for her to turn around.
"I can't believe your mother bought that for you."

Maria laughed. "I know. Me either."

"I wonder how it's going to hold up in the
water."

"That's something I don't have to worry about.
This suit's not gettin' anywhere near any water. I
can't swim." She rarely admitted she couldn't do
something that people who lived outside her
neighborhood took for granted. Anyone with any
sense would realize she didn't swim because people like her didn't have the opportunity to learn.
There weren't a lot of swimming pools on her
block. And the buses that stopped on the corner
didn't make connections to any beaches.

Cheryl handed her a towel and sunscreen. "I'm
going to stop next door to see if Andrew wants to
join us."

"Hold up, I'll go with you. I need to talk to
him about work. I want to see if he'll let me start
tomorrow."

"Tomorrow is Sunday, Maria."

"Yeah, but the plants don't know that. I'll bet there's somebody who takes care of them all the time." She wrapped the towel around her waist and stepped into her shoes. "Might as well be me." She stopped and eyed Cheryl. "Or did you want to see him alone?"

Cheryl flushed, leaving pink circles on both cheeks. "What's that supposed to mean?"

The question surprised Maria. "Hey, it's okay with me if you two are gettin' it on. You're old enough. You don't need nobody's permission."

"We're *friends*, Maria."

She shrugged. "If that's what you want to call it."

"That's what it is. And that's the way it has to be while we're here." She reached in and turned out the light in the hall bathroom as they passed. "Even though the agency isn't officially involved, they took a chance giving me the time off so I could bring you girls down here. The last thing I need is for word to get back that I'm fooling around with the next-door neighbor."

Cheryl wasn't like the social workers Maria and her mother had dealt with in the five years since her father died. She never made them feel like charity cases or like they lived the way they did because they didn't care or know any better.

Of course they knew better. They had a television. They saw how other people lived. And they wanted that kind of life just as much as everyone else did. But there wasn't a lot of time or energy or money to paint walls or fix up the yard when you spent the whole day washing and ironing other people's clothes for fifty cents a shirt the way her mother did.

"Why did you bring us here?" Maria asked. "What are you getting out of it?"

Cheryl didn't rise to the challenge in Maria's voice. But then she never did. "I want to show you some of the world outside Oakland," she said simply. "I'm hoping it will encourage you to want to see more."

"Why should we care? We have everything we need where we are." She worked hard to sound dismissive, but wanted Cheryl to give an answer worth hearing. There was a fire to learn and see things that burned so hot sometimes it almost overwhelmed her. Her frustration became anger that she turned on the people who deserved it the least. No one understood because she never gave them a chance. She knew what she had to do, and talking about it wasn't going to change anything, so why bother?

"It's easy to talk to you about this because I know you don't believe what you just said," Cheryl said.

"What makes you think I don't?"

Cheryl held the door for Maria to go through first, then followed and locked it behind them. "If you did, you wouldn't be working so hard to make sure your brother and sisters have a better life."

"I don't want them to end up like Fernando. It almost kills my mother when she goes to see him. She has this crazy idea that it's her fault, that she let my father down because she didn't keep Fernando out of trouble."

"How much longer will he be in prison?"

"Twenty-six years." She had trouble saying the words. "He'll be an old man when he gets out. Older than my mother is now."

"What a waste. For everyone."

Whenever she started to feel sorry for her brother, she thought about the little girl who had been playing on the porch of the house Fernando and his friends had showered with bullets. The girl's brother had died, and she'd been left blind and in a wheelchair for life. She would not regain her sight in twenty-six years, nor would she get up and walk. Of the two, Fernando got the better deal. Even knowing that, it broke her heart when she thought about her brother being locked away until he was an old man. She missed him as much as she was mad at him.

Maria hiked her towel up and pulled it tighter around her waist. She didn't like talking about Fernando. It always left her angry and sad and frustrated because there was nothing she could do, no way she could make it better. It just was.

They crossed the path to Andrew's house and knocked on the front door. He didn't answer. Cheryl went around the side to check the back deck, but he wasn't there either. "I guess he left."

Maria almost laughed. Cheryl was the worst person she'd ever seen try to hide her feelings.

They started down the stairs. "Maybe he had to go back to work," Maria suggested.

"Yeah, maybe," Cheryl said. She put a hand out to stop Maria. "Just look at that," she said in awe.

"What?"

"The ocean. Isn't it breathtaking?"

Maria gazed at the beach and the water and the birds, even a half dozen guys playing volleyball. They were only a few hours from Oakland, but this was another world.

⌐MARIA STOOD IN THE MIDDLE OF THE GREEN-house waiting for Andrew to finish talking to someone on the phone. Cheryl had dropped her off that morning, supposedly because the nursery was on the way to Fremont Peak, where the rest of them were going on a hike and having a picnic lunch. She suspected it had more to do with Cheryl wanting her to have a chance to meet Paul Williams before she was stuck in a car with him for twenty minutes. Cheryl did things like that all the time and never owned up to them.

Her hands shoved in the pockets of her shorts, she craned her neck to take everything in. The building was huge and made out of thick, hard plastic sheeting. Enormous fans, controlled by a thermostat, were at one end. Pipes ran overhead with sprinkler heads on them. A long tube of collapsed soft plastic with holes the size of a quarters hung suspended from the ceiling. The air was warm and heavy with moisture, but not as uncomfortable as Maria had anticipated.

She was surrounded by thousands of plants on metal mesh tables, some with incredible flowers in pinks and reds and yellows and purples and oranges. The smell coming from the flowers was better than any perfume she'd ever sampled, kind of sweet and fruity and sharp, all at the same time.

Long strands of gray moss grew on racks that lined the back section of the greenhouse. Every corner was used, every counter filled, every person busy.

A woman with black-and-gray hair pulled back into a ponytail sat at a bench. She took plants out of one pot, cleaned the roots, grabbed a handful of stuff that looked like small pieces of bark mixed with something white, and stuffed it and the plant into a new pot, slightly larger than the one it had just left.

Another woman moved between the tables studying the plants, stopping every once in a while to pluck off a dead leaf or flower and then moving on. When she reached the end of the aisle, she twisted a knob and the table she'd been working on rolled two feet to the side, bumping into the table next to it, opening up another aisle.

The third worker, a tall blond guy with broad shoulders and powerful-looking arms, stood at another table. He pulled plants no bigger than a piece of grass from a flask, wrapped them in moss, and put them in a flat. He wore headphones and moved to the rhythm of a song only he could hear. Maria smiled as he stopped to play invisible drums before moving on to another flask.

"That's Paul," Andrew said, coming up behind her. "I'm going to have him show you around and help you get started. If you have any questions and I'm not around, he or Alfonso—you'll meet him later—can answer them for you."

"He's the one who's going to give me a ride in the mornings?" She'd expected someone older, like Andrew. It had never occurred to her there might be someone her own age working at the nursery.

"I haven't talked to him about it yet, but I'm sure there won't be any problem. He comes in five days a week, and has Sunday and Monday off. If it's okay with you, I'll set you up on the same schedule."

"Yeah, that's fine with me. How long do I stay?"

"I can give you eight hours a day with a half hour for lunch and a couple of fifteen-minute breaks, if that's what you're looking for. If you don't want that many hours, I can—"

"No, that's fine. The more the better."

"I thought you were here on vacation."

She smiled. "I am—Sundays and Mondays."

Andrew looked at Paul and decided not to interrupt him. Instead, he motioned for Maria to follow. They left the first greenhouse and walked through three more. Each one was built the same way, but contained different plants, or at least different-looking plants.

"Are all of these buildings yours?" she asked.

"These and one more about half this size that I use for specimen plants and breeding. That greenhouse is kept locked and isn't open to the public."

"Why?"

"As ridiculous as it sounds, orchid people have been known to go to extraordinary lengths to steal pollen from a unique or award-winning plant."

"Why don't they just buy one of these?"

"The ones they want are one-of-a-kind or extremely rare or extremely fine specimens. Some are the parent stock of crosses I've made. Without them, the plants can't be duplicated except by cloning."

She'd come there thinking she was going to spend a month in the world's most boring job and was beginning to change her mind. Taking care of plants might not be exciting, but the background was. "How do they steal the pollen?"

"They'll either snap off a flower and stuff it in their pocket, or use something small, like a toothpick or matchstick to gather the pollen, leaving the flower intact."

"Amazing." She stopped to smell a deep red bloom that was larger than her outstretched hand. "How many plants do you have here?"

"Right now a couple of million. We're inventoried pretty heavily because we're getting stock ready to ship to the fall shows. Fall and spring are our big selling seasons. We don't ship many plants in summer because of the heat."

"A couple of *million*?" She did some quick calculating. Figuring each plant was worth ten to twenty dollars wholesale—a number Cheryl had given her—even subtracting labor and everything else, Andrew had one healthy bank account.

"That figure includes the starter flats, and we normally lose about half of them."

"They die?"

"We throw them away."

"You throw them away?" Her voice betrayed her horror. "Why?"

"There's a dozen reasons. They could be stunted or haven't developed properly or the flower isn't up to our standards."

He slid open the door to the fourth greenhouse, waited for her to step inside, then closed it snugly to prevent the temperature controlled air from escaping. "This is it," he said. "I wish I could give you something more interesting to do, but everyone who comes to work here starts the same way."

"It's okay. I don't want special treatment. The job's enough."

Andrew stopped to talk to a man who looked so much like her mother's brother, Juan, Maria did a double take. "Maria, this is Alfonso Martinez. He's in charge when I'm not around—and most of the time when I am."

"Hi." She smiled and nodded. "I'm ready. Just tell me what you want me to do."

Alfonso sent Andrew a long-suffering look. "When are you going to send me someone who knows what they're doing?"

"I'm a quick learner," she said. "And I'm good. By the time I leave here, you're going to be begging me to stay. I guarantee it." She reached up and twisted her long hair into a knot on top of her head. "Now, I'm ready to get started."

Andrew headed for the door. "She's all yours," he said, chuckling as he left.

"What do you know about orchids?" Alfonso asked when Andrew was gone.

"Nothing."

"About plants?"

"Nothing."

He sighed. "At least you don't have bad habits to overcome."

She grinned. "I didn't say that."

She'd gotten through to him, and he laughed. "Come on. I'll show you how to tell a good leaf from a bad one."

Although Maria had openly fought going to Santa Cruz with Cheryl, Deanna, and Karen, she'd secretly, desperately, wanted to come. Finally, she'd let her mother and Cheryl convince her, but insisted she had to have a job while she was there, hoping some miracle would happen to keep her from taking it so she could have a real vacation like the others. Like almost everything else in her life, she got some of what she wanted, but not enough to make her think anything had changed.

Now that she was here and learning something new, she wasn't sure she minded so much. If she had to work, this place wasn't bad. At least it was different. And it wasn't fast food.

⌒ "HEY, MARIA," PAUL CALLED FROM ACROSS the greenhouse.

She looked up from the plant she'd been inspecting. "Yeah?"

"Time for a break."

She waved him off. "I'll take one later. I'm busy now."

"It's lunchtime. Later's no good. You have to take it when it's your turn."

She glanced at her watch. *Twelve-thirty.* She would have sworn she'd only been there an hour, and the morning was gone. Now, with her concentration broken, she realized she was hungry. Before she left the table she'd been working on, she picked up a rock and laid it on the edge to mark her spot.

She'd tossed an apple, water, and package of cookies in her purse on her way out the door that morning, and now wished she'd taken the time to make a sandwich. "Where do we go? Is there a lunchroom?"

"For you, today is Fred's Place. It's a tradition

around here that Andrew takes you to lunch on
your first day. That way you can ask him any
questions you've come up with after working
here a couple of hours."

"Seems to me it'd be better to wait until I'd
been here a couple of days." She made her way toward him, holding her hands above her waist to
keep from accidentally bumping one of the plants
along the narrow pathway.

She tried not to look directly at him. She'd already seen enough to know he was someone she
wasn't interested in. Men with blond hair and
blue eyes had never appealed to her, not even
when they had a body like Ricky Martin's and a
smile like Brad Pitt's. And it wasn't just his looks
that turned her off. It was obvious he came from
money, his parents the kind of people who lived
in the hills in Oakland. Her kind lived in the flats.
He worked for pocket change. She worked for
sustenance. The two didn't mix.

Paul chuckled. "Not everyone makes it a week.
Some don't come back from lunch."

"Tryin' to scare me?" she asked.

"Now why would I do that?"

She stopped in front of him, wiping her hands
on her shorts, then folding her arms across her
chest. His eyes weren't blue, they were brown—
with gold flecks. Challenging. And . . . *sexy*.

He was looking at her as if he could read her
mind, almost as if her assessment of his looks was
his due. She didn't like that. Instantly, she decided

she didn't like him either. "Maybe you think it's funny."

"To scare people?" He shook his head. "Yeah, that's me all right. I live for that kind of stuff." He grabbed the handle and slid the door to the side. Instead of opening it just wide enough for them to go through, he pushed it all the way open.

She gave him a questioning look.

"For the chip on your shoulder."

"And here I thought it was your ego."

She expected him to be angry, but he seemed to toss it off. It was on the tip of her tongue to say something, to push a little harder, when she remembered he was her ride to work in the mornings, and it would be stupid to mess that up. She went for something neutral. "How long have you been working here?"

"A couple of years, off and on. Full-time in summer, but when I'm in school I only come in when there's a big order or Andrew's shorthanded."

They left the greenhouses and walked thirty yards to the nursery's main office, a converted three-bedroom house. "Must be nice."

"What's that?"

"To work when it's convenient."

"Actually it's a drag. But my folks won't pay the speeding tickets I get in my BMW, so it's either work or walk."

Before she had a chance to answer, Andrew looked up and motioned for them to join him. He shifted the phone from one ear to the other and held up a finger asking for one more minute. "Call me back when you've hired someone who knows what they're doing." He paused. "No, I'm not kidding. I told you in the beginning that I'm not wholesaling to anyone who can't or won't take care of the plants. If you want cheap plants that you can toss, get them someplace else."

Paul leaned close and whispered, "Andrew's particular about his quality stuff. When it goes out with his name on it, he wants to be sure whoever buys it is getting what they pay for and not some plant that's been so stressed it won't grow or bloom the way it's supposed to."

It was hard for her to work up much sympathy for someone who had to wait around longer than expected for an orchid to bloom. Still, she'd rather work for someone with integrity than without. She'd been a hostess at a restaurant that recycled its bread and made sauces from used butter. It was all she could do to keep from telling customers to eat somewhere else.

"How do they get stressed?" she asked.

"Too much or too little water. Too much or too little light. Sticking the plant under an airconditioning vent or near a heater. Wrong pot, wrong medium, planted too loose or too tight. They aren't as delicate as most people think, but they aren't philodendrons."

"My mother has a thing for African violets." She picked them up on sale, the plants so neglected that no one else wanted them. Through some magic Maria didn't understand, her mother brought the violets back to life.

"You'll have to take her a couple of the miniature cattleyas Andrew has developed. They bloom a couple of times a year, and the flower can last for a month or more. The retail nurseries are advertising them as the first real orchid houseplant."

"You sound like a commercial." Giving her mother an orchid would be more burden than gift. Elena Ramos could never see an orchid as just another plant. She would worry any pleasure away and grieve if the plant died.

She looked around while she waited. Not much had been done to the house to convert it into an office. The living room was outfitted with bookshelves, filing cabinets, and a desk, but the remaining rooms held little or no furniture. With a little paint and furniture, someone could easily live there full-time.

Andrew ended his telephone call and turned his attention to Maria and Paul. "I'm sorry, but I'm going to have to back out of lunch." He tossed his pencil on the desk. "That bark order we've been waiting for finally came in, and it's the wrong size. If I don't get it taken care of today, we're not going to be able to start the repotting tomorrow."

"You want me to see if Klein's has some they can sell us? I could go over there now to pick it up."

"Let me see what I can do here first."

"Don't worry about the lunch thing," Maria

said, trying not to show how relieved she was. "I brought something to eat."

"Just because I'm not going doesn't mean you aren't," Andrew said. "Paul can fill in for me."

Before she could come up with a reason for not going, Paul said, "Great. I love Fred's place." He held out his hand. "I assume you're paying?"

Andrew opened his wallet and handed Paul several bills. "Bring me the usual." The phone rang. Andrew answered. He nodded and motioned for them to leave.

Maria followed Paul out of the office. "I think I'd just as soon eat here," she said when she was sure Andrew wouldn't overhear her. "I'm not that hungry."

"Afraid to be alone with me?" he challenged.

What a jerk. "I'm not afraid of anything."

He grinned. "Then grab your purse and let's get out of here."

He'd won. And she'd let him. The thought disgusted her. What came next—telling him she liked riding in his stupid BMW?

3

HE'D DONE IT TO HER AGAIN. PAUL DIDN'T have a BMW, he had a Honda. A red one. Ancient. Rusted through on one fender, dented on the other.

"Nice car," she said, adjusting her shoulder strap

"It gets me where I want to go."

"Does it get you back, too?"

He laughed. "Most of the time."

She really didn't want to like him, but he was making it hard. If she had to be around him while she was there, she might as well try to get along. Having a friend who was a rich white boy wasn't something she'd ever set out to do, but then she'd never thought she would be pulling down two dollars above minimum wage standing ass deep in orchids, either. "You live around here?"

"Down the street from you."

"From where I'm staying," she corrected him. "I live in Oakland."

He turned the opposite direction from the way Cheryl had come that morning. The houses around there were small but had large, well-tended yards, some with picket fences and plastic deer, others with detailed topiary. This was where the people who worked the fields and held the service jobs lived, the ocean miles away, the views unspectacular. Small grocery stores and fruit stands sat on corners, and the service stations were so old they actually had areas where mechanics worked on cars.

"How do you like the house?" Paul asked.

"It's okay." She loved everything about it, from the rock fireplace to the deck that overlooked the ocean, but to say so was too obvious. Only people who'd never been anyplace special or done anything out of the ordinary would make a big deal out of a house. "You ever been inside?"

"My family stayed there every August when I was a kid—for over ten years."

"So how come you don't stay there anymore?" she asked.

"My mom and dad were the ones who rented the house, and they're divorced now. Last year my mom married the guy who lives in the house where I'm staying now."

"Your mom was foolin' around with one of the

neighbors while she was on vacation with your dad?"

"Are you always so blunt?" He sent her a sideways glance. "And so wrong?"

"If you mean do I call it like it is—yeah, I do. What's the point pretending something isn't the way it is?" She looked out the window at a house painted bright pink with dark green shutters. "And I'm right a lot more than I'm wrong."

"The divorce was my dad's idea. My mom and Peter didn't get together until later."

"And it was okay with this Peter guy that you moved in with your mom?"

The question seemed to throw him. "Why wouldn't it be?"

"Most guys don't want anything to do with a woman's kids when they're as old as you are."

"I happen to be great company. And I'm useful."

"Yeah, I'll bet." She softened the words with a lopsided grin. "What do you do, mow the lawn?"

"Actually, I'm the only one who does any work around the house."

She studied him through narrowed eyes. "You're there alone, aren't you?"

"Damn, you're good."

She shouldn't have been so pleased. "So, where are they?"

"Europe for the summer."

"For *three months*?" She sometimes put herself to sleep at night fantasizing about the places she would go if she were rich, but this was beyond anything she'd imagined.

"Peter's an artist. He visits galleries and stops along the way to paint when the mood strikes him. It's all tax deductible."

"And what does your mother do while he's sitting around painting?"

"Right now she's taking a cooking class in Paris. Eventually she wants to open her own restaurant."

Paul's mother was in France going to school to learn how to cook while her mother stood over an ironing board all day to earn money to buy basic ingredients for food she barely had the energy to cook. It wasn't fair.

"Where are you going to school?" Paul asked conversationally, not picking up on Maria's mood shift.

Why would he want to know something like that? "Kelly Morgan High School."

"When you graduate."

"Oh, you mean college. I'm not. At least not right away."

He didn't react the way she'd expected. Instead of the stunned disbelief she usually got from his type, he simply asked, "Why?"

"Now why do you think?"

He didn't answer for several seconds. "It can't be because you're not smart enough."

There was no way he could know how smart

she was or wasn't, but she liked that he thought she was.

"And it can't be money. There are too many programs that—"

There was no way he could tell how much money she had, either, and it made her mad that he assumed she couldn't afford to go to school even if he was right. "And you can tell just by looking at me that I qualify for those welfare kinds of programs?"

"I'm going on what Andrew told me."

Now she really was mad. Andrew had no right to talk about her. "He doesn't even know me."

Paul pulled up to a stoplight and turned to look at her. "Are you always like this?"

"Like what?" she fired back.

"Pissed off at the world."

She glared at him. "It's not the world, just the people on it that I can't stand."

⌇ ANDREW THREW THE KITCHEN TOWEL OVER his shoulder and went to answer the knock at the door. "This is a surprise," he said to Cheryl. He moved to the side. "Come in."

She waited until he closed the door before asking, "Still mad at me?"

"I told you I wasn't mad."

"Disappointed, then."

"I'm getting over it."

"I brought you a peace offering."

He looked at her hands. They were empty. "What is it?" he asked suspiciously.

"Me. Or at least as much of me as you can take advantage of in five minutes."

He laughed. "I'm good, but I'm not that good."

She reached up and put her arms around his neck. "I've been dying to do this since I saw that scowl on your face when I got out of the van." She touched her lips to his and then her tongue, tasting whatever he had been tasting in the kitchen.

He deepened the kiss, then murmured, "Remind me to scowl more often."

"First I need to ask you something."

"Is this part of my five minutes?"

"Sorry, it's as long as I could get away. The girls are cleaning the kitchen, and I promised we'd get a video as soon as they were done."

"You want to know what happened at work today."

She didn't bother asking how he knew. "I've never seen Maria in such a bad mood."

"She met Paul."

Cheryl frowned. "And?"

"She likes Paul."

"I'm going to need more than that."

"Think *West Side Story*."

"Paul is in a gang?"

"Skip that." He struggled for another analogy. "Okay, think *Sabrina*."

"The movie?"

He nodded.

All she could remember was how mismatched she thought Humphrey Bogart and Audrey Hepburn were. "Paul's an old man?"

"He's from the privileged side of the tracks, Cheryl. His life is so comfortable he donates part of his paycheck to a charity his brother is involved with. Do you know any other nineteen-year-old who hasn't started his own dot com business who gives away money he had to work to earn?"

"Maria would—if she could."

"Precisely my point. She can't, he can. But it's more than that. He does it and doesn't even know it's not the norm. That's an insult to someone like Maria."

"And a barrier," she said sadly. "This is not what I wanted her to see. She already feels defensive."

"She's hungry, Cheryl. But she's scared, too. She's afraid of wanting something she thinks she can't have."

"You've known her less than a day, and you can see all this about her?" She didn't doubt him; she was curious how he'd gotten through Maria's shell so quickly.

"All you have to do is talk to her a few minutes and you can see how bright she is. She works hard, she's quick, she has a smart mouth with a lot of anger and intelligence behind what she says, and she's passionate about things that interest her. She also has a way of looking at someone that makes them—makes *me*—feel like a bug under a microscope."

"You're amazing." She looked at him with a mixture of awe and puzzlement. "Can you do this with everyone, or was Maria special?"

He shrugged. "When you're raised the way I was, getting a handle on people quickly is simply a matter of self-preservation. I've met military kids who moved around a lot when they were growing up who have the same ability."

"How could I not know this about you?"

"It's not the only thing."

She tilted her head and studied him. "That's why you wanted us to have this time alone. It wasn't just to become lovers again."

"*Just?*"

"All right, poor choice of words. I misjudged you. I'm sorry."

"It gives us something to talk about in our old age."

She smiled. "I love being right—even when I'm being given credit for something I don't deserve." She stretched up and kissed him again. "Gotta go. I don't want them to come looking for me."

⌒CHERYL MOTIONED FOR DEANNA TO PASS THE popcorn, took a handful, and passed it on to Maria. She'd talked them into renting *Casablanca* as much to hear their reaction as to save herself from having to watch *Scream II*. When it ended,

Deanna was crying, Karen said she thought the clothes were fantastic, especially the beaded top Rick's girlfriend wore in the opening, and Maria didn't say anything.

"So, what do you think, Maria?" Cheryl asked, as soon as Karen stopped to take a breath.

She unfolded her legs and stretched. "Any woman who lets a man think for her is an idiot."

Deanna reached for another tissue. "She told him to."

"It was another time," Cheryl said. "That was how men and women saw each other then, the way they interacted."

"I think it was sexy," Deanna said. "Rick sacrificed everything to make sure she was safe. I wish someone loved me enough to do that for me."

"Did you notice how much he smoked?" Karen said. "And he always had a drink in his hand. I'll bet he was an alcoholic."

"How do you think it should have ended?" Cheryl asked Maria.

"She should have gone with her husband because she wanted to."

Karen snorted. "You're just saying that because you're Catholic and don't believe in divorce."

"Her husband was more interesting and braver than Rick. And a lot cuter, too."

Cheryl perked up. "Why do you think he was more interesting?"

"Look at all the stuff he'd done and how he wanted to get to America so he could keep fighting for the resistance. Another thing—Rick didn't have to get on that train in Paris. Her husband wouldn't have. He would have gone after her. What did Rick do? He went to Casablanca and bought a bar."

"You have a point," Cheryl said. It wasn't one she'd ever heard anyone else make, which made it even more interesting.

"But he never forgot her," Deanna said. "And in the end he gave her up because he wanted her to be safe and she wouldn't have been if she stayed with him."

"Can we get back to the clothes?" Karen said.

"Anyone want to talk about what was going on in the world when this movie was made?" Cheryl asked.

All three of them, in chorus, said, "No."

Cheryl laughed. She'd made her point and started them thinking. What more could you ask of a simple movie?

4

MARIA YAWNED AS PAUL BACKED OUT OF the driveway. Six-thirty was getting earlier and earlier every morning. It seemed the harder she tried to go to bed by ten, the more reasons there were to stay up. Deanna and Karen were like windup dolls with flapping jaws, always talking about what they'd done that day, where they'd gone, what they'd seen. Like she was interested in old missions and hiking out on some point to see seals. What good was that kind of thing going to do them when they got home? At least she'd have money to show for the time she was there.

"Late night?" Paul asked.

They'd been riding together for almost two weeks, and he obviously took that to mean he had

a right to ask questions. "Bad weed does that to
me sometimes."

"Yeah, me too."

She shot him a sideways glance. There was no
way Paul Williams's lips ever sucked on grass.
"Maybe you could hook me up with someone
who has a better stash."

His answer was too slow to be believable. "My
guy's out of town."

She laughed. "Probably visiting my brother."

"Okay, so you don't believe me any more than I
believe you."

"You're a cube, Paul."

"Thanks."

"You don't thank someone for calling you a
cube. It means you're six times worse than square."

"I know what it means. I'm a preacher's kid.
You're not the first person who's slammed me
with that."

"How can you be a preacher's kid? You said
your parents were divorced."

"So what?"

"Preachers can't get divorced."

"Obviously you don't know as much as you
think you do."

She could either tell him to go to hell—which
meant she would have to stop talking to him—or
find out more. "So it's okay? Nobody cares?"

"I didn't say that. In my mom and dad's case, it
split the congregation. Some even left to go to
other churches."

"How did you feel about it?"

He braked to let a car merge in front of him. "I hated it. For a time, I hated both of them, too. But I got over it."

"My dad died. He was late to work one morning and got hit by a car. It was his fault, he was jaywalking. There wasn't any insurance money, and my mom wouldn't let the lawyers who kept calling her sue anyone. I used to get mad at him sometimes, too, but it didn't do any good so I stopped."

Paul looked at her, back to the road, and then back to her again. "I have a feeling I'm going to regret this, but I've been invited to a party tonight and I'm supposed to bring someone. You want to go?"

"You must be desperate."

"I don't *have* to have a date to go."

"How many girls turned you down already?"

"Why do you care?"

"I just want to know."

"Two—they already had something else planned."

"Yeah, right."

"Do you want to go or don't you?"

"Let me think about it. I'll get back to you later."

"Don't do me any favors."

She smiled sweetly. "Don't worry, I won't." To make sure he didn't get the wrong idea, she added, "If I go with you, it's hands off."

"As if I'd want it any other way."

She eyed him. She either went to Paul's friend's party or sat through another one of Cheryl's old movies. Cheryl thought she was clever sneaking in history lessons with her vintage films. None of them wanted to hurt her feelings by telling her they weren't fooled, and it wasn't working. "Yeah, okay, I'll go. What time?"

"Six. It's a barbecue."

"You want me to meet you there?"

"Considering I live five doors down, I don't think it would be too far out of my way to pick you up. That's what we do when we go out on dates around here."

"This isn't a date." She didn't want him thinking this was the beginning of something between them. Two more weeks and she was gone. They would never see each other again. There was no way she was going home thinking about him, wishing for something that couldn't be. "I'm doing you a favor—to pay you back for giving me a ride to work every morning. That's all."

"Thank God. I was beginning to worry you might be developing a thing for me and that I'd have to break your heart."

"You wish."

⟶WHEN THE ROOM ASSIGNMENTS AT THE beach house put Maria in one by herself, she'd felt left out. Now she was glad. She didn't have to put up with Deanna and Karen teasing her for trying on every piece of clothing she'd brought with her as she looked for something special to wear for the party that night. She finally settled on a pair of white jeans and a dark green backless top with ties around the neck.

She stood in front of the mirror, turned sideways, hunched her shoulders, and reached over her head to make sure the top was tied snug enough to keep her covered when she moved. She wanted to be the one who controlled how much was on display.

She spread glitter gel over her shoulders and combed her hair, pinning one side up to expose the tiny green peridot earrings Carlos had given her for Christmas the year before. He'd asked for them back when they broke up, telling her he'd only given them to her because he thought she was going to be a "real" girlfriend. She'd refused out of spite. Now she wore them as a reminder.

"Whoa—look at you," Deanna said in a singsong voice when Maria joined her and Karen in the living room.

Maria ignored the compliment. She didn't want them thinking she cared how she looked, or they'd get the idea Paul was important. She'd never get them off her back then. "Where's Cheryl?"

"Next door," Karen said. "We're out of something, but I can't remember what."

"Tomato sauce," Deanna supplied.

"She's borrowing some from Andrew."

Maria glanced at her watch. Paul was late. What if he'd changed his mind and didn't come? She'd die. No, she'd kill him. "What movie did you get for tonight?"

"*Scream I* and *II*," Karen said smugly.

Deanna nodded. "Karen told Cheryl it was our turn to pick, and she gave in."

Maria groaned, putting on a show of frustration over missing the evening. "You couldn't have waited until tomorrow night when I'd be here?"

Cheryl came in carrying a can in one hand and a brilliant red miniature cattleya with a yellow throat in the other. She stopped and motioned for Maria to turn around. "Great outfit."

This she hadn't expected. "Thanks."

When Cheryl came out of the kitchen, she was carrying the flower but not the plant. She handed the cattleya to Maria. "Put this in your hair."

Maria's jaw dropped. "That's Andrew's new cross. It's the first one that's bloomed. Alfonso said it's worth thousands of dollars. *And you want me to wear it in my hair?*"

Cheryl studied the bloom closer. "He didn't tell me. But there's another bud." She smiled confidently. "And I know he wouldn't mind."

Maria stared at the flower, torn between getting rid of the evidence and putting it in her hair. There was no way to reattach it to the stem and it would be a shame to throw a perfectly good flower away.

She and Paul would be the only ones at the party who knew how special it was.

"Go on," Cheryl said. "I'll explain it to Andrew."

"Do it," Karen prompted. "I would."

"No one will guess you're from Oakland," Deanna chimed in. "They'll think you're from Hawaii."

She had no idea why, but she suddenly wanted that flower in her hair. She smiled her thanks and went into the bathroom to put it on in front of the mirror.

The effect was stunning. She looked older and exotic and even a little mysterious. More important, she looked as if she belonged at the kind of party she imagined a friend of Paul's would have.

Mesmerized by her reflection, she jumped when she heard a knock on the front door. Her mouth went dry, and her throat tried to close. What had possessed her to agree to go with him? She had no more business at one of his friends' parties than he did at one of hers. What would she say to these people? She had nothing in common with them. She would make a fool of herself and never hear the end of it, at least for the two weeks she had left. After that she'd have the memory of making a fool of herself, like the time she fell asleep on Carlos's shoulder and drooled all over his shirt.

And then he would know she really didn't belong.

Cheryl tapped on the bathroom door. "Paul's here."

"I'll be right there." She hadn't been this scared the first time she'd gone to the prison with her mother to visit Fernando.

After several seconds, Cheryl asked softly, "Are you okay?"

Maria closed her eyes, took another deep breath, and opened the door. "I'm fine," she said brightly. "Why wouldn't I be?"

She went ahead of Cheryl. Grabbing her purse off the coffee table, she made a point of not looking directly at Paul. She didn't want to see him looking back, didn't want to see his reaction reflected in his eyes, didn't want to be disappointed if he was, and didn't want to return his smile if he approved.

She did see Karen's and Deanna's reactions to Paul. Before now they'd only seen him at a distance. Up close he was pretty impressive. Karen did everything but lick her lips. Maria sent her a disgusted look that Karen ignored.

Cheryl walked them to the door. "Have a good time," she said. "And—"

"Don't be comin' home late," Maria finished for her.

"I'll have her back early," Paul said.

He'd already decided the evening was going to be a bust. Maria was tempted to tell him to go by himself, that way he could stay as long as he wanted.

"What I was going to say is that Andrew told

me to tell you not to come in until ten tomorrow," Cheryl said. "The shipment of ceramic pots that he's been waiting for is supposed to arrive in the morning, and he would like you to start work a couple of hours later and stay a couple of hours longer, if you can."

Paul thought a minute. "Yeah, I can do that. I just need to call a couple of people."

She could work every day all day and not have to rearrange anything. "Me too," she said.

"I'll let him know."

Maria continued to avoid looking directly at Paul until they were in the car and she could do it casually. When she did, her confidence rose a notch. "So, where is your friend's place?"

"Up the hill about a half mile. We could have walked, but I figured you'd be wearing the wrong shoes, so I brought the car."

He was right. She'd worn sandals held on by thin straps around her big toes and thinner ones around her ankle.

"By the way—the flower looks great in your hair."

She didn't know how to respond. Was he complimenting the flower or her hair or both? "Andrew gave Cheryl the plant and she gave me the flower."

He smiled. "He must not have told her what it's worth. But then from what I've heard about her, I don't know that it would have made a difference."

He had a beautiful smile, one that involved his

whole face. And she didn't even mind that he had blond hair all that much anymore. Not that she'd ever tell him. His ego was big enough already.

They were in the middle of the forest when Paul pulled up to a metal gate so cleverly hidden from the main road that Maria had never noticed it. He leaned out the car window and pressed a button attached to a speaker. When someone answered, he gave his name and the gate swung open.

Maria had seen places like this in the movies and in the Berkeley hills. In her neighborhood, metal bars were on the windows, not the driveways. "Who is this friend of yours?"

"Chris Sadler." Paul drove through the gate and made a quick turn that took them up a hill through more pines and eucalyptus.

The name took a second to register. Even then she figured it had to be a coincidence. Still, she said, "You're not talking about Chris Sadler the movie star."

"Uh-huh."

"Why didn't you tell me?" she asked evenly, feeling a seed of panic take root in the middle of her chest. Chris Sadler was only the hottest thing going. He was always on the cover of some magazine, and his poster was everywhere, including her sister's bedroom wall. Last she'd heard he'd dumped Jewel and was dating Kelly McIntire, lead singer for Broken Circuit. What if Kelly was there? What was she supposed to say to someone like Chris Sadler and Kelly McIntire? How was she supposed to act?

"He doesn't like people knowing when he's up here. This is where he goes to get away from crowds. I respect his privacy."

"Take me home."

It was plainly not the reaction he'd expected. He pulled to the side of the road and turned to look at her. "Are you serious?"

She was furious with him for putting her in this position. "I don't belong here."

"What are you talking about?"

"These are your kind of people, not mine."

"My kind of people? What in the hell is that supposed to mean?"

"Movie stars. Rich people. People who hire my kind of people to do their laundry. People who take and take and take and never bother to say thank you."

"I wash my own clothes, and so does everyone else I know."

"Including Chris Sadler?"

Frustrated, he ran one hand through his hair and wrapped the other around the steering wheel. "All right, I'll give you that one. But it hasn't been that long since he was staying in the house where you are right now and picking up change on the beach to spend at the boardwalk."

That caught her attention. "Chris Sadler stayed in our house?"

"Every June for over ten years. He came here the whole time my family came."

"That's how you met?" Somehow it made a difference.

"We didn't actually meet each other until a couple of years ago, before Chris made it big in L.A. Staying in the same house all those years gave us something in common, and we became friends."

"It doesn't bother you that he's so famous?"

"Why should it? Take away the hype, and he's just another guy."

She was past feeling foolish and on her way to feeling like an idiot. She'd reacted out of fear. Now she was curious. And a little excited. "I don't suppose you could forget this happened?"

"I'd sure like to try."

"I'll make you a deal."

"Why do I think this is going to benefit you more than it does me?"

"Because under that candy-ass exterior, you're a fairly sharp guy."

He stared at her, trying to look pissed, but then he laughed and ruined the effect. "Lay it on me."

"I'll stop putting your name on all the flats I find that were planted wrong, if just this one night you treat me like you don't think I'm the dullest penny in the stack." Every time the plants were repotted at the nursery the person who did the work put his or her name on a tag. That tag stayed with the plants until they were repotted again.

"You've been putting my name on—"

"Not really. But I think about it. A lot. Especially when you're giving me a hard time." She gave him her best smile. "Consider that fair warning."

"I knew better," he mumbled. "I told myself not to get involved with you, that you were trouble, but no, I had to invite you to this party."

"You're not involved with me, Paul. We're not even friends. So let's just go to the party and get it over with, and then you can forget you ever met me. Well, you can in two weeks, after I'm gone."

"Now that's a deal I can live with."

She shouldn't have been disappointed, he'd given her what she wanted. Still, it would have been nice if he'd argued just a little.

5

CHRIS SADLER'S HOUSE SAT AT THE southernmost tip of the cove on a rocky outcropping that overlooked the entire Monterey Bay. The rock-and-brick house wasn't as big as Maria had expected—she'd pictured something along the lines of the houses that sat on the side of the Berkeley hills—but it was still impressive. The shiny wood floors and fancy carpets, the white sofa and watercolors painted by Paul's stepfather, Peter Wylie, and the huge windows that looked out on the ocean all spelled money. Not splashy money, like things people bought when they won the lottery, but money that was spent a little at a time because the person waited until he found just what he wanted.

If Maria ever allowed herself to dream about such things, this would be what she dreamed of.

A house far away from everything and everyone. A place where the only sounds came from birds and wind and water. No guns. No babies crying because no one cared enough to pick them up. No people yelling at each other.

Paul had made quick introductions when they arrived, and Maria had tried to remember some of the names, but the only one that stuck, other than Chris's, was Janice Carlson. She had short dark hair, an athletic build, and was open and friendly with everyone. She seemed more like a "local" than the rest of the people there. Maria automatically gravitated toward her, sensing a social lifeline.

"That flower you're wearing almost makes me regret cutting my hair," Janice said. She handed Maria her requested soda.

Maria's hand went to the flower and then her hair. "I've thought about having mine cut, but every time I get in the chair I chicken out."

"It took me a whole year before I could work up the nerve, but I've never been sorry." She smiled. "Until now."

"Are you from around here?" Maria asked.

"Not originally." She sat on a cushioned wrought-iron chair. Maria took the matching one opposite hers. "But I've been going to school out here for the past three years."

"Oh? Where?"

"Stanford."

Maria knew the school. You couldn't live in

California and not know Stanford. It was one of those colleges so far out of her league she didn't even allow it into her dreams. So much for the hope she and Janice would have something in common. Trying for a conversational tone, one that would make her sound as if she discussed this kind of thing all the time, she asked, "What are you studying?"

"I thought I wanted to be a lawyer, but wound up in economics." She smiled. "I know, pretty boring stuff, but I find it fascinating."

Maria had no idea what someone who majored in economics did. "What made you think you wanted to be a lawyer?"

"Actually, it was my dad's suggestion. He said it was the perfect job for someone who liked to argue and wanted to be in charge. But then I moved out here and realized that part of my personality had more to do with what was going on at home than with who I really am inside."

The simple statement was like opening a door for Maria. All her life her dreams had focused on what she didn't want to become and where she didn't want to be. She'd been running away instead of toward something, willing to settle for anything that would get her where she wanted to go. In a lot of ways, her dream had become her burden.

But it didn't have to be that way. There was a world of possibilities, and there were dozens of roads she could travel to get where she wanted to go, roads that would let her enjoy the journey. Andrew loved what he did . . . and so did Cheryl. She wanted to be like them.

Chris came over, bent down, and gave Janice a kiss. She smiled and reached up to take his hand. "Did your mom ever call?" she asked.

"I forgot to tell you. There was a message on the answering machine when we got back from the store. She said they arrived safely and were on their way to buy a raincoat for Charlie."

Janice looked at Maria. "Chris's mother and Charlie are in London on their honeymoon."

"How nice," Maria said, wishing she could come up with something better. "London is on my list of places I want to see someday." A list she'd just started.

"I visited Chris when he was there for a movie last fall and can't wait to go back," Janice said.

The moment, the people, the conversation were surreal. Was this really her, Maria Anna Ramos, sitting in this house, talking about Stanford University with someone who went there, acting as if a trip to England was a real possibility, casually listening to Chris Sadler's girlfriend mention a movie he'd made, sitting not three feet away from Chris Sadler himself?

Deanna and Karen were never going to swallow this story. She could take a picture, and they still wouldn't believe her. Evenings like this just didn't happen to people like them.

Paul spotted them and came over. He handed

Maria a small plate with bite-size snacks that looked like miniature works of art. "I've been looking everywhere for you," he said. "I was beginning to think you'd cut out on me."

Cringing at the thought of what he would say next, she felt a flush of embarrassment sweep across her chest and up her neck. He must have noticed because he covered for her with a gentle kindness that took her by surprise.

"I gave Maria a hard time on the way here and never got around to an apology."

Chris tugged on Janice's hand and brought her out of her seat. "Seems to me these two need some time alone."

Janice gave Maria a conspiratorial wink. "Don't let him off too easy."

Maria swallowed her protest that she and Paul weren't the couple Chris and Janice thought they were. Instead she smiled, and said, "I won't."

Paul took Janice's vacated seat and reached over to her plate to take a cracker with a dab of something white topped with a dab of something black. "So what do you think of Janice?"

"I like her. A lot." She hesitated about saying the rest, but plunged ahead. "Does she know Chris is seeing someone else, too?"

Paul frowned. "Who?"

"Kelly McIntire."

He laughed. "That's not real. He only goes places with her as a favor and because they have the same publicist. She was afraid she was going to come across looking like a loser when she and that Hansen guy broke up, so Chris agreed to help out."

Maria glanced at Chris and Janice and saw that they were still holding hands. "And Janice doesn't mind?"

"They've been going together since he was seventeen and moved to L.A. to make his first movie. I guess she figures if he's stuck with her all that time, there's no reason to think he won't keep sticking."

She tried a cracker like the one Paul had eaten. It wasn't like anything she'd ever tasted. "What is this?"

He looked at her warily. "Caviar."

She didn't say anything.

"Well?"

"What?"

"What do you think? Do you like it?"

"I think so, but I'm not sure." It wasn't something she ever expected to have again, so she tried another, wanting to remember what it was like. "Yeah, I do like it."

He leaned forward, his elbows on his knees, and pointed to another cracker with something pinkish red on a mound of white. "Try that one. It's smoked salmon."

When she hesitated he picked up the cracker and held it up to her mouth. "Come on—no guts, no glory."

She'd never backed down from a challenge in

her life, and it was just a little cracker. She came forward and opened her mouth. His fingers touched her lips naturally and easily, as if he fed her like this all the time. Acutely aware of the intimacy, she looked into his eyes to see if he'd felt anything and was pleased to see he wasn't as indifferent as he would have her believe.

"What's this one?" She pointed to a pastry with a sprig of something that looked like a weed on top.

"I'm not sure, but I think it's a miniature quiche."

"What's a quiche?"

He told her what he knew, admitting it was probably wrong, and then went on to try to identify the remaining hors d'oeuvres on her plate. Some had to be tasted first. If there was only one, he took a bite and offered her the rest. She'd never shared food this way and decided it was one of the most innocent, yet intimate things she'd ever done with a guy. It was a dumb way to feel, and she was making way too big a deal out of it, but his easy familiarity made her feel special.

By the end of the evening she was almost as comfortable in this new environment as she was in her own. She liked these people, Chris and Janice in particular.

Chris saw them to the door when they were leaving. "Paul told me you're staying in the beach house. How do you like it?"

"I love it," she answered truthfully. "I'd stay there forever if I could."

"I felt the same way. I tried to talk Julia and Eric into selling it to me, but they weren't ready to let go." He smiled. "I had to settle for this place."

"Give me a couple of years, and I might be able to work up some sympathy," Paul said.

Chris laughed. "Not buying it, huh?"

Janice joined them. "Chris has some work he has to do tomorrow, so I thought I'd go to Carmel to do some shopping," she told Maria. "Want to come?"

More than anything. "I would—but I can't," she stammered. "I have to work, too."

Paul added, "She's helping out at the nursery. Andrew's shorthanded, and that's put us way behind repotting for the fall shows. He really needs Maria there."

"Maybe next time," Janice said.

She could have told Janice how much she wanted there to be a next time or how special the evening was to her or how important their conversation had been, but none of it could be said without making her sound needy. "Yes," she said softly. "Maybe next time."

She was quiet the five minutes it took Paul to drive her home. To thank him for all he had said and hadn't said that night would be to acknowledge her insecurities. Experience told her he would expect a kiss, probably more. If she went along, it would change everything between them ... again. They'd moved past adversarial into something she didn't know what to call. It was the first time she'd ever felt this way about a guy and didn't want to mess it up trying to make it into something it wasn't.

Paul pulled into the driveway and turned off the car. He started to get out, and she put her hand on his arm to stop him. "I had a better time than I thought I would. I'm glad the other two girls turned you down."

He looked at her for several seconds before admitting, "I didn't ask anyone else."

She wished he hadn't told her. "You were right. Chris is just a regular guy."

He nodded and reached for the key to restart the car. "See you in the morning?"

His eagerness to leave took her by surprise. She either got out of the car or gave him the impression she was waiting for the very thing she'd decided she didn't want, for him to kiss her. "Yeah ... What time? About nine-thirty?"

He frowned as if confused, and then remembered. "Don't panic if I'm a little late. If there's no fog, I'm going to catch a couple of waves before we go in."

She got out of the car and stood on the porch until he drove away. How could she have been afraid he would want to kiss her and feel this bad that he hadn't even tried? Something was wrong with her.

She needed to talk to someone, someone who would ground her in the reality of who she was and where she came from, someone who would get her head out of the fantasy of thinking she could ever be a part of the world she had seen that night. She didn't belong there. She would never belong there. Not only didn't she have the money to pay for the ticket, she didn't know where to stand in line for the ride.

Cheryl had left a light on for her in the living room. Maria turned it off and quietly made her way down the hall to her bedroom. As she started to open the door, she heard voices coming from Deanna and Karen's room.

Needing to be around people she understood and who understood her, Maria softly tapped on their door. Karen opened it just enough to see who was there. When she saw it was Maria, she opened the door a little farther and glanced down the hall toward Cheryl's room.

"Home from your date already?" Karen hissed unpleasantly.

"What's the matter with you?" Maria asked.

She glanced behind her. "Deanna's driving me crazy."

"What's wrong?"

"Who knows."

With a sigh, Maria said, "Let me in."

Deanna was sitting on the bed, her legs drawn up to her chest, her chin on her knees. It was obvious she'd been crying. She wiped her eyes with a well-used tissue when she saw Maria. "Date didn't work out?" she said sarcastically.

Maria looked from Deanna to Karen. Neither were dressed for bed. "If you two have got a bitch over me goin' out tonight, let's hear it."

"We don't give a flyin' fuck what you do," Deanna said, her lower lip quivering.

"Yeah, we like nothin' better than baby-sitting Cheryl while you're out screwing the locals," Karen added.

Deanna straightened her legs and crossed her arms over her chest. She'd always worn her clothes tight, but with the weight she'd gained, they looked painted on. "How come you get to go out and we don't?"

She went to work, watched movies, and sat on the beach when she had a day off. They went somewhere every day and made sure she heard what she'd missed. "Maybe because someone asked me."

"I'm sick of this shit," Karen said. "I'm going home tomorrow."

Deanna let out a soft wail and burst into tears. "If you go, we all have to go. And I don't want to. I like it here."

Karen gave her a disgusted look. "You like it because you get to eat all the time, and no one's on your case. Wait till Jake sees you. He's gonna take one look and that's the last one you'll ever get from him."

"Whatever."

Maria didn't believe Deanna's attempt at disinterest for a second. She'd had a thing for Jake since the second grade and had almost dropped out of school the year before, despite making the honor roll, just because he dropped out. Something wasn't right. She sat on the end of the bed, bringing her legs up and tucking them under her.

"So what's up with you and Jake?" Maria asked.

"Nothing."

"Like hell," Karen said, the words harsher than the tone.

Deanna bit her lower lip when it started quivering again, but she couldn't stop the tears. "He dumped me," she said, barely above a whisper.

Maria wished she could act more surprised. She'd seen Jake out with other girls for months and knew it was only a matter of time before he broke it off with Deanna. "You're better off without him."

"I love him."

"He's a bastard," Karen said. "You can do better."

"I don't want to do better," Deanna wailed. "Jake's the only guy I've ever wanted."

Maria and Karen exchanged glances. If they told her about Jake, they'd risk hurting her even more. "What did he say when he broke up with you?" Maria asked.

"I can't tell you." She covered her face with her hands.

Maria got up to find a tissue and spotted the box on the floor. She bent to retrieve it and saw a candy bar sticking out from under the bed. Her heart sank. Deanna was going to be huge if she didn't stop eating. She reached for the candy and saw something behind it. Bending lower she saw an enormous stash of cookies and candy and chips. "What is this?"

"What?" Karen asked.

"All this food."

Karen came around the bed to look. "Shit—" She gave Deanna a disgusted look. "I'm trashin' this stuff. You're goin' on a diet right now."

Maria stood and stared at Deanna. "This isn't new. It's what you've been taking from the kitchen since we got here." Why would she hide food and not eat it? And why would she put up with the abuse from Karen about how much she was eating when she obviously wasn't?

"Is that true?" Karen asked.

"What I do and what I eat or don't eat is none of your business." She snatched the Butterfinger candy bar Maria was holding, tore it open, and took a bite that filled half her mouth. "Satisfied?"

How could Deanna *not* be eating and still gain weight? And then it all made sense. "Oh my God," Maria breathed.

Karen turned on her. "What?"

Deanna tossed what was left of the Butterfinger on the nightstand. "Go ahead—tell her," she sobbed. "Tell the whole friggin' world for all I care."

"Tell me *what*?" Karen insisted, her voice raised, forgetting they were trying not to wake Cheryl.

Hoping that she'd somehow gotten it wrong, Maria made it a question instead of a statement. "You're pregnant?"

"Give the girl a prize." Tears formed twin streams from her eyes to her chin.

Stunned, Karen echoed, "Oh my God."

"Jake?" Maria asked already knowing the answer.

Deanna nodded.

"I *hate* that bastard," Karen said. "I hope that bitch Sally Ryker gives him a disease."

Deanna fixed Karen with a stare. "Jake is seeing Sally?"

If there had been even a faint hope, Maria would have protected her, but it was time Deanna faced the truth. "He's been taking her to parties for months now. And when she's not available, he finds someone who is."

"I was available." She said it so softly Maria had to strain to hear.

"Not anymore," Karen said. "The only thing you're gonna be givin' him from now on is a bill for child support."

"He says it isn't his."

"Like you been sleepin' around behind his back. There's no way you would—"

"But I did," she whispered. "Once. It was after we had this big fight where he said I was lucky he let me fuck him once in a while because I was so butt ugly there wasn't no one else who would."

Maria felt sick. "Who was it?"

Deanna took a long time to answer. "I don't know. It was at a party. I was drunk. All I remember is going into the bedroom with some guy."

Karen sat on the bed next to Deanna. "What makes you think it was him and not Jake who got you pregnant?"

"All I know is that I skipped my period the next month."

"*Could* it have been Jake?" Karen asked.

"Yes."

"Then it probably was. Although you'd probably be better off if it wasn't. If he's not the father, you and the baby won't be tied to that two-timing son of a bitch."

Maria sat on the opposite side of the bed. "Have you seen a doctor?"

She shook her head. "I was going to make an appointment at the clinic, but then chickened out."

It was Karen's turn. "How far along are you?"

"Five months."

Maria and Karen exchanged glances.

"I thought about an abortion, but I couldn't do it. I kept thinking what if my mom had done that to me?"

Instead of abandoning her daughter before she was born, Deanna's mother had abandoned her when she was seven years old, walking out on her and the man she'd been living with to go on tour with a soundman for the Grateful Dead.

"Okay, so you've decided to have the baby," Maria said. It was useless to talk about what she could have or should have done. It was the now, and the future, they had to deal with. "First thing we have to do is get you to a doctor."

"Yeah," Karen said. "If you're going to have it, you sure don't want it to be sick."

A fresh wave of tears spilled from Deanna's eyes. "What if Bill and Amy find out?"

Maria blinked in surprise. Bill and Amy Hutchins were Deanna's foster parents. They were hard-assed about a lot of stuff but basically good people—so good they let Deanna stay with them after her eighteenth birthday when the state stopped paying them. "How long did you think you could keep them from finding out?"

"I don't know. I can't face telling them." She hugged herself, grabbing her elbows and pulling them close as if she could squeeze until she disappeared. "What if they make me move out? Where will I go?"

"Couldn't you get welfare to help you out for a couple of years so you could finish school?" Karen asked. Before Deanna could answer, she added, "I'd ask my mom if you could stay with us, but there's no way my dad would let you. He told me if I ever got pregnant when I was still at home, he was buyin' me a one-way ticket to Florida."

"You could stay with us," Maria said. "You'd have to sleep with me and Alma, but at least you wouldn't be out on the streets."

"What would your mother say?" Deanna asked, the unexpected offer of help momentarily stemming her tears.

For the first time Maria was able to smile. "Once she finds out you're not eating like we all thought you were eating, she won't mind feeding you."

"What are we gonna tell Cheryl?" Karen asked.

"Please don't tell her," Deanna said. "She'll make me go back, and I love it here. I don't want to go home until we have to."

"What're we gonna do about getting you to a doctor if we don't tell her?" Karen asked.

After several seconds, they both looked at Maria expectantly. "What?"

"You're good at this kind of thing," Karen said. "Think of something."

As much as she didn't want to admit it, she was better at coming up with answers than they were. Too bad they were always other people's questions and not her own. "I'll think about it."

"How was your date?" Deanna asked shyly.

How could she tell them what she'd seen and heard that night, the food she'd eaten, the people she'd met, the longings that now filled her mind and heart?

She couldn't.

"It wasn't anything special," she said finally.

6

MARIA TRIED TO GATHER HER COURAGE on her way to work with Paul Tuesday morning. Given a choice, she would have walked the fifteen miles to the free clinic in Santa Cruz, but there was no way Deanna could make it. A taxi was out of the question. Even with their best lie they'd never convince Cheryl they weren't trying to hide something. Besides, Maria only had the extra money she had earned working overtime to pay for the appointment and whatever medicines Deanna might need. Taxis weren't an option.

"Why so quiet?" Paul asked after they'd gone several miles in silence.

She took a deep breath. "I need a favor."

"Uh-oh."

"It's a big favor, and it's serious, and I don't need any crap from you about it."

"Lay it on me."

"My friend needs a ride into town on Thursday."

Paul looked at her. "That's it?"

"You can't tell anyone where you take her, and you have to take me and another friend, too." She waited. "And we have to ask Andrew to give us a couple of hours off."

"Okay."

Again she waited. When he didn't say anything more, she said, "You don't want to know where we're going?"

"I figure you'll tell me when you're ready. And if you don't, then it's none of my business."

She really didn't want to like him any more than she already did, but he kept doing things like this and chipping away at her resolve. "We're going to have to lie to Andrew and Cheryl. Well, maybe not lie, but not tell the whole truth." After several seconds she added, "You don't have to do the lying, I'll take care of that. But you do have to go along with what I say." She looked at him. "Can you do that?"

"What are you going to say?"

"That you're taking us shopping to buy something for Cheryl to thank her for bringing us here."

"Isn't she going to wonder what's going on when you come home empty-handed?"

"We're not. I figured you and I can pick something up while Karen and Deanna are at the clinic."

"Have you thought about what you're going to say when Andrew asks why we're taking time off to go on Thursday instead of Sunday or Monday when we'd have the whole day off?"

"It can't be helped. The clinic is closed Mondays."

"I take it that means you don't have an answer?"

"Not yet. But I will."

"Why don't I tell him I have to take care of a mix-up with my schedule for next semester and that you and your friends are going with me to look at the campus? Everyone knows UC Santa Cruz isn't like anyplace else, so it won't seem strange that you and your friends want to check it out."

She stared at him. "You'd do that?"

"I figure you wouldn't ask if it weren't important."

She owed him an explanation, especially for involving him in a lie. "My friend is pregnant."

He let out a long breath. "I see."

"Five months, and she hasn't seen a doctor."

"I take it she hasn't told her folks."

"She doesn't have any real parents. Right now she's living with the people who have been her foster parents since eighth grade and she's afraid they're going to throw her out when she tells them she's pregnant. They're not getting paid to keep her anymore because she's going to turn nineteen before she graduates high school. There's no reason they'd go out of their way for her now." She didn't expect him to understand, it wasn't the kind of thing that happened to the people he knew.

"There's one thing you haven't thought of. Andrew and Cheryl are going to ask you about the campus."

"I can fake it. I've been to Berkeley. Lots of times." She'd only been there twice, once on a field trip with her advanced English class and once because she wanted to see the buildings she'd missed the first time. A stupid subterfuge, but a matter of pride.

"They're nothing alike."

"So you can tell me what it's like."

"It's not the same. Why don't I just take you there after we get off work tonight? You can call Cheryl and tell her we're going for hamburgers."

It sounded too much like a date. Still, what choice did she have? "When should I tell her I'll be back?"

"Make it seven. That will give us plenty of time." He thought a minute. "Better make it eight. We'll have to stop someplace to eat or she'll wonder why you're hungry when you get home."

‿PAUL WAS RIGHT. UC SANTA CRUZ WAS nothing like Berkeley. Maria felt comfortable in this atmosphere, not like an outsider pretending she had a right to be there. At Berkeley she'd been in awe of everything from the students to the enormous classrooms. No one was in a rush here. Some students even smiled, and a couple greeted her as if she belonged.

The libraries took her breath away and made her hands and mind itch to touch and feel and learn. She wasn't intimidated by the classrooms and could easily imagine herself sliding into a seat and waiting for a lecture to begin. She loved the quiet of the forest and the spectacular views of the ocean and the way the buildings looked as if they blended into their surroundings.

She'd fought coming, and she fought leaving, asking to see the dorms and cafeteria and even the administration buildings. They walked up hills and through the forest where they were rained on by moisture-laden pines. At one point she stopped under a redwood tree too tall for her to see to the top, closed her eyes, and stood perfectly still.

"Listen," she told Paul, her voice filled with wonder.

"That's a woodpecker," he said.

"No—listen to the quiet." Several moments passed before she added, "No cars, no radios, no people. I've never heard anything so beautiful."

He leaned back against the rough, fragrant tree trunk and studied her. "You belong here, you know."

"Yeah, right. Like that's something you would know about me."

"So what are you saying, that you think you're going to do better at Berkeley?"

It took a second for her to figure out what he was talking about. Because she'd told him she'd visited Berkeley, he thought she was planning to go to school there when she finally got around to going. She would have laughed but was afraid she might cry. He was the only person she knew who could make such a dumb mistake.

"We should get going." She started up the path before he had a chance to answer.

"It really is beautiful here," she told Paul, as they drove down the hill away from the campus. "I wish it were possible." She didn't realize she'd said the second sentence out loud until he responded.

"What do you mean?"

"I could never afford to go to a place like this."

"After what happened last time I brought it up, I'm almost afraid to say this. I started to tell you that first day that you don't need to afford it. This is part of the California system. All you need are decent grades and it's free—as long as your family income is low enough."

"Trust me, that's not a problem. But it doesn't matter. Even if you did know what you were talking about, I still couldn't come here."

"Why not?"

"I don't work for play money the way you do. My family needs what I make. I have to get my brother and sisters through school before it's my turn. And that's at least twelve years away."

"Why can't you work and go to school? Isn't that what you're doing now?"

He really had no idea what her life was like or how much effort she had put in to get where she was. And she would never tell him. Pride was a foolish road, but she'd been on it so long she didn't know how to get off. "You ask a lot of questions that are none of your business."

"How am I supposed to know where you draw the line?" he snapped. He turned into a residential section of the city and drove past houses with manicured lawns and expensive cars in the driveways. Neither of them said anything until the silence became a third passenger that took up more space than the two of them together.

Maria was the first to give in. "You don't have to stop anywhere for us to eat. I'm not hungry."

"What if I am?"

"Then stop. I can wait in the car."

He gave her a dirty look. "You know you can be a real pain in the ass."

"So I've heard."

"Oh, so it's not just me who thinks so."

"Get in line." She was confused and frustrated and angry. Three weeks ago she'd known exactly where she was headed and why. Her life might not have been what she would have chosen, but at least it had direction. Now she had dreams, wishes, desires—none of them practical or even remotely possible. "Okay, I'll have a hamburger with you. Just don't make a big thing out of it."

"Wow. What a favor."

"I'll make you a deal." She was tired of fighting him, tired of fighting her feelings for him.

"I can hardly wait."

"I won't give you a hard time . . . if you don't make me."

He actually laughed. "I can live with that."

He took her to Carpos in Soquel and talked her into ordering a loganberry milk shake to go with her hamburger and fries.

"Well?" he asked after her first taste, a smug smile in place.

She couldn't fake it. "This is sooo good."

"Wait till you try the fries."

She did. "Not as good as the milk shake, but close."

"I probably shouldn't tell you this—"

"But you're going to anyway."

"Do you want to hear it or not?"

"How can I know until you tell me?"

"I'll take that as a yes." He popped a fry in his mouth. "I overheard Alfonso talking about you to Andrew this morning."

Alfonso was the toughest boss she'd ever had. She put her hamburger down to listen. "What did he say?"

"That you were a natural, and Andrew should do whatever it took to keep you."

Until then high praise from Alfonso had been a rare grunt of approval as he walked by a table where she was working. "He really said that?"

"He said other stuff, too, but I don't want you getting a big head."

"Like what?"

"Like how you could spot a flat that was planted wrong before it started showing signs of stress."

"That's easy."

"And how you knew it was time to water by the change in the leaves."

"That's easy, too."

"It's not easy for me."

She shrugged. "All you have to do is look. The leaves change color when they start to dry out."

He smiled. "You and Andrew are the only ones who see it."

"You're kidding." But she could see that he wasn't. "It's so obvious."

"Every time he leaves for more than a week, the plants suffer because there's no one left who can read them the way he does. Too much or too little water, and it can set them back months. Instead of a plant setting its first bloom a year out of the flask, it could take two." He stopped to take a bite of hamburger. "Don't be surprised if Andrew tries to talk you into moving down here when you graduate."

"I can't," she said automatically. "There's no way I could live here when my family is in Oakland."

"You want me to tell him?"

"Then he would know you told me."

"I'd find a way that he wouldn't have to know." Finished with his own fries, he reached over to take one of hers.

"Are you going to keep working when school starts?"

"I'll cut back to a couple of days a week—until Andrew tells me he doesn't need me anymore."

"You don't need the money. Why bother?"

"He bailed me out of trouble a couple of years ago. I figure I owe him."

"What kind of trouble?" The question made him uncomfortable. At first she thought he wasn't going to answer.

Finally, reluctantly, he said, "My mom had moved down here to be with Peter, and I had to come with her because my dad had moved into a studio apartment. I was pissed because I had to change schools my senior year and stole some stuff from a grocery store thinking she would send me back if I got in trouble. Andrew was there when it happened. The owner was a friend of his and wanted to make an example out of me because he'd been losing so much stuff to shoplifters. Andrew talked him into dropping the charges if I agreed to come to work for him."

Second chances didn't come so easily in her neighborhood. "You were lucky."

"I didn't think so at the time. My dad threw a fit. He said my mom was too busy with Peter to pay any attention to me and that I was going to wind up in jail. He wanted to ship me off to boarding school. My mom talked him into giving me another chance. I lost my car, my freedom, and my girlfriend that summer."

"How old were you?"

"Almost eighteen."

"What did you miss the most?"

He grinned. "No contest, the car. It was a midnight blue 1985 Mustang. Some guy in San Jose bought it and totaled it three days later. It still makes me sick thinking about it."

"I love old Mustangs."

"What else do you love?" He took another fry.

She thought about it. "Spring days, long walks on the beach, curling up with a good book, and drinking champagne in front of a roaring fire."

The smile he gave her started at the corner of his mouth and ended with a knowing wink. "Got those single ads down pat, I see."

She really liked that he was quick and funny and didn't mind being teased. "I love the way rain makes everything look better than it really is and, I'll deny it if you tell Cheryl, I'm beginning to love old movies. I *like* chocolate milk, not the kind you make yourself, but the thick kind that comes in a carton. And popcorn and Junior Mints eaten together."

"How do you do that?"

"Take a handful of popcorn and put it in your mouth then pop in a Junior Mint." When he made a face, she added, "Don't knock it till you've tried it."

"What else?"

"Long skirts and boots. Stephen King and Harry Potter and Nora Roberts. Christmas and my birthday." She saw his hand moving toward her plate and picked up a fry and handed it to him. "What about you?"

"I'm partial to fog. Not the kind we get around here in the summer, but the valley fog where I grew up in Woodland. Sometimes it's so thick you can't see the white line in the middle of the road. I don't have a favorite candy—I'll eat just about anything except the M&Ms with the crispy stuff in the middle."

"Holidays?"

"I don't care about my birthday, but the Fourth of July ranks right up there with Christmas. The only thing I read anymore is stuff for school, but I used to like King and McCaffery." He smiled. "As for long skirts and boots, they're okay, but short skirts and boots are better."

"Movies?"

"Anything with Chris and nothing with subtitles."

"He's nice." The next came harder. "I can't remember if I thanked you for taking me to his party, but I should have."

"You did. But it's nice to hear it again."

She glanced at the clock on the wall over the salad bar. "We should be going," she said reluctantly. "I don't want to push things with Cheryl."

He stood and waited for her to come around

the table. "How does your being here with her work? Is she a friend or what?"

"She's one of the people who help run an after-school group where Deanna and Karen and I volunteer a couple of times a month. We look out for the kids who come by, organize games, things like that. We used to go there when we were kids, and now we all have sisters or brothers who do."

"That will look good on your application."

"What application?"

"To college." He held up his hand to stop her before she could say anything. "*When* you decide to go."

"They want to know things like that? I thought they just looked at grades."

"We need to talk about this—for the future. *Should* you change your mind and decide you want to go to college." He put his arm around her shoulder as they walked to the car.

He opened the door but she looked at him before she got in. "Why are you doing this?"

"What?"

"Pushing me to go to college? Why do you care what I do? Another week and a half and I'm out of here and we never see each other again."

"How do you know? Maybe Andrew will talk you into coming back next summer."

Her first reaction was anger. He was doing it to her again, giving her something to dream about. But then she looked into his eyes and saw that he really cared. *He wanted her to come back.* Impulsively, she leaned forward and kissed him, quick and clean.

Stunned, it took him a second to respond. "Is that a yes, or a maybe?"

She smiled. "I don't know."

He put his hands on the sides of her head and brought her forward for another kiss. This time it was long and slow and deliberate. "That was my vote. Do I need to explain?"

She shook her head, for the moment not caring that she was traveling a road she'd sworn she would not take. She had ten days to enjoy the ride. If the destination was a broken heart, at least she would always have the memory of the journey.

7

ANDREW DIDN'T SEE CHERYL SITTING ON his front step until he pulled into the driveway. She had on white shorts and a red tube top that set off her newly acquired tan and made her skin seem to glow. She had a bottle of wine in one hand and a bouquet of nasturtiums in the other. He parked his car and met her on the walkway. "I was hoping I got the message right."

"It's just you and me for two whole hours. Paul took the girls to town to do some shopping and to show them the campus."

While he'd been invited to dinner twice and had joined Cheryl and the girls on the beach a couple of times, the two of them hadn't had ten minutes alone the entire three weeks she'd been there. "Just two hours, huh?"

"I'm sorry. I really thought we'd have more time while I was here."

He took her in his arms for a quick hug. "Me too."

She looked up at him, "You've been wonderful about all this."

"You really think so?"

"Oh, yes."

"Then I have to tell you, it's worked out exactly as I'd planned."

She laughed. "How clever you are to have arranged for me to bring the girls without my knowing you were involved."

"I'm good. What can I say?"

"How about—come in, Cheryl, I have some fantastic cheese and crackers to go with that wine you brought."

"That would be a lie, I'm down to my last can of beans and quart of milk, but I'm sure if we dig around long enough we'll come up with something."

They went inside. While Andrew changed out of his work clothes, Cheryl put the flowers in a vase and opened the wine. She stared out the kitchen window while she waited for Andrew, remembering the first night he'd brought her there. They'd come a long way since, rebuilding the shattered trust of their relationship brick by brick.

Seventeen years had changed him. He was more patient and slower to anger. He was still idealistic, but more tolerant of those who weren't. At times a wanderlust still shone from his eyes, but now it was couched in a way that didn't frighten her. When he talked about faraway places, he always talked about seeing them with her.

But he worked too hard. It was something he'd never talked about, and she wouldn't have believed it if she hadn't moved next door and seen for herself how many hours he put in each day. He left home at six in the morning and was gone most nights until eight or nine. If she asked him for dinner or mentioned she and the girls were staying home to spend time on the beach, he stayed home to be with her. Then, as often as not, she would see him leaving to go back to work later that night.

She'd asked him if he still sailed, and he'd told her that he hadn't been out in over a year, that he'd rented the boat to a friend who had taken it to Hawaii. He no longer surfed or hiked or took off on his bike for the weeklong camping trips he'd taken for years along the coast. When she asked why, the answer was always the same. No time.

Why had he changed?

She heard him come up behind her and willed him to touch her. Lately she could think of little else. The forced separation had sharpened her longing for him until it had become a physical ache. All she had to do was think about him and her skin flushed.

As if reading her mind, he slipped his arms around her waist. She leaned her head against his shoulder. "I love it here," she said. "And I love being here with you."

He turned her around and lifted her to sit on the tile counter. She parted her legs and he stepped between them, resting his hands on her bare thighs. "I talked to Eric this morning, and he said they aren't going to get here in September after all. We can have the house if we want it. Now the only question is, can you get away for another week?"

She put her arms around his neck and moved closer. She felt his instant response and wrapped her legs around his waist. "I assume you mean alone?"

He nuzzled her neck, touching his tongue to the hollow at her collarbone. "Preferably."

"What about you? I thought you were a speaker at some conference in Florida."

"I'll get out of it." He moved higher, kissing her throat, behind her ear, then nipping at her earlobe. "I know a dozen growers who will take my place. All I have to do is ask."

"Are you sure?" she breathed.

He stopped to look at her. "Oh, yes."

Her heart drummed in her ears. She touched her tongue to her lips. "Me too."

He kissed her then, slow and deep and with growing urgency. His lips were soft and hard in turn as he coaxed, then promised. His tongue swept her mouth, tasting and inviting. A deep moan of desire rumbled in his chest. To Cheryl it was a primitive call destroying order and propriety. She knew, she felt, she wanted only one thing—to feel him inside her. She moved against him, rocking her hips hard.

Andrew caught the edge of her top and swept it down to her waist. He took a nipple in his mouth and pulled until she arched her back and pushed against him, mutely asking him to take more. His hands moved to her inner thighs, his thumbs slipped under the hem of her shorts, exploring, seeking soft, wet folds.

She cried out when he succeeded. He stopped her cries with his mouth, his tongue mimicking the rhythm of his hands. She moved to give him freer access and he touched and stroked and lapped until he felt her nearing a peak, then grasped her legs and carried her into the bedroom.

Their clothes came off in an awkward rush, landing on tables and bed and the floor. When they were finally naked, Cheryl lay on the bed and opened herself to him. He joined her and was inside in a single thrust. The climax was explosive, building on the cries and moans and movements of the other until nothing would have convinced them that fireworks had not gone off in the bedroom.

Still, there was as much frustration at the end as there had been in the beginning. After seventeen years of mental longing and foreplay, once was not enough. A lifetime would not be enough.

Her hand on his chest, Cheryl pushed herself

up to look at him. "I forgot how good you are—out of self-preservation, I think." She smiled seductively. "Now, you do realize that there's no going back."

He put his hand on the nape of her neck and brought her down to him for a kiss. His voice husky, he said, "Anytime, anyplace."

She glanced at the clock on the nightstand and groaned. "The girls are due back in half an hour."

He grinned. "I would suggest you do something to wipe that look off your face if you don't want them to know what we've been doing."

"What look?"

"The satisfied one."

"We could take a cold shower and pretend we've been swimming."

He cupped her breast with his hand. "It's going to take more than a cold shower, Cheryl."

She moved out of his reach. "If you keep doing things like that it will."

He sat up and tenderly touched her cheek. "I love you, Cheryl Cunningham."

"I've waited a long time, not just to hear that, but to believe it. Tell me again."

"I love you. I want to spend the rest of my life with you."

"Is that a proposal?"

"Yes."

She smiled. "Maybe it's a good thing we can't have children. Think how awkward it would be to tell them where we were and what we were doing when their father proposed."

Some of the light left his eyes. He took her hand, turned it over, and pressed a kiss to her palm. "I'm sorry. You would have made a terrific mother."

"And you a father."

"We have each other," he said. "That in itself is a miracle."

"Can something be destiny and a miracle?"

"It can if you answer my question."

For an instant she didn't understand. Then she did, and she smiled. "Yes—I will marry you. This afternoon, tomorrow, next week. Pick a time and place, and I'll be there."

CHERYL COULDN'T SLEEP. SHE ROLLED FROM side to side until her nightgown was so twisted she had to get out of bed to straighten it. She, Deanna, and Karen were getting up early tomorrow to take Karen to a hairdresser they'd found in Santa Cruz. The platinum spikes were scheduled to be toned down to a sexy blond shade. Cheryl had no idea why Karen had decided to make the change. It wasn't as if Santa Cruz didn't have its share of people with in-your-face hair and the attitude that went with it. Besides, Karen had never worried about fitting in. At least she hadn't before now.

Rolling to her back, Cheryl tried counting waves instead of sheep but couldn't stop thinking about Andrew and how much she loved him, how happy she was, and how her life had gone from mere contentment to perfect.

She'd wondered if Andrew's surgery would make a difference when they made love, but had been hesitant to ask. Then she'd forgotten all about it until afterward, when it was a moot point. The memory brought a flush of pleasure and a yearning so intense she caught her breath until it passed. Crazy thoughts went through her mind, the kind she'd had when she was nineteen and new to the intense physical response even thoughts of making love with Andrew brought. As she had then, she imagined herself sneaking out of the house to be with him, only this time it was to keep from being caught by three eighteen-year-olds instead of her parents. She calculated how long she would be gone if she went to his house, what they would do while she was there, how she would get back without being seen. A teenager's game. One she never would have believed she could indulge in again.

That afternoon, while they'd waited for the girls to come home, they'd made plans for the week she would come back in September, the places they would go, the people she would meet, the friends they would entertain as a couple. She smiled to herself. There would be no friends or entertaining. That would come later. For now all they needed was each other. They had seventeen years to make up.

Cheryl tucked her hands under her head and thought about how hard it was going to be to tell her family that she and Andrew were back together. She would have to do it in stages to give them time to get used to the idea. Then she would spring the news that she and Andrew were going to get married. Maybe they could make the announcement at Christmas if she brought Andrew to Thanksgiving dinner and—

Something, *someone* was on the deck. She sat up and turned her ear in that direction. A low metal-on-metal sound came next. The sliding glass door.

Grabbing her bathrobe, Cheryl put it on and silently crossed the bedroom. She quietly turned the doorknob and stepped into the hall. Swallowing the knot of fear stuck in her throat, she made her way toward the living room. She was about to peer around the corner when she heard the sounds of someone softly crying.

Convinced it was one of the girls, she listened for another minute, trying to decide if she should give whoever it was her privacy or offer a shoulder. The crying continued. Cheryl finally gave in to her first instinct and went to see what was wrong.

She found Deanna on the floor by the back door, leaning against the glass, her hands covering her face. Cheryl crossed the room and sat on the floor next to her. She touched her hair and Deanna came into Cheryl's arms. Her tears turned to deep, heart-wrenching sobs.

There was nothing pretty or genteel about Deanna's grief. Cheryl held her and rocked her and waited. For now it was enough to give comfort.

Time passed. Cheryl had no idea how much, only that she couldn't put off talking to Deanna any longer. Whatever had put her in this state had to be dealt with.

"We need to talk," she said.

"I can't . . ."

"Why?"

"Because." It was a child's answer.

Cheryl waited. "That's not good enough, Deanna."

"You'll be disappointed in me." The sob that followed was almost a wail.

Cheryl leaned back to reach for the box of tissues on the end table. She handed the box to Deanna. "Whatever it is, we'll find a way to deal with it."

"There isn't anything you can do. There isn't anything anyone can do."

"How do you know?"

"I just do."

"Does whatever's bothering you have something to do with the weight you've gained?"

Deanna glanced up from blowing her nose. She looked as if she were about to burst into tears again. "Who told you?"

"No one. It was a guess."

"You guessed I was pregnant?"

Somehow Cheryl managed to catch herself before the shock showed on her face. "No," she said carefully. "I thought it was something else."

Realizing her mistake, Deanna started crying again. "Now you hate me."

Mentally trying to deal with the news, Cheryl scrambled for the right words. "You know I would never do that, so let's not go down that road."

"You're mad at me."

"No, I'm not."

"Then you're disappointed."

"I'm not going to play that game with you either." She stood and held out her hand to help Deanna to her feet. "I could use a cup of tea. You look like you could, too."

They went into the kitchen, where Cheryl put Deanna in a chair at the table. She took her time making the tea, giving them both an opportunity to think about what would come next. Seated across from each other, Cheryl dunking her tea bag and Deanna swirling hers by the string, Cheryl took a deep breath and began. "Who have you told about this?"

"Maria and Karen."

"No one else?"

"Paul knows."

Cheryl waited for the pieces to form a whole. "You didn't go shopping or to see the campus today." She'd thought it strange none of them came back with anything. "Where did you go?"

"To the doctor."

"First things first. Is everything okay?"

She nodded. "They did some tests, but I won't know about those until next week."

"What did the doctor say?"

Her lip trembled and her eyes filled with tears. "It's a girl."

"That's not what I meant," Cheryl said gently. "I know you're concerned about the baby, but right now you're the one I'm worried about."

Deanna looked at her. "I don't know what to do," she whispered. "I thought about having an abortion, but I couldn't do it. And now it's too late." She buried her face in her hands. "I can't have this baby. How will I take care of her? I can't even take care of myself."

"We'll get you the help you need," Cheryl said. "There are all kinds of—"

"I don't want help." She gave Cheryl a pleading look. "I want it to go away. I want my life back. I want everything to be the way it was. I can't be a mother to this baby. I don't know how." She stopped to wipe her eyes and blow her nose. "Where will I live? When Bill and Amy find out, they won't let me stay with them anymore."

"You don't know that for sure. They love you, Deanna. They will want to help."

"They already told me I have to move out as soon as I graduate. I said I would sleep on the couch if they needed to use my room, but they said that wouldn't look good to the foster care people."

There were agencies to help Deanna, ways for her to keep her baby and finish school and get a job that would enable her to provide for them both. But it was going to be a long, slow struggle. "You need to talk to someone who has more answers than I do," Cheryl said. "As soon as we get back, we'll get you in to see someone."

"It's not fair. I made one mistake. I'm sorry. Why do I have to pay for it the rest of my life? I don't want a baby. Not now. I'm not ready."

"What about the father?"

For the first time Deanna showed a glimmer of certainty and strength. "He doesn't count. If it's Jake, he would just wind up hurting her the way my mother hurt me. I'll do anything to make sure that doesn't happen. I might not want this baby, but that doesn't mean I don't love it."

"What do you mean 'if' it's Jake's?"

"I don't want to talk about it."

Cheryl's heart broke a little at Deanna's revelation. "You'll get through this," she promised. "I'll help you every way I can."

"Do you mean that? Do you *really* mean it, or is it just something you're saying?"

It wasn't the time for speeches or details. "Yes, I really meant it," she said simply, sincerely.

Deanna stared at her for a long time before she said, "Will you adopt my baby?"

8

THE PHONE RANG, GIVING CHERYL A MOmentary reprieve from answering Deanna. She was so dazed by the question she didn't think to be concerned over a phone call at four in the morning until she heard Juanita Ramos's frantic voice on the line.

"Is Maria there? I need to speak to her please. Right away."

"Of course. I'll get her for you."

Cheryl put her hand over the receiver and said to Deanna, "Get Maria. It's her mother." When she was gone, Cheryl asked, "Are you all right, Mrs. Ramos?"

"No—yes. It isn't me, it's Alma. I don't know what happened to her. She went to a party and someone brought her here to the hospital. She's unconscious. The doctor said he thinks it's drugs, but it can't be. Alma's a good girl. She doesn't do drugs. Ask Maria. She will tell you. Alma is a good girl."

Maria came into the kitchen, her nightgown askew, her hair disheveled. Blinking against the light, she reached for the phone. "Mama? What's wrong?" She listened for several seconds. "Don't cry, Mama. She's going to be okay. You're right, Mama, Alma wouldn't take drugs—someone must have given her something. Who did she go with?" She paused then flinched. "Shit—I told her he was trouble. She *promised* me she wouldn't go out with him again."

Maria leaned her forehead against the wall. "He is not a nice boy, Mama. He was the one I told you about who got caught selling roofies at school."

Cheryl met Deanna's worried glance. Roofie was the street name for rohypnol, the date rape drug. If he'd given it to Alma, he either gave her too much or she'd had a bad reaction. If she was still alive, chances were she would come out of it in a couple of hours. But she would always wonder what had happened to her while she was unconscious. The wait to find out if she was pregnant or diseased would be horrific.

The possibilities made Cheryl sick to her stomach. She'd been living in Montana when stories about rohypnol first surfaced. Her outrage had been fueled by an astonishing apathy among legislators. Since that time attitudes had changed and drug companies and Congress had finally acted. Roofies were still frighteningly easy to get, but girls weren't as trusting and vulnerable as they used to be.

She would never understand the kind of man who drugged an unsuspecting woman senseless to have sex with her. It was so far beyond her comprehension that she found it impossible to think of them as fathers or brothers or sons. She recoiled at the idea she might actually know one of them and yet had a morbid curiosity, a desire even, to question someone who could do such a thing, to hear the rationale they gave for their behavior.

Maria looked devastated when she hung up the phone and turned to Cheryl. "I have to go home."

"Of course." She turned to Deanna. "Wake up Karen and tell her to get dressed."

"No—" Maria said. "That's not fair. You don't all have to come with me."

"I can't leave Deanna and Karen here alone," Cheryl said.

Maria ran her hand across her forehead as she thought. "Alma's only thirteen . . ." When she looked at Cheryl again there were tears in her eyes. "How could he do this to her?" Her breath caught in a sob. *"She's thirteen years old."*

"I'll get Karen," Deanna said.

Maria gave Cheryl a frantic look. As much as she would need her friends for support later, she needed time alone now. "Why don't I call Andrew?" Cheryl asked. "He can drive you to Oakland."

Maria took a second to consider the idea. "What about Paul? I know he would take me. Would that be okay with you?"

Cheryl was sure there were at least a dozen reasons she should say no, but she'd deal with them when and if they became a problem later. "I'll call him. You get ready."

Maria started to leave, then came back for a quick hug. "Thank you."

"Alma is going to be all right," Cheryl told her.

Maria silently nodded.

━━PAUL SAT IN A PLASTIC CHAIR AT THE END OF the hallway. Maria drifted back and forth between sitting with him and maintaining a vigil in Alma's room. He'd told her he didn't mind waiting alone, but she continued to come out to check on him as did Juanita, her mother.

He liked Juanita. She was a lot like Maria, and he was long gone on Maria. For a while he'd tried to put his feelings off to the fact she was a challenge, but it was more than that. He thought about her all the time—he nagged her about going to college at UC Santa Cruz, a cover for getting her within dating range.

Now that she was opening up to him, he understood what she meant about leaving her family being complicated. When they'd gone to the house to pick up Enrique, he'd understood why she was worried. If his family lived where they lived, he'd worry about them, too.

He glanced down the hall and saw Maria coming toward him. "How is she?"

She sat next to him. "Starting to wake up. The test they did came back positive. It is rohypnol. A policewoman came by to take a report."

"Was she . . ." He couldn't say the word. It was as if saying it aloud would make it true.

"No. Whoever dropped her off outside the emergency room door must have panicked when she started having trouble breathing."

"Did anyone see him?"

"It's supposedly on one of the security cameras."

He took her hand, entwining his fingers with hers. "How's your mom doing?"

"She's scared. She'd never heard of roofies before tonight. Now she says Alma and Rosa aren't going to any more parties—ever. And they can't go out with any guy she doesn't know. Like it's only guys you don't know who do things like this."

"Maybe you should move to another neighborhood." He sensed it was a mistake the minute the words were out. She let go of his hand and folded her arms across her chest.

"Where did you have in mind?" she asked, finding a new target for her anger. "Maybe down the street from you in one of those million-dollar houses that only have one bedroom? How much do you suppose the rent would be for a place like that? How much more ironing would my mother have to take in to pay for it? How many more hours would I have to work at the nursery?" Her voice quavered, and tears welled in her eyes. "Or maybe you were thinking Chris Sadler would let us stay in his house when he wasn't there. Of course it might be a problem when he did want to use it, but then we could always camp out on the beach until he was gone again."

"That's not fair. I'm only trying to help."

Now she was crying for real. "You can't. No one can."

There had to be a way. "If your mother could leave here, would she?"

She looked at him as if he'd asked the question in a foreign language. "Do you think we *want* to live like this?"

Enrique came down the hall and motioned to Maria. "Alma's awake. She wants to see you."

Maria stood and started to leave then turned back to Paul. "You don't have to stay. Go home. I'll call you later."

She wasn't simply sending him away from the hospital, she was dismissing him from her life. "I don't want to go home," he said.

"Andrew needs you at work."

She was right. Losing one of them was bad enough, losing them both would put Andrew in a real bind. "I'll call him and tell him we'll come in Sunday."

A profoundly sad look came into her eyes. "I can't go back. My mother needs me here."

He could see it was useless to argue, and selfish. "Okay, I'll tell him that it'll just be me," he said, defeated.

"And that I'm sorry?"

He nodded.

Enrique impatiently shifted from one foot to the other. "Alma's waiting."

Maria tried to give Paul a smile but couldn't pull it off. "Thank you," she whispered, then turned and followed her brother down the hall.

⟶MARIA STAYED WITH ALMA, TALKING TO HER, reassuring her, and crying with her until she was exhausted and fell into a natural sleep. Because she'd developed a fever, the doctor had decided to keep her another day. Juanita took Enrique and Rosa home to feed them and let them sleep in their own beds. She was due back at ten to relieve Maria.

She was curled into an uncomfortable chair beside Alma's bed, deep into memories of her three weeks at the beach house when she looked up and saw her mother standing in the doorway.

"You look so sad," Juanita said softly as she crossed the room. "Is Alma all right?"

"She's fine." Maria unfolded her legs and stretched. "Her fever's gone. The doctor said she can go home in the morning."

Juanita went to the bed and looked closely at her sleeping daughter, touching her fingers to her lips and then to Alma's forehead. She said a silent prayer and made the sign of the cross, then went to Maria and touched the side of her face. "What is it? Why are you still so troubled?"

Maria came forward and put her arms around her mother's waist, her head against her chest. "I'm afraid, Mama. Enrique is so angry. He's convinced he knows who did this to Alma. What if he does something stupid and winds up like Fernando? How are we going to stop him?"

"You think it would be better if we left?"

The question threw Maria. She put her head back to look at her mother. "Where would we go?"

"To Santa Cruz."

"Why would we do that?"

Juanita frowned. "Because of your friend."

"What friend?"

"Paul."

Now she really was confused. "What has Paul got to do with us moving?"

"He didn't talk to you about this?"

"About what?"

Juanita put her finger to her lips, motioning for Maria to speak softer. "Maybe he should tell you about it himself."

Maria glanced at the clock. "It's too late to call him tonight."

Juanita shook her head. "Why would you call him when he's right down the hall?"

"Paul's here? At the hospital?" She stood and ran her hands through her hair. "I told him to go home."

"He didn't listen. He said he was waiting for you."

Her heart did a funny skipping beat. She couldn't believe he'd stayed. "I don't know what to say to him."

She smiled and made a shooing gesture to get Maria out of the room. "Go see him. You'll think of something."

Paul was at the window staring at the night sky, his back to Maria. She came up behind him without saying anything. Without turning, he asked, "Have you ever seen the Milky Way?"

"I don't think so."

"It's amazing. There are so many stars you think you're looking at a cloud." He moved to make room for her. "You have to get away from the city to really see it in all its glory, like somewhere deep in the mountains, where there are no lights."

"Why are you telling me this?"

He took her hand. "Because I want to see it again. With you."

All her life happiness had been doled out in small, manageable pieces. This was big. Maybe too big. "What did you say to my mother?"

"It was just an idea I had. You don't have to do anything you don't want to do." He smiled. "As if you would."

"What did you do, Paul?"

"I called Andrew."

"And?"

"Asked him if he needed that house for his office."

At first she didn't understand, and then it came to her in a rush. It couldn't be true. Things like that didn't happen to people like her. If she didn't say anything, she could hold on to the fantasy a little longer, but not even that could keep her from asking, "What did he say?"

"The house is yours, if you want it. I told Andrew that your mother might be willing to come to work for him and that you would probably come in a couple of times a week, too." Before she could say anything he held up his hand to stop her. "I know—it's none of my business, and I had no right to interfere, but I don't care. This was too important. I wasn't going to let you—"

"My mother would be so good with the plants." Maria didn't even try to contain her enthusiasm. "She can make anything grow. And she will love the ocean. So will Rosa and Alma. I don't know about Enrique. He can be so stubborn sometimes."

"Gee, I wonder where he got that."

She looked at him wide-eyed. "I'm not stubborn." He didn't seem convinced. "Really, I'm not."

"Prove it."

"How?"

"Go out with me."

"I did go out with you."

"On a real date, not one where you have to pretend you're doing me a favor."

"Pretend?" she teased, happier than she knew how to be.

"You know what I mean."

"I do," she said. "And I will." She came up on her toes to give him a kiss.

When she was little she'd thought *Cinderella* was an especially stupid fairy tale and that any girl who waited around for Prince Charming to rescue her didn't deserve to be rescued. She was obviously going to have to rethink her position.

September

1

ANDREW WENT FROM THE LIVING ROOM into the kitchen, a paintbrush in one hand, a damp rag in the other. It was his final pass-through. He looked for places that still needed touching up with the trim color they'd used on the windowsills and baseboards. He wanted the painting finished by that afternoon to give it a few days to dry before the new carpet was installed.

Paul came out of the bedroom, his face sprinkled with sunshine yellow freckles from the roller he'd been using on the ceiling. "Done," he announced. "And another career choice bites the dust."

Andrew smiled. "Decided painting's not your thing, huh?"

He looked down at his paint-splattered T-shirt

and jeans. "If I had to pay for the paint I spilled, I'd never be able to make a living."

They'd had to use the last drop in the bucket after Paul stepped off the ladder and into the freshly filled roller pan. "It's the finished product that counts, and the room looks great."

He grinned. "Yeah, it does."

Spotting a bare corner on the window over the sink, Andrew made a quick swipe with the brush, checked the coverage, and stood back to check the other corners. "Have you talked to Maria in the past couple of days?"

"Yesterday."

"Did she say whether Enrique was coming around yet?" Initially, only Maria and Juanita had come to talk to Andrew and see the house. Maria had been a nervous wreck when she introduced her mother to Andrew and during the entire time he showed her around the greenhouses. Juanita was hesitant in the beginning, looking for reasons the move wouldn't work and asking a hundred questions about working for Andrew.

Instead of being put off by her questions, Andrew was encouraged. Juanita was interested and enthusiastic and looking for something long term. If she had the same innate feel for plants that Maria demonstrated, in a couple of years she would be as invaluable as Alfonso, allowing Andrew to be away from the nursery for more than a week at a time.

Just when it looked as if the job and house were a done deal, Enrique announced he wasn't moving. He didn't want to leave his friends in Oakland.

Paul took the roller to the sink and dropped it in a bucket of water. "Maria said she talked him into giving Santa Cruz a year. After that, if he still wanted to go back, she would help him find a way."

"If he's anything like I was, all he has to do is meet the right girl, and he's here for the duration."

Paul laughed. "Ain't that the truth."

⌒CHERYL STOOD BACK AND LOOKED AT THE table setting. Everything was perfect, from the linen to the crystal to the silver. The candles were ready to be lit, the champagne cooled and ready to open, the lobster casserole ready to put in the oven.

The only thing missing was Andrew. He was late. But then he had no idea she was at his house waiting for him. She'd come down a day early as a surprise and was beginning to wonder if he'd gone to Oakland a day early to surprise her.

She was about to call the nursery when she spotted his truck coming through the forest. After a quick check of her reflection in the front window, she went outside to greet him.

He parked behind her car, got out, and stopped

midway down the driveway to look at her. "Have I ever told you how beautiful you are?" He shook his head in wonder. "How did I get so lucky?"

She smiled. "Luck had nothing to do with it. I put a spell on you."

He came forward and took her in his arms for a long, slow kiss. "Nice surprise. Thank you."

"I couldn't wait." She touched a streak of white in his hair. "Been painting?"

"Getting the house ready for Maria and her family."

"Have I thanked you enough for what you're doing for them?"

"Purely self-interest. If Juanita works out as well as I think she's going to, I could turn the place over to her in a couple of years . . ." He tucked his chin under hers and nuzzled her neck. "Then I can spend all my free time doing things like this with you."

She tilted her head to make it easier for him to kiss her, sighing when he caught her earlobe between his teeth. "Sounds like a plan to me."

He let her go, took her hand, and led her into the house. Spotting the table setting, he smiled. "Give me five minutes for a shower, and I'm all yours."

He was out in four, dressed in khaki slacks and a chambray shirt, his damp hair finger combed. Cheryl was at the kitchen window staring at the beginning of what promised to be a spectacular sunset. Andrew came up behind her and slipped his arms around her waist. She leaned into him. "Hungry?" she asked.

"For a lot of things," he murmured against her hair. "Want me to make a list?"

"It scares me to think how easily we could have missed this moment. If I hadn't gone to the reunion, if you had listened when I told you I didn't want to get back together."

"None of that matters," he said. "I've decided we were destined to find each other again."

She turned to look at him. "Do you really believe that?"

"I wouldn't be here if I didn't. There isn't one logical reason I chose this place to settle and start a business except that I wanted you to be able to find me if you ever came looking. I was willing to wait forever."

"You know you could have looked for me."

"I talked myself into believing I gave up that right." He gave her a lopsided grin. "However, I'm not sure how much longer I would have gone down that noble road."

She put her arms around his neck and kissed him. "I don't care how we got here. All that matters is that we did."

He put his hands on her arms. "Mother Nature is putting on an amazing show for us out there." He'd wanted the perfect time and setting for this night, and nothing he could have come up with could match what was happening outside. "I think we should show our appreciation."

Instead of watching from the deck, Andrew grabbed a throw off the sofa, and they headed for the beach. He spread the plaid blanket in the shelter between two large rocks, sat down, and held out his hand for Cheryl to join him.

"I'll bet you think I don't remember this place," she said, sitting between his legs and leaning her back into his chest, her head into his shoulder.

"I'd be disappointed if you didn't."

This was where they'd made love for the first time, where they'd vowed to love each other forever. The sunset that night had been glorious, too.

The sun wore a belt of dark blue clouds and the sky around it was awash in pink and orange and purple. A slowly moving line of pelicans flapped and glided in silhouette against the finger-painted background. In seconds the sea would reach up and snag the brilliant ball. Cheryl waited for the magical moment when they would meet and merge and let out a soft sigh.

Andrew leaned to his side to dig something out of his pocket. His chin on her shoulder, he held an open velvet box in front of Cheryl. In it, a large blue sapphire caught the light, and for a moment it seemed as if it, too, belonged in the sky.

"You remembered," she said, her voice a low, emotion-filled whisper.

The last time they'd been together in San Diego, they'd window-shopped while waiting for the bus that would take Cheryl home. She'd stopped to look at wedding sets in a jewelry store window and loftily told him she'd decided diamonds were for ordinary people and ordinary lovers. She wanted a sapphire, dark blue and emerald cut.

The very ring he held in front of her now.

"I guess I should make this official," he said. "Will you marry me?"

She nodded.

"Is that a yes?"

She nodded again, afraid to trust her voice.

Andrew took the ring out of the box. She held up her hand for him to slip the two-carat sapphire on her finger.

She held her hand against the vivid sky. "It's even more beautiful than I imagined." She shifted to face him. "And I'm happier than I thought possible."

"Do you need more than a week to plan a wedding?"

"One week?" She couldn't have heard him right. "*This* week?"

"If that's too soon, we could make it the end of the month. I just figured the adoption would go easier if we were married a month or two first."

She put her hand to her chest in an attempt to still her wildly beating heart. She had never loved him more than she did at that moment. "Are you sure?"

He smiled. "Yes, I'm sure."

"We don't have to do this. I'd understand if you didn't want to. It's a big step. We've only just found each other again. It may be too soon."

"Who are you worried about, Cheryl, me or you?"

"You," she admitted. "Me, a little, too. I don't know if I have it in me to be the mother this baby needs. What if I mess it up?"

"I'll be there to help you."

"You sound so confident."

He considered what she'd said before answering. "I learned firsthand the wrong way to raise a child. I'd like a chance to do it right."

"The baby will be here in three months. Do you realize what that means?"

"That she's going to feel cheated because her birthday is so close to Christmas?"

"You're serious about this," she said, dumbfounded.

"Given a choice, I would have given us a year or two alone, but life has a way of setting its own timetable. We either act now or regret not acting for the rest of our lives."

She came up on her knees and threw her arms around him. He fell backward. Raining kisses on his eyes, his cheeks, his chin, and finally his lips, she breathlessly said, "I love you, Andrew Wells."

He caught her face between his hands and kissed her long and deep. She responded with a soft moan, moving against him suggestively. Her hand went to his thigh and then to the front of his khakis. He stopped her.

"Not here," he said, pressing his lips to her palm.

"Why not?"

He gave her a wicked grin. "Because you don't want sand to get in the way for what I have in mind."

Cheryl immediately stood and smiled. "Race you."

"And if I win?" He stood beside her, suddenly serious. "Never mind," he said, looking deep into her eyes. "I already did."

They tumbled into bed as the last drop of sun dripped into the horizon . . . unnoticed.

Rita Award-winning author
Georgia Bockoven

"Bockoven is magic."
New York Times bestselling author Catherine Coulter

ANOTHER SUMMER
0-380-81865-5/$6.99 US/$9.99 Can
"*Another Summer* is Georgia Bockoven at her very best.
Heartbreaking and uplifting, poignant and triumphant . . .
it will appeal to anyone who believes
in the healing power of love."
Kristin Hannah

Also by the author

THE BEACH HOUSE
0-06-108440-9/$6.50 US/$8.50 Can

DISGUISED BLESSING
0-06-103020-1/$6.50 US/$8.99 Can